# Pinky
# Swear

## ALSO BY DANIELLE GIRARD

*Savage Art*

*Ruthless Game*

*Chasing Darkness*

*Cold Silence*

### BADLANDS SERIES

*White Out*

*Far Gone*

*Up Close*

### DR. SCHWARTZMAN SERIES

*Exhume*

*Excise*

*Expose*

*Expire*

*The Ex: An Annabelle Schwartzman Story*

### ROOKIE CLUB SERIES

*Dead Center*

*One Clean Shot*

*Dark Passage*

*Everything to Lose*

*Grave Danger*

*Too Close to Home: A Rookie Short Story*

# Pinky Swear

A Novel

## DANIELLE GIRARD

**EMILY BESTLER BOOKS**

**ATRIA**

NEW YORK   AMSTERDAM/ANTWERP   LONDON
TORONTO   SYDNEY/MELBOURNE   NEW DELHI

*For Danya Kukafka and Sarah Grill;*
*Lexi, Mara, and Cate couldn't have been in better hands*

Of course I feel too much, I'm a universe of exploding stars.

—Sara Ajna

# PROLOGUE

*1 day before due date*

THE HAND THAT holds the knife is mine but feels like a stranger's.

Pinned between the soot-stained wall and a dumpster, its blue-painted exterior dented and streaked, the man is on his knees, hands raised in surrender. The blade touches his neck where the pale folds of his skin contrast with his tan face, like rings on a tree.

I am prepared to cut this man. To kill him. This is not me; I am not this person.

But here I am.

The smells of piss and garbage and stale alcohol mix with night air and the scent of rain. My fingers are unfamiliar, nails black with grime, palms scraped and sore and soiled with something that, in the dark, might be grease or dried blood.

I regain focus as the light of the caged bulb overhead flashes across the metal blade.

"Where is Mara?" I demand.

"I'm not lying, I swear. I don't know where she is."

I press harder and the tip of the knife dents his skin, its tension holding the blade on the surface. Any harder, the knife will slice through.

"You don't have to do this," the man says. "This ain't going to solve nothing."

"Where would she go?"

"I haven't seen her in years. I swear—" He starts to turn, twisting away from the blade.

"Don't move," I warn, shifting the long edge of the knife against his skin. "You knew her."

"I did. But it's been years since I seen her. Most peaceful years I ever spent." He inches farther from the blade, driving his shoulder into the dumpster.

"No," I snap. That's not Mara. My partner in the biggest undertaking of my life, Mara is my oldest and most loyal friend. *I would do anything for you, Lexi.* From the start of our friendship in middle school—the three of us. Together every lunch, huddled at the cafeteria table we'd claimed junior year. Friday night sleepovers. The notebook we passed between us with confessions about our crushes, dreaming of our futures. First drinks. Double dates. Whispered plans to attend the same college, to be roommates in the dorms.

The knife slips and I clench it tighter, drawing the point into his skin. He cries out as blood beads at the site, swelling into a fat droplet before rolling down his neck. I don't recognize myself, but I have no choice. Everything depends on finding her.

"Where did she work?" I ask.

"It's been years since—"

"Where?" I interrupt.

"Mostly at bars—she had jobs six, sometimes seven days a week, on and off." He motions down the darkened alley, toward the street. "She's worked at most of these places."

I'm focused on my next question, calculating how to unlock a memory from this man that will lead me to Mara when he grips my wrist and twists toward me, bending my arm until I cry out and release the weapon. He snatches it off the ground and wields it like an expert.

"You want to know about Mara Vannatta? She's a user. She used me like she used everyone." He talks so fast I can barely keep track of his words. The knife hovers in my face as he fires anger like darts. That blade makes it impossible to focus, to hear his words.

"Whatever she took, you're not getting it back." Spittle sprays from his lips and strikes my cheek. Lunging, he shoves me with his free hand, and I land hard on my tailbone. I expect him to turn away, but instead he swings around, swiping the blade at my chest, so close that I lurch backward and slam into the dumpster. He grabs a fistful of my hair and throws me down on the eroded asphalt, pebbles shredding my hands and knees. The impact expels the air from my lungs, and I struggle to inhale.

"Come to my club and fucking threaten me," he sneers and kicks hard into my ribs. "Get the fuck out of here."

Curled on my side, I wait for the next blow.

It doesn't come.

Something clatters to the ground, and I spot the discarded knife as the man slips back into the club.

A line of scalding heat burns across my chest, my own panic alongside something else. Still lying on the asphalt, I finger the damp fabric of my shirt, a tacky sensation. Blood. The knife sliced the skin. Tenderly, I tug the neckline away to see how much blood has soaked into the fabric.

I stretch to reach the knife, the motion sending a lancing pain where his shoe connected with my ribs. With shallow breaths, I wipe the knife clean on my jeans and press the lever along its ridge to close the blade. I will have to learn to be better with it. Or get another weapon.

I am going to find Mara Vannatta if it kills me.

I touch the bloody cotton of my shirt and wonder if it might.

# CHAPTER

# 1

16 days before due date

THAT FIRST STEP is like entering an airport hangar, a line of plane engines roaring in my ears. I have to remind myself that it's just a baby store. Albeit a giant one.

I'm stopped, mouth agape at the oceanic expanse of baby supplies while people stroll past as though we're in a Target. But the reality of a baby—my baby—has me paralyzed and stunned to silence.

How long I've wanted this. How many times I've tried to be a mother and failed.

And now it's happening. Because of Mara.

And then she is beside me, parking a cart in front of us. "We could start with bottles."

"Bottles?"

She bumps my hip with hers. "You know, be like Tim Palmer and check out all the different nipple shapes," she says, referring to a boob-obsessed middle school classmate.

How she ever remembered his name is beyond me, and I can't help but laugh as she lets out a sigh.

"This place is huge."

"Massive," I agree. And a little scary. I meet the blue-button stares of two dozen teddy bears on a shelf, all of them peering at me in a way that suggests I'm ill-prepared to be a mother. They're not wrong.

I've never been pregnant longer than eleven weeks, never changed a diaper, never so much as held an infant—yet in two weeks' time, I will be a mother. A single mother, the *single* twitching in my spine with the shame of a teen pregnancy, though I am thirty-five. Instead, it's my best friend who carries my baby, stepping in when my body has failed what, to me at least, is its most crucial biological task.

Mara edges the shopping cart forward, the bulge of her pregnant belly—of my child—almost touching the handle. "You drive," she says, motioning to the cart.

I look around for something smaller, like a basket. The cart feels overwhelming. "Didn't you say all we need is a couple of outfits and some diapers?"

Mara laughs and links her arm through mine, shaking her head as though I'm making a joke. But the laid-back reaction punctures the swell of my worry, deflating it, if only temporarily. I won't be alone, Mara's presence reminds me. Mara has no plans to move out in the next few months, and even when she does, she'll still be in Denver.

And there's Henry . . . but my marriage is more complicated.

Mara has been urging me to come here, pick out onesies and bottles and pacifiers, but the experience of losing my every pregnancy sprouted a paralyzing fear that it would happen to Mara, too. Six times I allowed hope to plant its promise and grow, believing that I was on the path to motherhood. Six times, hope died—miscarriage, IVF procedures that didn't take, a surrogate who changed her mind.

Even seeing Mara every day since her procedure, being in the bathroom (facing the wall in terror) when she peed on the first stick, attending every appointment, still I can't uproot the worry that something will go wrong and we'll lose the baby. *We.* As if *we* are pregnant. I used to roll my eyes at would-be fathers who talked about a pregnancy in ways that suggested *they*, along with their wives, carried their future child. One in particular, a young lawyer at the firm where I worked in Seattle, prattled on endlessly about how *the pregnancy is giving us a bit of heartburn.* And *our feet are swollen. We've had to get new shoes.* How ridiculous he sounded.

Sixteen days until the baby's due date and I'm finally daring to buy supplies. It isn't that I haven't planned. On the wall of the nursery, which is painted a light mossy green, hangs a three-foot-long needle-point of animals that has taken me months to complete, squinting hunchbacked on the couch with a needle and a dozen colors of thread, trying to follow the pattern to perfection. In the center of the room is a round floral rug, where the baby and I will play. There is a rocking chair where I will hold her and inhale her sweet, milky scent. When she's older, we will stick glow-in-the-dark constellations on her ceiling. A small stack of books lines one shelf with my favorite on top—*Owl Babies*, the first story I remember loving as a child myself, the one I checked out from the kindergarten library and read until its pages frayed. While the little things are ready, I still haven't purchased a car seat to take her home from the hospital.

Every time I imagine the nursery filled with baby toys and clothes and diapers, I remember my brother Simon. I can still smell his room beside mine, fresh paint and wood shavings. The mobile over his crib, painted black and white after my parents researched what would best stimulate his young brain. Even at five years old, I sensed the shift in attention away from me and toward the baby growing inside my mom. Dinner conversations revolved around articles about brain develop-ment in a baby's first year, ways to help a child foster a calm demeanor. Words exchanged over my head but with the occasional glance in my direction, divulging their meaning: The next baby would be superior to their first.

One Saturday, my parents invited me to go to the baby store, and I pictured rows of cribs with babies to choose from. *Go put on your nice clothes*, my mother had said, shooing me up the stairs. I donned my blue holiday dress, the nicest thing I owned, ready to make a good first impression on my baby brother. As I crept down the stairs, I heard my mother's voice.

"He's going to be perfect, Gil."

"He will," my dad agreed. "He'll be everything we wanted, our fresh start."

Every little girl dreams of being someone else—a princess or a rock star, an actress or her favorite teacher—but never was that desire so fierce and unwieldy as the moment I longed to be Simon.

Now, standing under the yellow glare of the big-box-store lights, I can't remember going to the baby store with my parents to shop for Simon. It's possible that I went, but just as likely that I'd broken down and cried, the very thing my parents most despised. A little girl unable to control my emotions, as my parents celebrated a child who would be a better version of me. When my mom went into labor, I stayed with Mrs. Lewis, a stooped, hook-nosed neighbor. The way my dad swung Mom's little gray suitcase, holding her elbow with the other hand, they might have been going on vacation.

My parents returned home a day later. My dad rounded the car, red-eyed and exhausted, and helped my mother onto the curb. Stony-faced and grim, she was tucked under his arm as the two struggled up the walkway, the suitcase like an anvil in his grip. With a firm palm on my shoulder, Mrs. Lewis stopped me from running to them. *You don't mention your brother*, she whispered. *Not ever.*

"Come on, this is going to be fun," Mara says now, giving me another little hip bump.

She leads and I follow, marveling at her determined optimism. In our trio of friends, she'd always been the dreamer, the one who could imagine the best outcome to any situation. With no children of her own, Mara is as clueless about this as I am, but she doesn't seem the least bit nervous.

I work to inject my own thoughts with the same energy by reminding myself how much I've learned as a stepmother—though Henry's boys were eight and ten when we met. We pass a couple in an aisle lined with high chairs and bouncy seats, the man at his wife's side while she asks Siri to recommend the best baby swing. Her husband is focused, his hand protective on her lower back. His gaze radiates reverence, and she glows with an unearthly light. His awe is obvious, the miracle of her body nothing short of magic. I share his awe, though it comes with the bitter aftertaste of envy.

Henry would know what to make of this place, how to navigate it, what to choose. At this moment, he is surely in his office, studying some spreadsheet. I could call; he would come.

My next inhale catches in my throat. I miss my husband.

A matronly woman, wearing slacks and a pink sweater, approaches as I take hold of the cart and inch it forward.

"Welcome to Everything Babies," the woman says. "Are you looking for something in particular?"

"Literally, we're here for everything babies," Mara responds with a chuckle.

My palm grows damp on the cart's plastic handle as I eye the immense store and imagine how many things I need, how much it will all cost. Six months after moving out, Henry still pays the bills, but I'm not sure how he'll react to purchases made for a child that isn't his. I have my inheritance. My parents were planners, and what they left will tide me over while the baby is little and I figure out what to do next.

"Is this your first?" the woman asks.

Can she tell I'm unprepared? I have no idea how to answer the simple question. *Yes, Mara and I were best friends in high school and she's agreed to carry the baby because I can't, but it isn't actually my husband's sperm because he has two grown boys and didn't want more kids.* The only people who know the situation in its entirety are me, Mara, Henry, and the doctor who implanted the sperm bank–fertilized eggs.

"It is," Mara says, grinning as she leans over to kiss my cheek. "This is our first baby."

Mara has always had a mischievous side, saying things for shock value or as a joke to laugh about later. "We met in high school, if you can believe it," she goes on, tucking a loose strand of hair behind my ear. "It was love at first sight."

I smile and shake my head at the antics. There's no stopping her; it's best to play along.

The woman claps her hands and grips them together as though in prayer. "Wonderful. And do you know what you're having?"

"A girl," Mara exclaims.

"You absolutely are," the woman says. "Look how high you're carrying. I know the first can be quite overwhelming—by the second, you'll be an old pro." She touches Mara's arm and adds, with a wink: "I've got four." Then, as though to banish the thought she has just planted, she waves a hand in the air and laughs. "No need to get ahead of ourselves," she continues, walking to the first checkout lane. "We have a starter list; it can be helpful to see the basics written out."

The woman ducks behind a register and returns with a trifold pamphlet in a cheery, gender-neutral yellow.

"First up, cribs. A lot of people start with something like this," she says, leading us to the aisle where a dozen cribs are set up and pausing at a blue net playpen. "This has a bassinet feature," she explains, stooping down to lift the base of the crib and clicking it in place below the top rail. "You can use it by the bed when the baby is brand-new and then, as she grows, it's a travel crib and a playpen." She waves with a flourish, like a magician completing a trick. "I'll leave you to it. Just holler if you need help."

Mara reaches out a hand as the saleswoman steps away. "Give me your phone."

"Who are you calling?" I ask.

"I'm taking your picture, Lexi. Stand next to it. Or better, pretend you're putting Goose down."

"Don't let people hear you calling the baby Goose," I whisper. "They'll think we're nuts."

"Come on," she says. "It's a cute nickname." She waves her hands at her massive bulge. "Here I am, the Goose Oven, at your service."

"I think I prefer Mother Goose," I say.

"I still like the original—Womb Auntie—though I'm happy to call her by her real name if you'd tell me what that is," Mara says, hiking up her eyebrows.

"I don't know her name yet," I insist. It's partially true. My parents called my brother Simon from the moment they knew he was a boy. Maybe it's superstitious, but I won't call my baby by her name until she's safely in this world. "I don't need a picture with a playpen."

"You don't have to post it. Save it for her baby book; it's a memory!"

I stand with one hand on the playpen and offer a barely tolerant smile. Mara isn't on social media, one of the things she abandoned when she left her abusive husband back in Philadelphia. From the moment she showed up on my front porch fifteen months ago, Mara has been vigilant about keeping her name and location out of the public domain. Even more so since the pregnancy. She rarely speaks about her marriage anymore, but whatever inconveniences she's suffered from staying off social media are surely a small price to pay for her safety.

Henry was hesitant to welcome her into our home; after all, she was a stranger to him. Though I'd told him about Mara, I rarely talked about high school, the period before I left home for Seattle. How to even explain the bizarre bond between teenage girls, the inseparability of me and Mara and Cate all those years ago. In the most general terms, Henry knew that I'd had two best friends in high school, and that Mara needed help.

His boys were grown, and the furnished coach house in the back sat empty. In a rare moment of persistence, I pushed and Henry conceded.

"This thing is a great idea," Mara tells me. "It's a playpen, a crib, and a changing table all in one, and it's a hundred bucks." She points to a beautiful wooden crib a few feet away. "That one is twelve hundred."

Reading my expression, she drapes an arm over my shoulder. "Goose doesn't need much. It's not like our mothers had all this stuff. Can you imagine? I probably slept on the floor for the first three years. I can't remember even seeing a picture of a crib."

"I'm sure you had one," I say, recalling a single photograph of me in a crib, my hands clenched on the top rail, my face crumpled. I was crying. *You cried all the time*, my mother once said when she found me looking at the few pictures she'd put in an album.

Mara and I load the Pack 'n Play box onto the cart, and the squeaking wheels take me back to high school trips to Walmart, where the three of us spent hours in the aisles horsing around, sharing a soft-serve ice cream or french fries, the store preferable to any of our houses. Hers, small and crowded when her parents were fighting, which was often; mine, cavernous and dismal; and Cate never wanted to be at her house, blaming it mostly on her younger twin sisters.

"Crib, check," Mara says, leaning across the handle of the cart to run her finger down the list. "Next is a car seat, then we definitely need one of those front pack things, so you can carry her around and still have your hands free."

Mara, rubbing her belly, admires a pink car seat with a leopard-print cover.

"Navy," I say, fighting the flare of envy as she strokes her baby bump. Ashamed of my reaction, I lift the navy car seat, averting my gaze. "It's much more practical."

"Screw practical," Mara says. "You're having a sweet baby girl. Let's spoil her." As I push the stroller down the aisle, Mara picks up a small stuffed tiger on a plastic clip and attaches it to the handle of the car seat. "From me," she says, and I know we're both thinking of Cate.

I sense Mara is about to say something when a little girl with blond curls runs up to the leopard-print car seat on display. "Mom, can we get this one? Please."

"We already have a car seat for the baby, Elsie, remember? It's the same one that you used," her mother says, taking her hand. "Come on."

As I watch her go, I imagine Goose as a toddler, chubby hand in mine as little feet stumble awkwardly across a floor in her new Mary Janes. Then, as a three- or four-year-old, tongue held between her teeth, as she focuses on putting a wooden puzzle piece in place. Five years old, gripping my hand tightly, tears brimming in big brown eyes, on the first day of school.

There is so much unknown ahead, and so much to look forward to.

# CHAPTER

# 2

OUTSIDE THE BEDROOM, the ink ebbs from the sky, a bright magenta. Never a particularly sound sleeper, I wake four or five times a night now, flipping from one side to the other, swapping out pillows, unable to get comfortable—as though *I* am the pregnant one.

From the day we got word of Mara's pregnancy, the joy of this dream coming true has been shadowed by a shame that cloaks me like a second skin. When I was so fixated on finding a way to *have* a baby, I didn't allow myself to dwell on my own body's failure. But now, watching Mara's belly grow is a constant reminder of my defect. There is guilt, too—that I asked so much of my friend, fear that it was my desperation that made her agree to be my surrogate. If she resents me for it.

In recent months, the preoccupation around the pregnancy itself has absorbed the guilt; jealousy is a frequent visitor. But the shame never leaves. Shame that I couldn't get pregnant, but also shame for how I feel now: that I am not simply flooded with gratitude both for Mara's ability and her willingness to do this for me. Shame for feeling shame, like Russian dolls, each nesting an emotion uglier than the last.

With Henry gone, the house is quiet and I often wake to the

haunting silence of the bedroom. The absence of his purring snore, the white noise he plays at night. When I can't sleep, I watch videos of labor and birth on YouTube. First, the natural births—in homes, in baths, in the forest. Women split open with pain one moment, joyfully cradling an infant the next. Then, the hospital videos.

One night, I searched for cesarean sections and held my breath as the surgeon made her initial incision across the pinkish globe of the woman's belly, the skin stained yellow from antiseptic. I studied the path of the scalpel as it sliced, cutting deeper. The doctor lifted a small power tool that began to whir, tiny wisps of smoke rising from its tip. I reversed the video and rewatched as the tool cauterized the small vessels bleeding along the line of the incision. I was mesmerized by the surgery, the calm efficiency with which the doctor worked, how the team answered her curt directives, an artful choreography. I cried as the nurses used retractors to hold open the uterus and the doctor pulled the baby's head free, her movements strong and assured.

This fascination is not something I share with Mara. Nor do I tell her that, alone in my bedroom, I sometimes talk to Goose as though she can hear me—as though Goose's soul is residing within me, even if her body is not. I make promises. I promise that I will be strong so she can fall apart when she needs to. And I promise to be better, to practice my mantras and calm my brain, so that my child can see what it means to overcome.

I shift in the bed to look at the clock where the numbers bleed a fuzzy blue. Seven twenty-nine. We have an ultrasound today, where we will get to hear Goose's rapid little mouse heartbeat, count her fingers and toes. *Almost fully baked*, the doctor told us last time.

Our appointment isn't until nine, but I can't go back to sleep, so I decide to surprise Mara with some grapefruit juice, her favorite, and a scone. There are still a few left over from the low-sugar batch I made over the weekend.

In the kitchen, I start the coffee maker, thinking of how Henry would wake first and bring a cup of coffee to me in bed. He always predicted what I would like most off a restaurant menu. He supported us wholly, happy for me to work at the flower shop because I enjoyed it, despite the abysmal pay. *We have plenty of money*, he always said.

All things I took for granted.

At twenty-four to Henry's thirty-eight, I entered our relationship an anxious, overgrown adolescent, a half step beyond the panic-ridden child I'd once been. Henry's confidence, his utter calm, made the transition easy. He was safe, protective. The introduction to his kids, the way he coordinated the move of my things from Seattle to Denver upon our engagement—everything was designed to make my life stress-free. Like a new book on a shelf, Henry slid me into his life. After all, he had the career, the house, the kids. All I had was a secretarial job, working for a lawyer who had a temper that was his least likable quality aside from his wretched breath, and a tiny studio apartment I could hardly afford with mold that crawled along the baseboard like a slow-moving infestation.

Arriving in Denver, I was happy to assimilate into Henry's life. Most of our friends are closer to Henry's age than mine. The couples we socialize with had their children young, and the kids—theirs and Henry's—were way past the diaper stage when I arrived. There were no baby showers to attend, no infants to hold. I said I didn't need children; Henry's were enough.

And they were. Until they weren't.

When I first brought up my desire to have a baby—almost five years ago now—Henry told me that he didn't want more children. Kyle and Nolan were his life. I understood. At the same time, I hoped—even expected—that he would change his mind. That loving me would mean being open to what *I* wanted, to sharing the experience of adding to the beautiful family we had with his sons.

I was wrong.

But Goose will be my future now. She will be Olivia or Emma, Oliver or Thomas (I can't help but prepare for the possibility of a boy, despite the doctor's confirmation of her gender). A nickname is one thing, but choosing Goose's permanent name is something I don't want to share with Mara. I've already been forced to share so much.

As the coffee brews, I pour the juice and heat a scone in the toaster oven, cutting it open and placing a thin pat of butter on the steaming pastry before carrying the plate out to the backyard. Down the stone path to the back of the property, the coach house is dark. Maybe Mara had trouble sleeping, too. She experienced a fair amount of nausea early on in the pregnancy, but things seemed easier after the first trimester. While she doesn't complain about aches or pains, she must feel them. Even as a kid, Mara slept like the dead, but I can tell she hasn't been sleeping well. Especially this last week. When I ask about it, she swears she's fine, but there are dark circles under her eyes, and she lies down to nap every afternoon.

The coach house door is unlocked, which is strange. When Mara moved in, we installed an interior latch so that even with a key, no one could enter. Our neighborhood is safe, but after what she'd been through, it was no surprise that she'd want extra security. She must have forgotten to lock up last night. Balancing the plate and glass in one hand, I enter the darkened living room. An undercounter light in the kitchen flashes on and off, reminding me of the electric fly traps Mara's dad used to hang in their yard. The little flash and zap as a fly struck the live wire.

"Mara?"

No answer.

Leaving the food on the counter, I go to her bedroom and listen at the door. It's silent and I imagine her sound asleep, splayed across the bed like a starfish, the same way she's slept since we were kids. There's no good reason to wake her so early, so I let myself out and return to my own kitchen where I pour coffee into an Oberlin mug, the crest of Nolan's alma mater faded from too many washings. The mug is Henry's favorite, a Christmas gift from Nolan five years ago when he came home from his first semester, and holding it makes me feel a little closer to my husband. Now graduated and working in Chicago, Nolan is in town for a week of vacation. The three of us had lunch together over the weekend, then he and Henry came for dinner last night. I was strangely nervous about having my stepson for dinner in his own home while his dad is living in a corporate apartment, so I made Nolan's favorite, a chicken cacciatore, and Mara baked a raspberry crisp.

In the end, the evening was lovely. Nolan asked about the baby and entertained us with stories of spending his days standing in pouring rain on his latest engineering project and the highlights of a corporate outing to a Bulls game. Henry and I mostly stayed quiet at dinner, but he helped me clear the table and, as I was standing at the sink, he leaned in behind me, the way he used to. "I miss you," he said and kissed my cheek, then turned and left before I could respond.

When I returned to the living room, Nolan was seated beside Mara, his palm on the flat of her pregnant belly, his head dipped close. A moment later, he jumped. "Wow, I totally felt her! That's crazy."

Mara laughed like it was a party trick, and from the ottoman across the table, Henry leaned in as though he would have liked to feel the baby, too. Mara caught it. "Henry?"

But he shook his head. "I'm good." He stood, and Nolan gave Mara a hug, following his dad into the entryway. "I can't wait to meet her," Nolan said, embracing me. "Dad said he'll get me a ticket to come home once she's here and settled in."

Henry's gaze flicked to mine with a flash of uncertainty, but I nodded. "Of course. You have to come. Kyle, too."

Nolan released me, and Henry gave me a one-armed hug like I was an old friend, but before he left he grabbed my hand and held it an extra beat.

As the sky outside grows bright, I top off my coffee and settle onto the couch, pushing thoughts of Henry from my mind. Book in my lap, I read a few pages, grateful for the escape as I keep one eye on the clock. Mara is almost always awake by seven thirty, so when the clock shows eight fifteen, I go to check on her.

The north-facing coach house remains dark.

Her bedroom is still quiet, so I give a perfunctory knock before letting myself in. The bed is unmade. Empty.

"Mara?"

The coach house is only one bedroom and bath plus a living/dining area and a small laundry room, so it takes no time at all to confirm she's not here. We did talk about the doctor's appointment last night, but it's possible she forgot. She's been complaining about pregnancy brain . . . My phone shows no missed calls or texts, so I dial Mara and listen as it rings once and goes straight to voicemail.

The doctor's office is only a ten-minute drive away, so technically we still have time. I return to the house and pour a fresh cup of coffee, but I can't focus, and the bitter smell is nauseating.

I check my phone again, dial Mara's number even though it's only been a few minutes. Again, voicemail. It strikes me that the message is not Mara's voice but the generic computerized one. The sound of the automated message makes me cold. Unnerved, I walk back to the guest house and enter Mara's room. The first thing I notice is a black cord dangling from an outlet behind the bedside table.

On my knees, I tug it free from the wall and stare at the unfamiliar metal tip, an adapter for something I can't identify. I look around the room, scanning for some other electronic device this cord might charge, but all I can think is that it's for another phone.

But that's impossible.

Mara told me that Lance, her ex-husband, had been known to track her, showing up when she least expected him or interrogating her about the places she'd gone. To protect herself, Mara had disposed of her cell phone when she left Philadelphia. I'd given her an old iPhone of mine, and we set her up with a new number in my name.

The charger must be for something else, but the cord has set off a spark, and I'm bombarded by tiny explosions of fear. Looking around again, the space seems so wrong. So un-Mara.

Over the months Mara has lived here, I've come to think of the coach house as hers, and while she added some personal touches to the main room, the bedroom is unchanged. The same beige damask duvet cover with matching shams, the same throw pillows—one with a needle-point pheasant, one a mallard.

I retrieve the juice and scone I left earlier and am turning to leave when I notice that the framed photograph on the side table, the one of Mara and Cate and me, is lying face down. The photograph was one of the few things Mara brought with her, the frame something she picked up at a flea market one weekend. Even without seeing the sun-faded image, I can picture our grins, recall the day with surprising clarity—

the three of us arm in arm in arm at the homecoming football game our junior year. I have long since gotten rid of anything from that time. For months after Mara's arrival, the sight of this photograph, framed on the table, was like catching tender skin against rough wood. It left little splinters.

Now that Mara is back in my life, Cate's death feels closer, too. The memory of that night in my parents' kitchen brushes my skin, like walking through strands of spider silk. The solid surface of the dining chair, legs folded beneath me, a cloth napkin under my ankle to pad the bone from the hard wood. The table a little too high to work at comfortably, I sat hunched over a handwritten draft of my senior paper for AP History. I had a desk in my room, but some nights I worked in the kitchen while Mom was doing dishes just for the sound of someone else's presence. Our phone rarely rang and, when it did, my parents acted like it was an unnecessary interruption. Mom's face had tightened into a series of lines as she listened to the caller—her brow and lips horizontal, eyes narrowed, the three lines between them straight as soldiers. Then she pivoted toward me, the receiver hanging off her hand like she considered throwing it in the trash.

"It's for you, Lexi. Mara is hysterical. I can't understand a word she is saying."

I grabbed the receiver. "Hello?"

"Lexi," Mara had sobbed. "It's Cate. Cate is dead."

Unable to speak, I'd turned for my mother, but she was gone. I was alone in the kitchen.

"How?" It came out as a wail.

I sank onto the kitchen floor and lowered my head onto bent knees. An image of the Vannattas' hot tub, usually filled with Caleb and his rowdy buddies, flashed in my head as Mara described finding Cate, the stain of blood on the fiberglass where our best friend had slipped and hit her head, the waxy texture of her skin as Mara dragged her out of the water. When she hung up, I was paralyzed on the linoleum floor, fighting to stave off a panic attack by focusing on the items that surrounded me—my parents' wineglasses, spotless and drying upside down beside the sink. The coffee maker put away for the night, the tiled counter immaculate. A single magnet in the shape of a flower—a gift I'd given my mother for her last birthday—stuck to the corner of the refrigerator. I'd imagined she might use it to pin up a picture of me, but the only thing I'd seen hung there was a grocery list.

Collapsed on the floor of my parents' sterile kitchen, I clawed at my T-shirt and surrendered to the panic rolling over me. I had never felt so alone.

Mara and I handled the loss of Cate very differently—while she celebrated her, kept her out in the open, I hid her away. There are so many things that Mara and I handle differently. Her optimism, her confidence. Even after what she went through in her marriage, Mara has remained steady, a beacon.

As I set the photograph upright, the back falls open, exposing the cardstock behind the photo. There's a dent in the paper, as though something was pressed into it. When I remove the picture to take a closer look, something else falls free. A folded piece of newspaper. The paper trembles as I unfold the brittle yellow page, but I already know what it is.

The article from the Cleveland paper, about Cate's accident. I have read these words so many times, I used to dream them at night, my imagination creating a vivid picture of Cate floating, lifeless in crimson-tinged water.

I refold the paper and study the imprint in the frame's cardboard, recognizing the jagged teeth of a key.

I remember the day Mara bought the frame, just a week or two after her arrival. I can't imagine why she's kept a key hidden here, what it unlocks.

I also can't imagine why it's missing.

# CHAPTER

## 3

*February 2008*

The excitement that vibrates through Cate makes her feel drunk,
even though she's only had a single sip from the box of Franzia
white zinfandel Mara swiped from the refrigerator. The tart aftertaste
that tingles on Cate's tongue adds to the sensation that she's stepping
out of childhood, that this night marks a beginning. She's been here
when Mara's hot older brother, Caleb, has thrown parties, but those
nights the girls stayed up in Mara's room, sneaking out for an occasional
peek at what the older kids were doing. And the three of them have
gotten tipsy a few times, either hanging out in the Vannattas' hot tub on
Friday nights or at Lexi's, but going to Seth Wilson's house will be her
first official high school party. Giddy and triumphant, Cate feels like she
could punch through a brick wall. She doesn't say any of this out loud,
just enjoys the way freedom heats her chest and hums, electric in her
limbs so she can remember it the next time she's stuck at home, being
lectured by her mother about what God expects of her.

The three of them—Cate, Lexi, and Mara—are most often together
at Mara's house since her parents are hardly ever around; although even
if they are, they're usually fighting too much to notice what the girls are
up to. Rather, her mother is yelling at her father and he's drinking beer

to ignore her. Lexi's house is nicer, but if her parents are home, any sound they make feels like talking during church. And Cate's own house is an actual nunnery because, at her age, her mother was going to be a nun. So now it's like she expects Cate to act like a nun, too. That and her twin sisters are totally annoying.

Cate's mother has no idea what it's like to be a regular teenager, and she's dead set against her daughter having normal teenage experiences. Which is why Cate comes here as often as she can get away. Mara's house is basically a free-for-all, and while it's much smaller than Cate's or Lexi's, there's nowhere Cate would rather be.

Mara is the coolest of their trio, maybe even the only cool one, but there is an awkwardness to Mara, too. Her aversion to being alone, her desire for little hits of physical contact. The way she is constantly bumping up against them, linking arms in the hallway, offering to paint their nails and do their makeup, as though those tiny moments of touch prevent some deep starvation she would otherwise suffer.

Oddly, Mara is not a hugger. Lexi is the one always embracing Cate and Mara when they leave. Though Cate and Mara are her closest friends, Lexi spends more time at school than either Cate or Mara, so she seems to know more people. Cate's surprised at how many random students greet Lexi in the halls and also a little surprised at the awkward way Lexi raises a hand and mumbles hello in response. Like looking at them directly might make her melt. Lexi's not like that when it's just the three of them. Mara once asked Lexi how she knew so many people, and Lexi made some joke that it was because her mother always forgot to pick her up, so she ended up spending most afternoons stuck on campus with one club or another. They all knew it wasn't really a joke.

Lexi's wide exposure to other kids makes her the reporter on school gossip. Without siblings or family aside from her parents, Lexi is also the most invested in the group. The notebook was her idea—and by Thursday, she's the one planning out their weekends. When Cate considers her own role in their trio, she feels like the tether. She keeps them connected—by her own need for them as much as anything. She also provides the sobering reminder of the tenuousness of their freedom. Her fear of getting stuck in Cleveland, in Ohio, in the life to which her own mother is bound—by marriage, by religion—propels her forward, so she's the constant nudge toward graduation and a future unleashed from their pasts.

By some unspoken agreement, Mara is leader of their little tribe. Cate suspects it's because of Caleb—Lexi is an only child and Cate only has the twins. Having an older brother offers unique access— primarily to other boys. From the time they were freshmen, Caleb's friends had acknowledged them in a way that other older boys hadn't. Plus, the boys' occasional banter about girls contained precious intel on how to act—or, more often, how not to. Caleb and his friends even provided a layer of protection against assholes. Cate and Lexi are happy to let Mara lead the group—after all, it's Mara who gets them invited places—like tonight's party, hosted by a college freshman.

Mara's brother is also around, keeping an eye on them and driving his mother nuts. She yells at Caleb almost as much as Mara's dad, but Caleb turns on the charm and his mom can't stay mad. It's kind of sweet how easily he calms her down. All the way through high school, he was always dating one of the senior cheerleaders. Now that he's at a local college, living at home to save money, Mara says it's an endless stream of sorority girls.

Lexi sits on Mara's bed, a nest of purple pillows surrounding her as she reads their shared notebook, the one that says *Physics* in Sharpie in Lexi's clean black handwriting, the one they all write in and exchange between them. This is their fourth notebook, the others burned in a silly ritual performed in a rarely used firepit in Lexi's backyard. Each one is labeled with that year's science course as a ruse, and it works— not once has a teacher confiscated the notebook. Hell, teachers don't even give it a second look. Instead, the girls are praised for their rapt attention in class, which provides endless entertainment afterward.

"Try this one," Mara calls from the closet where she's stooped over a pile of clothes before tossing something lacy and red in her direction.

Cate turns her back to Lexi to remove her T-shirt and pulls on the red camisole.

"What does this say?" Lexi reads aloud, "'Michael M. sat on the bleachers in those stupid jean shorts that cut so high they showed his—'"

"Ball sack," Mara said.

"Gross," Lexi says, her cheeks flushing in the way Cate knows she can't stand.

"It was," Cate adds. The note is hers. Lexi is always trying to sort out her handwriting, which she thinks is plenty legible but obviously not to Lexi. Lexi's own writing is neat and square, naturally, and Mara has a preference for colored ink, her writing unexpectedly round and girly, and she takes her time with every word as though the point isn't just what she says but how it looks.

Cate glances over her shoulder to see that Lexi is absorbed in the gossip about Michael M. Lexi had a crush on him last year and Cate wonders if she still does. She's barely turned around when Lexi says, "No way." Cate assumes she's talking about the lacy top, but when she glances back, Lexi is still reading. "Rachel and Tyler? What is she thinking? He's such a douche."

Cate feels a ripple of pleasure as she faces herself in the mirror; her long arms are pale, and she wishes she'd thought to sneak on some self-tanner. The last time she did, she'd ended up with weird streaks on her wrists and her mother threw a fit when she saw them while Cate was in her soccer jersey. But if she's honest, the pale skin of her chest and midsection that shows through the fabric doesn't look awful. With her eyes squinted a little, she's almost sexy.

She doesn't have the guts to wear it, but she gives the top an extra look in the mirror, imagining how it would feel to walk into the party in this. Until she spots her plain white cotton bra—the only kind her mother will buy—underneath. Like a kid playing dress-up.

Isn't that basically what this is? Half the reason she's excited about tonight is to wake up tomorrow morning, knowing she'd done something bold. Risky.

Mara pokes her head out of the closet, a black top in her fist. "You need a different bra," she says. "Get a black one from my drawer and try this," she adds, tossing over another shirt.

Lexi is watching her, but Cate doesn't look.

Mara emerges from the closet and lifts the box of wine to her lips, taking a long swallow. She offers it to Cate. "I just had some," she says, and Mara shrugs and puts it back on the dresser. The trio first drank from one of Mrs. Vannatta's wine boxes in the eighth grade, all three of them puking long before the adults came home from their party. Only Mara seems to have put the memory solidly in the past. Cate still shivers a little at the smell of wine and, when Lexi drinks, she looks like she's holding her breath.

Mara hands her the black bra, and Cate strips down again to put it on. The bra is padded and the cups are too big for Cate, no surprise since Mara has the best boobs of the three. Before Cate can remove it, Mara adjusts the straps and motions to the black top, which Cate puts on. Long-sleeved with a rounded neckline that dips to reveal a hint of cleavage, it actually looks pretty good.

"That's perfect," Mara announces just as Lexi says, "Ugh, I can't believe I can't come."

In a rare turn of events, Lexi has to go out with her parents for dinner, so for once it'll be Cate who gets Mara to herself. Cate turns to Lexi, who nods at the top, one brow raised. "You look hot."

Cate grins. "I do, don't I?"

"Our little Kitty Cat becomes a tiger," Mara pipes in.

Lexi lifts a pen and starts writing in the notebook, reading aloud as she goes. "Cate and Mara are going to kill it tonight. Jason J. will be there. Pray for that tight white tee. And Kyle, Tanner, Wyatt . . . I am totes jealous. Meanwhile, Lexi will be eating overcooked prime rib and listening to old people discuss the importance of compounding annual interest. If she gets any action, it'll be a slobbery cheek kiss from her dad's best client, Filthy Phil."

Cate groans.

"That sucks," Mara said. "If Filthy Phil comes for you, accidentally knock him in the nuts."

Lexi's laugh is awkward, and Cate knows her friend is miserable to be missing the party. Still, she keeps on a brave face as she lowers her head to write again. "Will keep a fork in one hand to aim into Filthy Phil's lap if he gets too close." Her hand continues across the page, and Cate wishes she could come. It's always better when the three of them are together.

It's rare that Lexi's parents insist she join them on a weekend night. In truth, Lexi's parents never seem to care if she's with them. She's lucky that way. But tonight they have a dinner with some of her dad's biggest clients and it's supposed to be a family thing, so Lexi has to be there.

She slaps the notebook closed and drops it on the bed. "I better go," she announces with a groan.

"Bummer," Cate says. "I wish you could come. You could tell them you're sick?"

Lexi shakes her head. "Better to suffer through it and keep them off my ass." She stands from the bed and adjusts the waistband of her jeans, then crosses to Cate and grips her shoulders, making a little delicious sound before giving her a hug. "Be careful tonight," she says, then raises an eyebrow. "Tiger."

Cate laughs, but she catches her reflection in the mirror. She could be a tiger.

"I want all the details tomorrow," Lexi adds, lifting her bag from the bed.

"Pinky swear," Cate says.

Lexi only nods, and Cate knows what she's feeling exactly. Usually, she's the one stuck at home when Lexi and Mara have Saturday night sleepovers. "Not on a church night," her mother says, as though God cares how much she's slept the night before service.

Even Cate's dad seems to think the rule is dumb, but he doesn't argue with her mom. Certainly not about church. Cate's mother was a nun—well, she was becoming a nun when Cate's dad met her and supposedly fell in love at first sight and then wooed her away from her faith, like the plot of a Brontë novel.

The saving grace is that her mother likes Mara. Maybe it's because Mara acts like she has nothing to hide, like she's the most honest, upstanding seventeen-year-old around. Not prim and proper, but responsible and conscientious. Or maybe it's because Mara doesn't look like the kind of girl to go to a party in a skimpy top. More like she'd hang out in sweats and watch a game.

Take this morning, for example. Her parents had gone out to look for a new dining room table, and Mara came over to keep Cate company, babysitting the twins. She was like a wizard, the way she lured Cate's mom in—not overselling it, inquiring about the shopping trip, acting like a new dining room table was a total thrill. Then, at just the right moment, Mara slipped in the request. "Please, Mrs. Murphy, can Cate spend the night? I got this really cool nail polish set for Christmas. It's all these light pinks and there are stickers you can put on. I'm dying to do pedicures and watch a movie. We're trying to decide between *Aladdin* or *Mulan*. Cate says she's never seen either."

Cate almost laughed, it was so obvious, but her mom bought it. Mara always knows exactly what to say to Cate's mother. The nails, for instance: Cate's mother does not approve of makeup or showing skin. Sometimes Cate suspects her parents have had sex twice—once for her and once for the twins. But nails are her mother's secret treat. Only pedicures and only in shades of pinks, because God forbid a grown woman have red fingernails; that was for prostitutes.

"Toes only," Cate's mom said.

"Oh, yeah. I never do my fingers," Mara agreed.

Once Lexi leaves, Mara puts on "Low" by Flo Rida and turns it up, taking another glug of wine before passing the box to Cate.

"Sit in front of the mirror and I'll do your makeup," Mara directs.

Cate grabs the notebook and sits, holding the wine in her lap, and savors that rush of freedom. She's seventeen years old and her life is finally starting.

As Mara lays out eyeshadow and blush and lipstick on the carpet, Cate reads what Lexi has written. About a fight between a popular couple in the hallway after school and a list of the boys she deems kissable—Lexi counts twelve boys, including four juniors and a sophomore. "Who's Trent Farrell?"

Mara looks over her shoulder and laughs. "New point guard on the basketball team. Total stud."

Lexi signs off, *Let's go, girls. Make it epic.*

# CHAPTER

# 4

A BREEZE CATCHES the door of the coach house and slams it shut, making me jump. The tapestry on the wall flutters as I return to the photograph, fingering the impression of the key again. Why would Mara feel the need to hide a key? What is it for—and why is it gone?

Gone. The word catches, sharp in my throat. Mara's not gone; she forgot our appointment and went out. She's on an errand, maybe. She probably took my car—

My car. I leave the apartment for the main house, breathless by the time I reach the kitchen and yank open the garage door so hard it slams into the wall of the laundry room. A desperate sound rips from my throat when I see my car parked in its normal spot. The hood is cool to the touch; wherever Mara went, she did it on foot.

*Stop.*

Any minute now, she'll walk in, hand on hip, joking about how her brain has stopped working with the pregnancy. These days a mile or two is about as far as she gets on foot, and it's too early for the library, but she may just be around the neighborhood. I take a sip of coffee in an effort to keep calm but set down the mug, my stomach too unsettled for more caffeine.

Mara, of all people, knows how I worry. We've talked about the idea that Lance is out there somewhere, possibly still looking for her, and this far into the pregnancy, she would never leave without letting me know. It feels like I've missed something, a note or a message. I check the living room, the kitchen, my bedroom and bath, get on hands and knees to see if something slid under the oven. Nothing.

I return to the coach house and scan the surfaces there. No note in the kitchen or dining room, under the furniture or the appliances. I pull myself off the linoleum floor and try to shake off the worry. There's a reasonable explanation. *Leave it to you to turn a gust of wind into a hurricane, Alexandra,* my mother used to say.

The coach house is only seven hundred square feet. In a couple of minutes, I have searched every possible place for a note and found nothing.

I could call the police, but surely, they'd laugh at me. It's barely eight thirty in the morning, and if Mara is actually missing, she's been missing at most for twelve hours. She isn't *gone* gone. Still, I've checked everywhere: the yard, both houses, the garage. She'll be back any minute now. Unless she went to our doctor's appointment early. Maybe she had labor pains and got worried, took a cab to the doctor's office? But surely she'd wake me if something was going on with Goose.

I cross the cold stone of the backyard and stand in my kitchen as I call the doctor's office.

"Dr. Lanier's office."

"Hi, I have an appointment at nine a.m. under the name Mara Vannatta. I was wondering if she's shown up yet?"

There is a pause. "If who has shown up?"

"Mara Vannatta."

"I thought you were Mara Vannatta."

How many times these past months have I wished to be Mara? Not just for her ability to carry a child but for her resilience, her calm, her humor. For her ability to put the past behind her, while I remain fettered by the childhood emotions—fear, shame, anger—that have kept me chained for as long as I can remember.

"Ma'am?"

"I'm the biological mom, Alexandra McNeil," I explain. "Mara is my surrogate."

Another pause, dead air.

"No one has arrived for that appointment yet."

The soft skin of hope is punctured, releasing disappointment into the air like a noxious cloud.

"Do you need to reschedule?" she asks, clipped.

As I fight to resuscitate the deflated balloon of hope, I hear the click of my mom's tongue, snapping in disapproval. As though my desire to believe makes me a fool. And maybe it does. But Mara knows we have our last ultrasound today.

"Ma'am?"

"No need to reschedule," I answer. "We'll be there."

The woman ends the call before I can thank her. If Mara isn't at the doctor's, she must be out for a walk. But if we're going to make it to the appointment on time, she should be home by now.

Upstairs, I brush my teeth, yank a comb through my hair before pulling it into a ponytail. I am holding my breath as I cross to the window to peer into the yard, but the coach house still looks empty.

I let myself imagine the places Mara might have gone if she forgot our appointment. She enjoys visiting the Denver Art Museum for their artist lecture series. She walks to the park a few days a week and, until the pregnancy made it tough, she volunteered at the animal shelter. She's come to the floral shop where I work part-time to help when I'm alone. Nothing like when we were in high school, forever attached at the hip. But that was adolescence, when being alone equated to being left out. Solitude feels different as an adult.

One of the most surprising discoveries I had after Henry moved out is how I often feel more at home in his absence. He never gave any impression that this wasn't my house, and I would never have said I felt that way—until the house was mine alone. Before, I gave him my full attention when he arrived home from work. Stepped out of the way if he was hurrying up the stairs. Chose to sit in the center of the couch to be near him when he took his regular seat at the end.

At first it felt foreign, to occupy the corner that had always been his. To lay stretched across the couch where we'd sat side by side. But then it felt good. Decadent. No towels on the bathroom floor, flung in a hurry before work. No subtle frown when I steamed broccoli, or suggested we order takeout on nights I didn't want to cook. I'd never considered these things a nuisance. They were trivial compromises in a happy marriage, but there is something delicious in thinking only of myself, a freedom in disregarding the rules, like eating dessert before dinner. Mara and I live together differently without a sense of marital hierarchy, the wife always a half step lower.

Maybe Mara is just doing her own thing this morning, but this doesn't feel benign the way the museum and the library do. There is something nefarious about the strange black cord and the key hidden behind the photograph, now missing—these facts are burrs in my shoes, digging in, impossible to ignore.

I leave a note on the counter.

*Heading to the appointment. Meet you there? Use Uber if you need, or call me.*

From the hall closet, I grab one of Henry's oversized jackets and pull it on over my clothes, seeking comfort in its bulk and his familiar smell.

On my way to the appointment, I drive past the parks and circle the paths we've walked, stop at the closest coffee shop since the library and the museum aren't open yet. No sign of her.

At the doctor's office, I skip the elevator, trying to burn off the nervous energy by taking the stairs. My shirt is damp under the arms and at the waistband. I can smell my own anxiety. Mara will be sitting in the waiting room, I tell myself; I don't want her to know how scared I was. More than a decade has passed since I've felt this panic—I rarely acknowledge how much I've grown into myself, until everything is yanked away and I'm floating in that same turbulent sea.

Despite my fervent hope, the waiting room is empty.

"Can I help you?" asks the receptionist.

"Yes," I say, breathless. "We have an appointment at nine a.m. with Dr. Lanier."

"Sure," she says. "Let's get you checked in. What is your name?"

"I'm Alexandra McNeil and the appointment is for my surrogate, Mara Vannatta."

"And is Ms. Vannatta here?"

"Not yet," I admit.

"Take a seat. As soon as she arrives, we'll take you back."

I remain at the desk, unmoving for several long seconds, weighing whether to admit that I don't actually know if Mara is coming. There is a compulsion to confess my fear to someone, to seek another woman's opinion. For all these months, I've accepted Mara's help—I've hidden the shame and the anger, too embarrassed to let her witness my ugliness.

But what if she was hiding something, too?

The woman looks up from her computer, and her expectant expression sends me into retreat. In the corner of the waiting room are two seats partially obscured by a large fig tree, and I sit in the farthest chair, hidden from the desk but in view of the entrance.

My phone shows no new messages. From my favorites list, I hit Mara's name, hoping beyond reason that she has returned to the coach house, her phone charged. Again, the line goes straight to voicemail.

To distract myself, I browse email: an ad from the baby store, promotional announcements from our local food cooperative, a reminder from the bank about an upcoming mortgage payment. Not one personal message. My phone used to buzz daily with emails and texts from local friends, ones I'd made in Henry's circle and through the kids, lovely but never particularly intimate. Shared articles or recipes, funny memes.

For the next fifteen minutes, I flip through magazines, pages blurring.

"Excuse me, do you know when Ms. Vannatta will be here?" the receptionist calls over.

The image on the page in front of me snaps into focus—a mother, infant in her arms, her gaze on the baby as a soft smile curves her lips.

"Ma'am?"

"I don't actually know," I admit, holding back the full extent of the situation while she stares at me from behind the desk. I focus on the green tint of her thick frames, avoiding her eyes. "I haven't been able to reach her this morning."

The receptionist's lips part, but she stops herself and says nothing. I hear the words anyway.

*You don't know where your baby is?*

# CHAPTER

# 5

ON THE DRIVE home, I wind slowly through the neighborhood, scanning the streets for Mara. I pass stately homes ranging in style from a sleek modern design with two-story windows to the petite hacienda with its curved tile roof, wisteria climbing the stucco walls. The red buds along the limbs of the Wasatch maples look like dragonfly wings, and on the manicured hedges, green sprouts of new growth stretch like unruly children. The Rockies rise in the distance, snow still capping their peaks. I've always loved spring in Denver, but today my anxiety is a blanket of gray, cold winter.

There is no sign of Mara, but around the corner from the house, I spot someone.

Known as the neighborhood watchdog, Molly Rowe keeps track of every house on the street. I pull over and give her a little wave, which earns me a deep-furrowed frown in response. Though I have spoken to Molly many times in the past decade, she is not an easy person to like. After Henry moved out last September, Molly would hover near the house, asking questions whenever I stepped outside. *Where is Henry? Are you two all right? Is that your sister who's moved in?*

"Hi, Molly," I call through the open window. "I was wondering if you've seen my friend Mara today."

"Mara?" she asks, brows raised and arms crossed.

"The friend who's been staying with me," I clarify, though she knows exactly who Mara is. "She's pregnant."

"Why would I know where she is?" The furrow in her brow carves deeper.

"I just thought you might've seen her. She isn't home and she forgot to take her phone."

Molly's expression shifts, opening in what looks like a flash of glee. As though my desperation thrills her. "Maybe she's out with that man."

A roil of heat in my gut. "Man?"

Her lips twist slightly, in humor or disdain. With Molly, the two seem to be close cousins. "The man who came to your house," she continues. "Sunday, I think it was."

Today is Wednesday. "This past Sunday?"

"Yes. I saw him go inside," she says, as though I've accused her of lying. "If you didn't let him in, Henry must have."

Henry wasn't at the house on Sunday. He was with me and Nolan.

"You're sure it was Sunday?"

"Positive." A Tesla drives past, and from Molly's disgusted expression, the driver might as well be Elon Musk himself.

"And he entered the main house? Or went through the yard toward the coach house?"

"The main house, Alexandra." Molly delivers the words with a sigh. "I can't see through the fence and I'm no peeping Tom. All I know is that a silver car parked in front of your house and a man walked up to the door. Either someone opened the door for him or he just walked in—"

"Did you see what he looked like?" I ask, thinking of Lance, though I realize I don't know what Mara's ex-husband looks like.

"I didn't see much. He was dressed in black, skulking around."

Skulking around? I glance down the block at my house, a relatively modest colonial for the neighborhood. Our subdivision is shaped like four coiled earthworms, their heads pressed together. A trail system runs through, but many of the streets end in cul-de-sacs, making accidental traffic rare. There are only two or three cars on the curb now. Most are parked in garages or circular drives in front of the larger homes.

"In the middle of the day on Sunday?" That was three days ago.

She releases a heavy breath. "I didn't take notes on the exact time, but yes, on Sunday. It's not like I make a point of watching the houses, but I didn't like the look of him." She waves at me, a dismissal. "Ask Henry."

"Thanks, Molly."

A man in my house.

Suddenly, everything about the empty coach house and Mara's absence feels dire.

I need to find her, and I can't do it alone.

Idling in my driveway, I dial Henry's cell number. The call goes to voicemail, his calm voice a reminder to take a breath. I consider what to say—how can I possibly relay what has happened? *Hey, I lost track of Mara and my baby?* I ask him to call me back and drive into the garage until the yellow tennis ball, hung from the ceiling by a strand of rope, bounces lightly on the windshield.

In the kitchen, the sound of the freezer dumping a fresh batch of ice makes me jump and spin toward the garage as though I've been followed. I shrug out of Henry's coat and hang it on a chair, straighten a stack of mail on the counter, and refold the dish towel that hangs from the oven handle. Everything is where it should be.

Everything except Mara and Goose.

When I came home from lunch with Henry and Nolan on Sunday, everything was normal. Monday and Tuesday, too. The visitor couldn't have been Lance. If he'd found Mara, come to threaten her and Goose, she would have told me.

Unless he threatened to hurt her if she said anything.

But then he left. He hasn't been here the last two days. Mara was right here and fine last night, so if he didn't come to take her, what did he want? Money? Unable to sit still, I pace beside the bookshelves in the living room. I adjust a photograph of Henry and me in Hawaii, in a mother-of-pearl frame I bought on the trip, scan the books and photos.

If Lance showed up demanding money, what could Mara even offer him? There's nothing valuable here. While Henry has money, and the house would sell for a lot—real estate in Denver, and especially our little neighborhood, has appreciated considerably since Henry bought—there is little of real value in it. His ex-wife got the silver and crystal. Our wedding was a quiet affair; we didn't register for gifts, and we're hardly art collectors. Even my wedding gown was a simple knee-length silk dress, which a friend helped me pick out at Nordstrom. There is the colorful oil painting of a cottage in the woods that Henry and I bought on a drive north from San Francisco after a conference, now hanging in our bedroom, and the brown leather coat he bought me our first Christmas together. When the boys were younger, Henry and I sometimes joked that if there were a house fire, we'd save the boys first and then the Nespresso machine.

The only object of real value is my engagement ring. I stopped wearing it this winter, when Henry had been gone a few months. I race upstairs to my bedroom and open the top drawer of the bureau where, nestled among bras and underwear, a small crystal dish rests, on which my ring has been sitting for the past six months.

The dish is empty.

Fear turns my stomach. Missing doesn't mean taken. More likely, the ring has been knocked from the dish. I push aside some clothes to search, but it doesn't immediately appear. I don't care about the ring. I'd have happily given it to Mara to pay off Lance.

But if she gave him my ring, why is she still gone?

Other than Molly's account, there is no reason to think a man has been in the house—yet the seed, now planted, blooms into a thorny bush. Henry would tell me Molly is a lonely old woman who invents gossip to feel involved. Still, I recognize the sensation of spinning in place, a top making no forward progress, growing dizzy. I take three long breaths and try to focus on doing something constructive.

To pass the time, I gather the laundry—mine from the hamper in my closet, the towels from my bath, and shove it all, with more force than necessary, into the washer and start the load. Relieved by the movement, I cross back to the coach house, a tiny hitch of hope in my throat that I will find Mara there, seated on the couch, flipping through a magazine. But she isn't, so I exhale past the disappointment to pull the towels off the racks in her bathroom. Arms loaded, I'm heading for the closet that houses the washer/dryer when it occurs to me that something is off in the bathroom. Dropping the towels in a heap, I circle back. The evil-eye mug that holds her toothbrush is empty, the toothbrush missing. And the toothpaste. Her face soap and the little exfoliating pad she uses are gone, too. The few items that remain are generic things I bought—hand soap, dental floss. Under the sink are the supplies I provided—toilet paper, a brush and cleaner, extra towels.

Not one thing is personal to Mara.

In the bedroom, I open the top drawer of the bureau and find several pairs of underwear and socks. In the second, a handful of T-shirts. The presence of her things should be reassuring, but it isn't. While the drawers are not empty, they aren't full either. Some items are definitely gone.

I know Mara keeps her driver's license in a small zippered wallet—I saw her pull it out once when a woman carded us at the grocery store—but there is no sign of it now. Surely, she has other papers. Henry's office has a whole cabinet of papers for the family—insurance, medical and marriage records. Could Mara really have shown up here with nothing more than her driver's license?

I shut the drawer, knocking my elbow as I turn from the bureau, wincing at the uncomfortable zing of pain. All of this has that same sensation—a pain that is both benign and paralyzing. One that comes from the most unexpected place, from the gentlest of bumps. Mara would never hurt me. Why, then, is she gone?

I shake out my tingling arm and turn to the closet floor where the worn duffel Mara carried when she arrived lies empty, save for a crumpled receipt.

On instinct, I pocket the receipt and continue my search. A pair of well-worn Steve Madden boots lay discarded on the floor of the closet, along with a pair of slippers I bought her at Marshalls. Several flowing dresses hang on the bar, all purchased by me, and on the shelf above, nothing but dust.

Aside from the book, the items that sit on the bedside table are generic, items provided by me—hand lotion, tissues, a nail file. The table has a small drawer that sticks when I pull the handle. I yank hard and it flies open, the drawer and its contents falling to the floor. I drop to my knees at the sight.

Mara's iPhone, the one I gave her, lies on the carpet, the charger wound around it like fingers on a neck.

# CHAPTER
# 6

I SLOWLY UNWIND the charger from the phone and hold it in my palm, afraid to touch it. I don't want to confirm that this is my phone, the one I gave Mara. I go to set it down and graze the screen, which comes alive.

The battery wasn't dead after all.

*Hello*, the screen reads, first in English and then in other languages, prompting me to continue the phone setup.

The phone has been restored to factory settings, a discovery which strikes with the same electricity-laced pain as striking my elbow on Mara's bureau. It seems impossible that this is the same day when I woke and put on a sweater, imagining the chill of the room where a tech would slather clear gel over the globe of Mara's belly and press the ultrasound paddle, where we would hear the scratch of static as the instrument adjusted to the contact, followed by the staccato woosh-woosh of Goose's perfect heart. Then, the watery images as the tech adjusted the device so that we could see her fingers and toes, her seashell ears and the small wave of her eyelashes.

The last ultrasound was the first time the tech had pointed out Goose's lashes. Initially, with the movement of the fluid, I didn't see them. As though she knew we were talking about her, Goose had shifted, offering her profile, and the curl of the lashes became clear. "Look how long they are," I'd said, already filled with the pride of a parent whose own child is the only perfect specimen.

"Like Cate's," Mara had said, and the two of us, without a beat, echoed each other's words. "Tiger lashes."

I stare down at the phone and try to connect the fact of it to the woman who carries my daughter.

Over the past few months, Mara has increasingly talked about getting set up on her own—finding work and eventually a place to live, but not before Goose gets here. She's surely feeling antsy; it shouldn't surprise me that she'd go out and buy herself a new phone. It's a logical first step in getting her life back, but I'm surprised she'd do it behind my back. Without sharing her new number. Plus, she doesn't have an income, hasn't had one since she arrived, so how would she afford it? I imagine her wanting to do this small thing on her own, a way to exert some bit of control over her life.

The life I've hijacked for a year.

Not that she'd ever say as much.

Being my surrogate was not Mara's idea, and she was hesitant at first. Not only worried about the potential risk if Lance found her but also concerned that she might be unable to get pregnant and would let me down. Even as I pushed the subject, I knew it was too much to ask.

I was also desperate enough to keep asking.

I've been so focused on the baby, I haven't really acknowledged that my life isn't the only one that's about to change in a major way. I also haven't considered that Mara might be ready to be on her own.

But if she's left now, it can't be that. If she's gone now, it has to be because someone found her. Took her.

Lance.

On the floor of Mara's room, I am suddenly underwater, unable to breathe, at once cold and burning up, sweating. The room blurs as I lose focus and, disoriented even in the familiar space, I fight the wave of vertigo.

I know all the signs of a panic attack, have experienced them for years. For a while, I had bested them, learned to ward them off by focusing on my breath, by shifting attention from what is happening inside my body to what I see and hear around me. The white-hot shame of childhood burns in my chest, the impatient voice saying I'm too old to fall apart. That I ought to be able to control myself by now, that something is wrong with me. I lay my forehead on the carpet and fight the self-recriminations, the sounds of my parents' voices. *You are in control*, I remind myself. *You alone.*

Panic used to rain down on me, hail striking until my solidity was fractured. Through the fissures came the inability to breathe, the nausea and dizziness, the spiraling thoughts. Now, it feels like the opposite— that panic is a weed that grows inside me. My thoughts seed the fear, then sprout every poison that comes after.

The heater kicks on and the smell of dust rises with the warmth from the grate on the floor. A car door closes down the block. The boy across the street, home from college for spring break, dribbles a basketball—*snap, snap, snap.* He shoots, striking the rim with a rattle.

Eventually the nausea dissipates and my chest loosens. I return to the surface, lifting my head as I rest on my heels.

Mara being forced to leave is the only reasonable explanation for her disappearance, for not taking her phone, not leaving me a message to say where she was going. Lance must be the man Molly saw. Lance McIntyre. Mara didn't like to talk about him and when she did, it was in broad terms, commenting how something reminded her of him— the sharp sound of a man's laugh at a restaurant, someone who looked momentarily familiar, until he turned and she saw that it wasn't the husband she'd escaped fifteen months ago.

When I answered the door that January day, I hadn't seen Mara in sixteen years, and her appearance was startling. Even through the layers of makeup, bruises formed dark shadows on her neck and face, and her left eye was swollen to a slit. She was thinner than I'd ever seen her, with a broken arm and a deep laceration on her thigh. Her appearance shifted something in me, as though a piece of my past had been returned, made more precious by its absence. After what we'd been through in high school, I was determined to care for her.

"He seemed so sweet when we met," she told me in one of the rare moments we spoke about him. "He'd grown up in Philadelphia and loved the city, shared it with me. He took care of me, and I could tell him anything. Then we were married, a simple wedding with a justice of the peace, and it was like he changed overnight. Everything I told him, he used against me. To trap me, control me. I didn't realize who he was, what he was. If he finds me here, he'll kill me. And he could— he could find me anywhere."

"How?" I'd asked. "How could he find you?"

Mara's gaze had flicked to mine and immediately away. She didn't want to answer.

"Mara?"

"He's . . . he's powerful."

As soon as the words were out, she'd shut down, fear in her eyes mixed with regret, like she wished she hadn't said so much.

It took two weeks of convincing Mara that she was safe before she'd allow me to take her to a doctor. For weeks afterward, I brought her food and books and magazines, insisting she rest until the last of the bruises faded from green to gray and eventually vanished, until the color and fullness returned to her cheeks and she was recognizable as the woman I'd known since childhood, the closest thing I have to a sister.

I am determined to find her, which means I should call the police, even if it's only been a few hours. She could have left just before I woke up, which would mean she'd barely been gone long enough to have breakfast with a friend, assuming Mara had friends here other than me. Or if she had a car. I have no proof she was taken—but her husband was abusive, and a strange man was seen at the house. That should be enough.

I text Henry. Could you come to the house?

I try to think like Henry would, retrieving a legal pad and pen from the desk in the upstairs office. I carry them downstairs to the kitchen to make a list of everything I know about Mara's life since we left high school. I write *Mara* at the top of the page.

Henry's reply: Hey, just out of a meeting. I can come now. Is everything okay?

There's little reason to lie.

Mara is gone. I can't reach her.

Three dots appear and roll across the screen for far too long. I can imagine him struggling with what to say, how to reassure me. When the message finally appears, it isn't at all reassuring. I'm on my way.

The fact that Henry is leaving in the middle of a workday—that he, too, seems concerned—only compounds my terror.

The legal pad remains blank. I know a thousand things about Mara, but I can't think of a single one to write down. I start with *Philadelphia. Married. Abusive husband. Lance McIntyre. Powerful. Escaped. Scared.* The pen hovers, unmoving, as I try to recall the stories she's shared. The pieces I collected like shells on the beach, some whole but many broken, only fragments of what they'd been.

Once upon a time, our lives had seemed like different ends of one wide pool, separate but also attached and in full view of one another. I'd known who Mara had hooked up with and wished she hadn't. Who she hadn't and wished she had. Her favorite foods, colors. The pair of broken-in Vans that she loved like old slippers.

What comes to me is the Mara of our childhood, the girl who preferred company to solitude, noise to quiet, who worked hard to make people smile and laugh. Who was fiercely protective of her friends.

When I moved to Seattle for college, I tried to convince her to come—we could live together, I'd told her. *School's not for me, Lexi. You know that.* And even when I argued that she was great at school, that with the way she absorbed math and science, she could probably be an engineer, she laughed me off. She didn't want to go to college and, not ready to settle into a job, had decided to travel through Europe. *For as long as it's fun*, she said, and I'd felt both terror and awe at the idea of taking off alone, without a plan.

Like jumping off a building.

Unlike Mara, I craved the enclosed universe of a small school, the schedule and predictability of classes and coursework. Both of us were still reeling from the loss of Cate, and there was logic in going our separate ways. How would we heal alongside a constant reminder of what we'd both lost?

So I let Mara go.

She sent postcards. Some featured skylines—from London to Amsterdam to someplace in Austria—while others showed paintings, statues, rolling green hills. Each included a short note. *You should be here. I miss you!* Or *I met the hottest guitar player!* Mara never wrote her name. Just the same signature, every time. *More soon. Pinky swear.* My first semester of college, I tacked the postcards to a corkboard in my tiny dorm room. When I moved out second semester, I taped them to the wall of my sad studio apartment with its yellow walls where the paint was stained in long streaks from moisture that, even in summer, never dried out. Eventually, the postcards stopped coming.

Looking back, I was never lonelier than the spring of my freshman year, having lost my two best friends. While I held tight to the image of Mara traveling the world, the brave adventurer, I also did my best to block memories of Cate from surfacing. The reality that she would never go to college or travel the world or fall in love was a weight too heavy to bear, so I closed that reality into a tight box and buried it deep.

As time passed, I thought less frequently about either of them. Or about home. It was a relief to relinquish everything from that time. To forget what happened.

And then she was on my doorstep and, within a few weeks, we'd picked up where we left off, the intervening years melting in the comfort of familiarity. Catching up was like drinking from a steaming cup of coffee—intense enough to burn if we drank quickly, so instead we exchanged small sips of each other's lives.

She told me about spending a week in Cleveland while her mother was in hospice, dying of emphysema right after she'd returned from Europe—how small her mother seemed, how unmoored she'd felt afterward. How she took a position right after that as a server on a Norwegian cruise ship to get as far as she could from her mother's death. On her first trip, she kicked a couple of septuagenarians out of a storage closet where they were having sex and got fired because, in the process, she'd unintentionally outed them to their respective spouses. She told me about going to Greece and working at a restaurant on the beach for almost a year before joining two friends to hike the Italian Alps. That it was turning twenty-nine that brought her back to the States. Deciding it was time to settle down, go back to school.

Years of working in restaurants and bars before enrolling in a local community college. The semester she studied accounting and business while working full-time, and the guy who convinced her to quit school and start a nightclub with him. How that all went sideways and she was forced to take a crappy job just to get her feet under her. Meeting Lance. We'd talked the same way we had as teenagers—trading trivial details, which, in number, seemed to amass a life. I realize now that what I'd actually collected were, at best, crumbs of an existence.

And I ignored the changes in her—the softer manner, the dimming of the confidence she'd had in high school, her new reservedness, the way she seemed no longer to yearn for casual touch or constant companionship. Only now do I realize how few times I heard her laugh— really laugh—in the months she's lived with me, and I'm filled with shame for how little I actually learned about the sixteen years of my best friend's life while we'd been apart.

And now, Mara is missing, maybe even in danger, and I have no idea how to find her.

# CHAPTER

# 7

S till in sweaty soccer clothes, Cate sits on her bed and stares at the notebook. Runs a finger across Lexi's handwriting. *Physics*. Mara had slid it into her backpack as they packed up, skipping Lexi even though it always went to her Monday, then to Cate Wednesday, and Mara on Friday—Mara's parents were the least likely to snoop and find it, so it spent weekends there.

But after Saturday night . . .

Lexi called the house phone at Cate's twice yesterday to hear what happened, but thankfully Cate's mom told her that Sunday was a family day. The first time Cate's ever been grateful for that—and for the fact that she doesn't have a cell phone. It's easy enough to avoid her MySpace page since they were all now half on Facebook anyway. Although knowing Lexi, she'd messaged both.

Lexi had finally pinned them down at lunch today, and if it wasn't all so fucked up, it would've been sweet to see their friend so excited about their night out. Not all jealous that she couldn't go, just psyched for her friends. Cate had watched Mara from the corner of her eye, impressed at how casually she talked about the boys at the party—how Wyatt looked hot, how Tom K. ended up puking down the front of his coveted Bon Jovi concert tee, that Michael M. looked good despite Mara still imagining his nut sack. That Devon Harding showed up baked out of his skull.

All Cate could think was how badly she wished Lexi had been there. That Lexi would never have lost track of Mara, of either of them. She would have kept them together, safe.

The beginning of the night had been so awesome—how electric she felt walking into Seth Wilson's house, the night air chilly and her blood warm from the boxed wine. Gone was the churning of her stomach, the sweat on the back of her neck and her upper lip that always came with being around the popular crowd. Instead she felt like one of them, and she was high on it.

Only once, passing through a huddle of smokers in the front yard, did Cate hear her mother's voice. *Good girls don't put themselves in dangerous situations. They don't wear clothes that invite impure thoughts. It isn't a man's job to contain himself—it's a woman's job to avoid becoming the object of his desire.*

And then she entered the house, leaving her mother behind. The rum and Sprite Mara handed her silenced the voice that usually taunted her about how out of place she was, too nerdy, too ugly. She felt beautiful—carefree and bold as the two of them wandered through the crowd. As Lexi had predicted, Jason J. was there, his *David*-like sculpted chest wrapped in a tight white T-shirt. Mara caught Cate's eye and nodded toward him, the two of them laughing in silent agreement to report to Lexi first thing. The others from Lexi's list were there, too—Tanner and Wyatt in a corner with a couple of cheerleaders and also Zack, the student council president and a track star, whom Cate never saw outside of school. And then, of course, the college kids—Seth and his class, including Caleb, though the older boys mostly ignored them.

After her second drink, or maybe her third, Cate ran into a couple of soccer girls who'd graduated the year before, and with the familiar banter of teammates, the party was easy. As she listened to their college stories, she noticed Kyle standing alone against the wall. Behind a raised beer bottle, he scanned the room as though he was looking for someone, and Cate recognized his expression, the unsettling sensation of casting about for a place in the crowd. Their eyes met, and he looked embarrassed as she smiled and he returned it, a genuine smile—caught but also relieved. She glanced at the soccer girls, and when she looked back, he was making his way toward Tanner and Wyatt, so she followed the girls into the kitchen for another drink.

She couldn't remember when Mara disappeared, when she'd last seen her friend.

When Cate noticed she was gone.

A car on the street outside her bedroom startles her as she holds her breath like cornered prey, relieved when it drives past.

Why didn't she go find Mara?

Everything would have been different if she had.

Suddenly cold, Cate climbs under the covers, reminded how much her mother hates when she gets into bed in dirty clothes. She doesn't care. Not today.

The covers up around her shoulders, she hugs her favorite stuffed tiger—the one whose neck is loose from so many washings—and opens the notebook, skipping the things she wrote at Mara's before they'd left for the party, childish notes about who they might kiss and in what order. Whether they would let a boy go to second base.

Sickening now.

She turns the page, filled with dread.

*I can't remember exactly how we started talking. Over the punch bowl on the back deck, I think. He looked good, tall and wiry and tan even though no one is tan in Cleveland in February. He grinned when he saw me. Like it lit up his whole face.*

*I ate it up, like an idiot. That's what I am, a fucking idiot. He invited me to sit out by the pool, filled our glasses. Kept filling them, sitting beside me on the chaise, bumping my shoulder, his thigh against mine. Touching but not coming on to me. Not pushing. Asking questions about me, getting me to talk.*

*I ended up telling him about the trip my mother promised for my birthday. I was maybe eight or nine–I haven't even told you guys this. It's so lame. Why would you want to hear about how my mom promised me a fucking trip to Disney World? Why would I want to go? I got all choked up, telling him. I was crying like a baby. God, why didn't he just walk away?*

*I can't remember now if it was my idea or Mom's—that we could go to Disney World, just the two of us. It would've been lame—she'd have been pissed to be there, grumpy about the cost of everything, about missing out on work, about the humidity and how it made her hair frizz. But god, I wanted that trip so badly. Wanted something that would belong to just the two of us. I don't even know why—just that it felt like it would give me a tiny sliver of her that was only mine. And even if it sucked—maybe especially if it sucked—we'd have something to laugh about, like a little secret, when things at home were so awful. I held on to that dream until freshman year when I finally realized what an idiot I was for believing she was going to take me.*

*I thought he was a gentleman. A gentleman because he didn't try anything and the way he listened—it was like he really got it. At some point, he said, "That must've been so hard." And I swear to god, it felt like I was in love. Like, finally, a boy who gets me.*

*He wiped my tears—it's like a cheesy movie—and I started to wonder if maybe he didn't like me like that, if it was just a friendship thing. And I was freezing, shivering, and he took my hands. Made a big deal of how cold I was and said we should go inside.*

*He pulled me up until our bodies were touching and then he kissed me—the sweetest kiss, not like making out with a garden hose, like with Jimmy Turner or that weird flicking tongue Jeremy did. It was like kissing a man, like he knew what he was doing. But then he stopped, pulled back, and ran his thumb down my jaw. I swear, my insides were on fire. I totally understand how girls get carried away, just give it all up. He stared at my face, then wrapped his arm around me, holding me as we returned to the house. Like he wanted people to know we were together. I told him I had to use the bathroom so we went upstairs, him behind me, his hand in mine. Like I was leading and he would follow me anywhere. It felt like the power was mine.*

*What a joke.*

*He opened a door and stuck his head in, then said something like, "This'll work."*

*I didn't even think about it. Work for what? How did I let him pull me into that room? But then we were there, in a bedroom, in the dark, and he was kissing me. And I started to sort of wake up, to pull away. I was ready to leave, but he pulled me down on the bed, so we were both sitting on the edge. There was a painting of a beach on the wall and it sort of helped. Made me feel calmer.*

*Then he handed me a metal flask, the top already off. I shook my head, but he pressed it into my hand and I didn't want to look like a loser. A taste, I thought, and took a sip. But he lifted the bottom and the liquid slid down my throat. I choked and coughed and he patted me on the back. Said he was sorry and he thought it was almost empty. I almost got up then and left. Why the hell didn't I leave?*

*But he took my hand. "Can I hold you?"*

*I said sure. What was the harm? So we lay down and he spooned me and I closed my eyes and thought this was what all the hype was for. Being held. Feeling small and safe and protected in his arms.*

*After that, it gets jumbled. I don't know if I fell asleep or what, but then we were kissing and his hands were in my hair, his mouth on my neck and I could feel him through my jeans. I remember thinking, fuck yeah. I did that.*

There is a spot on the page, the stain of a tear, and Cate runs a finger over it.

*My shirt was gone and then my jeans and I tried to get him to stop. I said it. I said stop. But he kept going. I didn't fight him. That's the worst part. I didn't do anything to save myself. My hands didn't work, my voice didn't work. I just lay there, wishing to hell that I'd disappear, silently begging for it to end, until someone pounded on the door. He shouted at them to fuck off, but the pounding just got louder, more frantic. The bed was rocking, making me seasick, and I was fighting not to throw up. I did not want to throw up in Seth Wilson's house—imagined people talking about it at school until after graduation. Eyes closed, I took sips of air and crossed my arms over my chest to roll away from him. There was a bang and his weight lifted off me.*

*And then you were there and I felt relief, actual relief. Like, okay, it's over now. Now I can get out of here, forget.*

*But I can't forget. I can't get out of there. Not even for a few minutes.*

*Every time I close my eyes, he's on top of me and I can't breathe.*

*I thought writing it down would help release the pressure of it. But it doesn't help.*

*Nothing will help. I know one thing for sure. No one can know.*

*You have to destroy these pages. Now.*

Cate clings to her stuffed tiger, pressing her face into the worn curve of his back, and sobs. The chill is gone and now she is burning up, sweating as she throws the covers off and rips the pages from the notebook, clawing at them as if the words are his face.

She will destroy the pages; of course she will. Burn them. And they will never speak of it.

Not even to Lexi.

# CHAPTER

# 8

WHEN THE DOORBELL rings twenty minutes later, I run, sliding in my socks to get there. I yank the door open, breathless, and see Henry standing on the front mat. Henry, who has a key, who owns this house. Why wouldn't he let himself in?

Mistaking my frustration for distress, Henry steps into the house and takes my hand. My hand in his, he closes the front door and faces me. "I thought dinner last night went well. Did something happen after Nolan and I left?"

"No." Mara looked comfortable, happy even. "Did Nolan say any-thing?"

"Just that he was looking forward to meeting his sister." Henry offers a soft smile that says a dozen things at once—that he's happy for me, that we're family, that he's here, and also a flash of something like regret. Does he wish he'd agreed to be my baby's father?

I pull my hand away, all of it too much in this moment. "I don't understand where she could be."

"We'll figure it out," he says, with all the confidence of a man who has never lost anything of value. In the kitchen, he eyes the notepad on the table, the short list about Mara. "Tell me exactly what happened."

The words come out in a torrent, but Henry just nods as I tell him about the coach house, her missing things, and Molly's report of the strange man. I skip over the possibility of my missing engagement ring before handing him the iPhone and charger. "It's the one I gave her."

Henry stares at it a beat. "The man Molly saw, are we sure it was her ex-husband?"

"Who else would it be?"

"A delivery guy?" he suggests. "Someone she met?"

"We didn't get any deliveries." I glance at him. "And what do you mean—someone she met? She's nine months pregnant."

"Okay," Henry says calmly. "Pregnant or not, she's a beautiful woman. Maybe she met someone and explained her situation."

"It still doesn't explain the phone."

Henry doesn't argue. "What was her ex-husband's name?"

I point to his name on the page. "Lance McIntyre."

He pauses a moment. "Tell me about before she came to Denver. Do you know where she worked?"

"She's always worked in restaurants—through Europe and then when she got back home." I had the impression that she worked hard, and there was no question that she'd be good in hospitality, keeping track of what everyone wanted, checking in. It was like the way she used to manage Cate's mother and my parents, always making everyone feel like she shared their worldview, their priorities. "She must've done well. Lance lost his job, so she was supporting them both for a while."

Henry's eyes narrowed. "Wait, he was unemployed?"

I replay the memory. "Yes. She said it was after that when things got bad."

"Lexi," he says in a tone that means I've missed something obvious.

"What?"

Henry grips the back of the chair, his gaze on the notepad. "She was worried he'd find her, right? That he had power, could use his network to track her down."

"Right," I say, remembering her words. *He's powerful.* When the conversation replays in my mind now, it isn't the mention of his power that stands out to me. The words that echo in my head, pulling strands of something like electricity down my spine, is what she said just before. That she didn't realize who he was, *what he was.* As though he wasn't human, not someone she could reason with or walk away from. Not just a man but something larger, more menacing—a monster.

"A guy with the power to track someone across the country isn't some unemployed bum. He's not being supported by his waitress wife. A guy like that has money, and a lot of it. Or he's some sort of celebrity— a politician, maybe?"

If that was true, why would Mara tell me that she'd supported him? It made no difference who paid the bills. Getting out of the relationship was the right decision, even if it came with substantial risk. But then, why lie about who he was?

"We should call the police," Henry says. "To be safe. To make sure nothing has happened to her."

"Doesn't she have to be gone for a couple of days before they'll start looking?" I ask.

"She's carrying your baby," Henry says. "Police don't wait two days to investigate a missing child, and that's essentially what this is."

His words are a warm rush of reassurance until he adds, "You can show them the surrogacy contract. It probably includes more information about Mara."

Oh, God.

I remember receiving the contract from the attorney, the weight of the pages in my hands as I left his office. Driving home, I thought of Henry, who always handled those things—not just household bills and accounts but also my parents' estate. Several weeks after my father's death, the attorney had called to inform me that my parents' estate was "as straightforward as they come." But when those documents had arrived, I couldn't understand what I was supposed to do. I didn't see where I could sign and be done, so I'd given them to Henry.

Henry sees my expression and sinks into a chair. "Oh, Lexi."

I don't answer, recalling the way the attorney Henry recommended had sat behind his massive oak desk and outlined what the surrogacy contract was meant to do, lobbing terms like *relinquishing parental rights* and *legal parentage, compensation and expenses*. And then I heard the words *termination clause* and for several long seconds, I was back standing in the kitchen, pressing the lever on the toaster to make breakfast when I'd felt that single, stabbing pain.

When I'd lost the pregnancy. The last one.

I took the contract and brought it home, set it in the inbox on Henry's desk in the office upstairs, waiting for him to look at it, to confirm that it was all we needed and nothing more, that we could sign it.

But that wasn't his inbox anymore or his desk, because he hadn't lived in our house in months. The more time that passed, the more I returned to what Mara said when the pregnancy test came back positive, our palms pressed to her still-flat belly: "I will carry your sweet baby, and I will do everything I can to protect your child."

Then she'd lifted her tiny finger and linked it with mine. "Pinky swear," she'd said.

Now, Henry turns his back to me and calls the nonemergency number at the local police department, and an hour later, the doorbell rings. Two detectives stand on the front porch and, miraculously, one is a woman. I scan her for signs of motherhood, though I don't know what I'm looking for. Peanut butter smeared on her sleeve, spit-up down her back, or just the weary look of the perpetually sleep-deprived. Of course, I can't tell.

Mother or not, a woman might better understand my plight. The detectives are polite enough when we invite them into the living room and I offer coffee or water, which they decline. The four of us sit across from one another, an awkward double date. The female detective, Sullivan, pulls out a notepad.

Mostly it is Henry who does the talking—not because he is overbearing but because every time I start to speak, my throat closes up. Sullivan writes everything down, and when he has told them all we know, she looks up at him. "The woman is your surrogate?"

Henry radiates discomfort in the extra moment it takes him to answer. "She's carrying my wife's baby."

"Your wife's baby," Sullivan repeats, her stare a sharp blade. "It's not *your* baby?"

The male detective, Bentley, watches Henry, too, as he shifts to sit up straighter.

"That is correct," he says finally, his cheeks crimson. Henry is a blusher, something he can't control, something he despises. Perhaps it's one of the reasons he chose a career in engineering, a job that rarely elicits a passionate response. Henry has never yelled at me, never yelled at his boys, but he looks like he wants to yell now.

Though they must see his discomfort, the officers continue to wait, neither speaking. Surely Henry knew the police would ask about the baby's parentage. He's chosen not to participate in this pregnancy but to support me while I live in this house, no questions asked, without filing for divorce or telling me to move out. We have not talked about the future. What will happen after Goose is born.

But this isn't about Henry. It's about my daughter. And my best friend.

"I don't think the baby's paternity is what matters here," I say, finding my voice. Henry cocks an eyebrow, and I realize with a burst of pride that it's what Mara would have said. I press on. "The baby is due in four days. We need to find Mara. I'm afraid she's in danger, which means the baby is in danger."

Sullivan doesn't write anything down, only studies Henry as though to gauge how he is handling this.

"Do you have a last known address for Ms. Vannatta?" Detective Bentley asks.

"I don't," I answer. "We grew up together in Cleveland, but neither of us has lived there in seventeen years."

There is something strange about inviting an old friend back into your life—with so much shared history, Mara and I fell into the comfort of knowing each other. Or, of *feeling* like we knew each other. In so many ways, our relationship is utterly familiar. We can finish each other's sentences, burst into laughter without saying a word, crave the same foods on the same nights.

The iceberg of those gap years floated between us, but we skirted around it, leveraging the shared knowledge of our past. That trust. But Henry isn't wrong—if I was going to trust this woman to carry my child, I should have done my due diligence. I also know that, had I pushed for more information, I could as easily have driven her away. As kids, we'd each had difficult home lives. None of us envied each other's situation, though we could point out bits we liked—the food at Cate's house, the freedom at Mara's, the television in the upstairs play-room that no one ever used at mine. And while we all dealt with diffi-cult parents, Mara's were the most combustible. At any moment, there was a real risk that her parents might separate and Mara could be dragged to an aunt's house in Michigan or her dad's cousin's in Arkan-sas. Or that her mother might finally kick Caleb out of the house and turn her anger on Mara. These were threats that loomed for years, ones Cate and I had heard during the epic shouting matches that oc-curred with regularity at Mara's house. Ones she alluded to in our note-books. Even then, she refused to talk about the possibility or discuss how the fighting impacted her.

When her parents fought in front of us, Mara just turned the music up to an ear-splitting level and rolled her eyes, like the horrible things they shouted at each other were part of a family schtick. When she ar-rived in Denver, she came with the same stubborn refusal to talk about her pain—physical or otherwise. She let me take care of her; she ac-cepted a place to stay and clothes and food, but there would be no pity. Not ever.

"Mrs. McNeil?" the detective repeats. "Do you know her last ad-dress?"

With the back of my hand, I blot the sweat forming on my upper lip. "No. I have her full name and date of birth."

"We'll need that," Sullivan says.

"Any cameras on the house? Outside or inside?" This from Bentley.

"No," Henry says, and I imagine he is remembering when the boys were young and I was regularly alone in the house with them while Henry traveled. I had asked about a security system, but the neighbor-hood was as safe as they came—deliveries never went missing from front porches, cars were left on the street overnight and not bothered. Never so much as a smashed pumpkin or egg on a window. In the end Henry had convinced me that cameras and alarms were unnecessary and we were lucky not to need them.

And I'd believed him. Until now.

"And what is the husband's name?" Bentley asks.

"Lance McIntyre."

"Spell it for me?" Sullivan asks.

I spell it out and realize I don't think I've ever seen it written. "That might be a guess on the spelling," I admit.

"A guess," Sullivan repeats, raising her brows. "How long has Ms. Vannatta lived here?"

Suddenly I hate that this woman is here. It's bad enough to be patronized by a man—what woman hasn't been patronized by a man? Stupidly, I had expected compassion from a woman, but aren't we as cruel to one another—or crueler—than men? The way we constantly criticize each other for decisions, as though there's only one right way to be female, or a mother.

"Mara has lived here since January of last year. She still goes by her maiden name."

"No car?" Bentley asks, blowing out a breath.

"No car," I confirm. "What will you do to find her?"

"We'll run a background check and put out a countywide ATL—attempt to locate," he explains. "We'll contact the hospitals, check for activity on her credit cards and her phone. See if we can locate the husband. He's obviously top priority."

There is some reassurance in hearing the steps, knowing someone will be looking for Mara. But it's unsettling, too, to hear the generic procedural terms. This is what the police do to look for missing people, but how many remain unfound?

"Do you have a photograph of Ms. Vannatta?" Bentley asks.

"I do," I say, with more relief than the moment warrants.

"Can you send that to me?" He reaches over and hands me a business card with an email address.

"I'll do it now."

"Does she have any distinguishing scars? Tattoos?"

I recall the tattoo on Mara's ankle, a blurred purplish ink. I'd wondered, briefly, where she'd gotten it. Was it from her European travels or something more recent? Why didn't I ask? Was that a detail she would have guarded? She certainly didn't make an effort to hide it. Another inch of iceberg I failed to explore.

"Lexi?" Henry prompts. "She does have a tattoo, doesn't she?"

"Yes. A flower on her ankle." I close my eyes to picture it. "It's blurry, but it looks sort of like a lotus inside a circle, only the petals are thinner." I describe it as best I can as Sullivan takes notes. When I'm done, she gives her partner a curt nod.

Bentley gets to his feet first. "We'd like to look at her apartment, if we could."

"Of course." I lead them to the coach house. Henry does not follow, and I wait outside while the officers walk around.

"This is how she left the apartment?" Detective Bentley asks.

"Mostly," I say, remembering the picture frame that I set upright. "I opened some drawers, to see if she'd taken anything."

The two detectives exchange a look. Disapproval. "So you've touched all the handles and such," Bentley says, scanning the room.

"Not all," I begin, trying to recall which ones I opened. Truthfully, it was most of them. Why wouldn't I? I was searching for any clue she might have left behind.

"No signs of struggle," Sullivan calls to her partner as she emerges from the bathroom. She glances at me. "You sure she wouldn't leave by choice?"

"I'm sure," I tell them, because I need it to be true.

"Anything else you can tell us?"

"Not that I can think of." There's the picture frame with the imprint in the cardstock, evidence of a hidden key, but I don't mention this. It feels instinctive to protect it, too close to Cate, even though I can't see what a key could have to do with our old friend.

They pass back through the yard and to the driveway, pausing until I catch up.

"We'll be in touch," Sullivan says. "Most times, people turn up on their own, so please keep us posted if you hear from her."

"I will. Absolutely."

As the detectives share a silent exchange over the top of their sedan, Sullivan rolls her eyes, and I slam the front door with more force than necessary.

# CHAPTER

# 9

HAPPY TO BE rid of the detectives, I march back inside to complain to Henry about the awful way they treated him. He emerges from the kitchen, pulling on his coat, the residual flush of pink still in his cheeks. He averts his gaze from mine, and there is a roundness to his spine, some combination of anger and embarrassment.

Henry is a deeply private person, and I have put him in a position where people are asking why my baby is not his. Where complete strangers know that his wife wants a baby but cannot get pregnant. That his wife has lost track of the surrogate carrying her child. That she failed to get a signed surrogacy contract.

He pauses in the entryway and zips up his coat.

"I'm sorry this is happening," he says, though the set of his jaw suggests it's not only remorse he feels but also disappointment, disdain—like the moment of Mara's arrival set these events in motion, and we've now reached their inevitable conclusion. *The baby wasn't Mara's idea*, I want to remind him. *I talked about wanting a baby long before she came.* But I don't argue, just watch as he fiddles with his car keys.

"Thank you for coming," I tell him.

"I have to go to New York tomorrow—there's a conference. I can't miss it. I'll be gone through the end of next week."

So Henry had planned to be gone when Goose is due. Goose isn't his baby—she isn't his problem. *Not my circus, not my monkeys,* as Cate used to say. How I wish I could call Cate.

"There's something I should tell you," he says, staring at the ground. I brace for the blow. "What?"

"When I came by last week, I called and you were at the shop, remember, and I told you I needed the mortgage records to call on the property taxes."

"I remember. What about it?"

"I didn't want to barge in, so I went around back first. Mara wasn't in the coach house, and when I came into the house, she wasn't down here either. Not in the kitchen or the living room."

"Henry," I say, gripping his arm. "What are you saying?"

"I found her in the office. She was looking through the file cabinet."

"I'm sure it wasn't—"

"She was thumbing through our files, Lexi," he says, taking hold of my hand. "She had your medical records open across the drawer in front of her."

All my inconsequential suspicions form a stack of blocks, and I can see the tower sway, ready to fall. "What did she say?"

"She didn't see me, so I went back down the stairs and pretended I was just arriving, called up to her. When she came down, she said she'd been looking for a pair of socks in your bureau."

"You didn't confront her about the files?"

"No," he says, but I sense he isn't finished.

"Henry?"

"I didn't know what to do. I didn't know if you'd appreciate my opinion, but I was worried. So I called an investigator."

"An investigator?" I repeat.

"A guy someone in my office used to look into his own adoption. I asked the investigator to do a background check on Mara." The words come out in a rush, like he's ripping off a Band-Aid, expecting pain.

"Henry." I'm frustrated at him for assuming the worst, but isn't that what's happened? The worst. Now I'm curious about what the report revealed. I can't come up with any reason Mara would be looking through my medical records. "What did you find?"

He shakes his head. "Nothing. I panicked and backed out. The guy ran the report, but when he called to collect payment, I told him I didn't want the file. I hope I'm wrong about this, and it's not my business—"

I wave him away, impatient. "Where's the report, then?"

"I never got it." He smooths the rug underfoot with this toe. "I mean, I paid for it, but I told him to trash it. I think I was afraid of what it might say, how I'd face you—and her—if I knew something I shouldn't. Plus, I felt guilty for going behind your back. I asked if there was anything in it to suggest she might be a danger to my family, and he said probably not. That's all I know."

*Probably not.* I don't want to admit to Henry that running a check on Mara was appropriate—or worse, that it was smart.

"Henry, I need to see that report," I say, the words barely a whisper. But I need to see it. Maybe it will explain something. "Can you get a copy for me?"

"I'll call and request it," he says, finally meeting my gaze and reaching out to touch my arm. "She's your best friend, Lexi. It's like the detective said: She'll show up."

I think about the detective's comment in the coach house. *You sure she wouldn't leave by choice?*

The question strikes a tender fear inside. I responded so quickly. But am I sure?

Once Henry is gone, I'm antsy for something to do, so I retreat to the office and pull my medical records from the file cabinet, skim through the pages for whatever Mara might have seen. Medical reports from blood tests and hormone levels, invoices, insurance information. None of it seems noteworthy. Next, I boot up the computer to Google Lance McIntyre. The home office is unchanged from when I moved in, with a large oak filing cabinet in one corner and an upholstered chair in denim and matching ottoman in another. Beside it is a small table with a short stack of coffee-table books about Denver. I gave Mara the login credentials so she could use the computer, though as far as I knew, she never had.

Now I wonder if she'd spent time here and just didn't tell me.

The home page is the same as always—a tropical shoreline, two bathers swimming in the clear sea. The bookmarked web pages are all mine and Henry's—our bank, Facebook, the remote login for Henry's work, Nolan's school, then Kyle's. Facebook is automatically logged in to my account, and I scroll through a dozen posts before noticing the search bar. When I click, my search history appears.

The first on the list is Caleb Vannatta, Mara's older brother. I hesitate a moment before clicking on his name, but his profile is private and we aren't friends, which seems odd. But stranger still is that his name appears in the search history at all. For years, I checked the site regularly, clicking through profiles, but I haven't been on in months. It's possible that I searched for Caleb when Mara first arrived. It had to have been me, right? Surely Mara doesn't need to check Facebook to know what her brother is doing. When I've asked her about him, she's given me brief updates: *He's doing the dad thing. Still working for the same company. He and Cheryl seem good.*

A Google search for Lance McIntyre brings up several obituaries and a law firm website in Louisiana. I try spelling the name *McIntire* and discover a decade-old shooting in Omaha. Adding Mara's name doesn't yield any additional matches. Thinking of Henry's private investigator, I search local firms and print the first page of results. If Henry can't get his hands on the report on Mara, maybe I'll hire someone else to do a background check. As I'm leaning down to retrieve the page off the printer, I spot a single sheet of paper that has fallen behind the desk and use two fingers to draw it out.

The formatting looks like a printout from a web page. A timetable. I spot a word that makes my vision swim. *Greyhound.*

A bus schedule.

Down the left edge are departure times from Denver's main bus terminal and, along the right, arrival times in Philadelphia. Mara ran *away* from Philadelphia. Why would she go back?

The paper could be old, something she printed shortly after her arrival.

But then I read the top banner, which lists the date for this particular bus schedule.

It's today's.

Mara printed out a bus schedule to Philadelphia.

What if she *wasn't* taken? What if leaving was *her* plan?

Suddenly, everything Mara has told me is shaded in doubt.

The one thing I know for certain is that I'm catching the first flight to Philadelphia tomorrow.

# CHAPTER

# 10

*February 2008*

The latest notebook entry is written in Lexi's square block writing, all caps. UMMM, NOTEBOOK FOUL!! I see evidence of a torn-out page. (Not pointing any fingers . . . Mara. LOL!)

A heavily inked arrow points to the metal spiral where several tiny tabs of white remain from the pages about Saturday night, the ones Cate had burned in an empty paint can in the garage, after her parents had gone to sleep, like a witch casting a spell. How she wishes there was a spell to make this go away.

It's been a few notebooks, so here's a refresher on the OG rules in case that boxed wine wiped them clean.

## NOTEBOOK RULES

1: Only the three—CML—are allowed access to this book. When it's in your possession, you'd better keep it hidden from nosy parents, younger sisters, or older brother.

Cate recalls Mara's reaction to that one, scribbled in the margin of their first notebook: *as if my jackass brother would be caught dead reading a girl's diary.*

2: No removing pages. If you wrote it, we all get to read it—no cutting pages out. Come on! It'll be good to let that shit out. We've got each other's backs.

That was Mara's idea. Seemed like a good idea at the time, but now it's idiotic. Of course they'd need to remove pages. They aren't freshmen anymore, when the biggest thing to freak out about was failing a pop quiz in earth science.

The next one was Cate's idea: Absolutely no passing notes to members of the group individually or outside of this notebook. Charlie's Angels, baby.

That one is idiotic, too. But none of them could have predicted they'd be keeping secrets from each other.

The rest of the page is filled with Lexi's tidy square font where she has rewritten the entire list of rules, like she's had it memorized this whole time, which she probably has. At the start, Lexi had been the keeper of the notebook, storing it at her house because they all agreed that her parents' total lack of interest in her life would extend to her bedroom. But Lexi came home from school one day last fall to find her mom recovering from the flu and going through a box of Lexi's old stuff. According to Lexi, her mother was an inch of Spanish homework away from the last notebook, the one they hadn't yet burned, marked Chemistry, when she got home. And Lexi didn't exaggerate. Mara liked to dramatize the truth and Cate wasn't above a little hyperbole, but if Lexi said it was that close, it was *that* close.

ANYWAY, Lexi continued on the next page.

My dad brought up my brother. It was like an episode from your mom's X-Files, M. No warning, I'm at the kitchen table at the crack of dawn, finishing the take home Pre calc test and he comes in to make coffee, glances at my paper, and points to the empty chair beside me. "Simon would be right there, converting fractions into percentages, and eating peanut butter on graham crackers for breakfast."

I swear, I don't think either of them have mentioned Simon since the day they came home from the hospital without him and the neighbor warned me never to so much as mention his name. How weird is it to have a dead brother that no one talks about? And the stupid, spacey look on my dad's face—like he was drunk and also about to cry. The math thing was weird enough, but peanut butter on graham crackers? I used to love those—I mean, LOVE them, but my mom thought I was getting fat in like third grade and stopped buying them.

I don't know if I ever told you guys how excited they were when Mom was pregnant? Like Simon was going to be the second coming.

I almost started bawling right there. I should've asked if he was okay, but Mom came in and like a damn switch, he was totally normal again. It made me realize how maybe there's this other side of my dad, one I could really talk to if my mom wasn't around . . .

I can't stop thinking about it. I mean, Simon was born in the fall, so what the hell? Why was he thinking about Simon now? I waited for it to come up again, but last night, he came into the living room while I was watching CSI and sat in his chair, like always, and opened his newspaper. What the hell? No way I'm telling my mom about it. Here, Lexi has drawn a face, mouth open, little X's for eyes.

Sounds like a stroke but wtf do I know, begins the next entry on the following page, written in swooping purple letters. It's kind of sweet that he still thinks about Simon. Did it make you sad, L? Imagining life without my brother doesn't make me sad. Does that make me a bitch? Probably but still true.

Moving away from thinking about my brother (barf) . . . Lexi, you got Trent Farrell in my head and now I see him everywhere. Is he following me around, ya think? Or maybe I'm following him? I even went into the gym to watch practice. Okay, I'm a creeper. Damn.

Cate turns the page to start her own entry. Already it feels like last weekend is behind them. They can do this. They can keep this secret.

Even if they can't forget it, at least they can bury it firmly in the past.

# CHAPTER
# 11

*3 days before due date*

MY FLIGHT TO Philadelphia is delayed, so I pass the time rereading every text Mara has sent me in the past fifteen months, searching for some message hidden among the generic missives.

> Went for a walk!! 🖤

> I'm at the library. Have you read A Little Life!? Is it too sad???😩

> Confirmed doctor's appointment for the 10th at 9:30 a.m. 🌱

> My turn to cook. We should invite Henry!!? 😜

When I've read our text thread so many times I have it memorized, I scroll through my calendar, looking for mementos of the path to Mara's surrogacy, replay the memories of our first appointment with the doctor, the blood draws and physicals, the morning we drove to the appointment for implantation. How quiet we both were. I skim back, week by week, until there are no appointments, no mention of Mara in my calendar at all.

And then I remember that spring morning, shortly after she arrived. The weather was cold but the sky a vivid blue, the sun bright as we walked, bundled up, to the Cherry Creek Mall to buy her a new pair of jeans. She'd only brought one pair with her and they were threadbare and dingy. The shops didn't open until ten, so we'd bought coffees and walked to a park. Seated on a bench under a sycamore tree, branches heavy with swelling buds, we'd watched as people jogged by and threw Frisbees for their dogs.

We'd been there a while when a woman showed up with a massive blanket, which she laid out twenty feet from our bench, before unloading baskets from her car—bouncy balls and plush toys. With each trip, I'd felt a growing sense of unease, as though she was setting up for a magic trick that would vanish some essential part of me.

Then, the mothers arrived. Babies in strollers, babies in slings. The women settled in a circle on the blanket, babies between their legs.

"We're in the ninth circle of hell," Mara had said.

"It's Mommy and me," I told her, unable to tear my gaze from the throng of babies. Mara and I hadn't talked about children—having them, wanting them. I had no desire to discuss the failed IVFs, the insulting nondiagnosis of idiopathic infertility. Watching those babies, I imagined my frozen embryos, sitting in tiny vials like sea monkeys, waiting for someone to add water. My insides churned with longing as the women held their children, kissed their necks, their cheeks, all milky breath. One baby scooted toward the center of the blanket, holding a ball in his chubby, dimpled hands and pressed his mouth to it, blowing raspberries against the orange rubber. I told myself to look away, as though the babies were the sun and I might go blind from staring directly at them. How I wanted to join the group, to feel that weight in my arms, sticky hands on my face, to know that one day the word *mama* would come, addressed to me, from a pair of tiny, rosy lips.

That day I told myself I had to stop wanting it so badly. There had to be some therapy, some drug, that could turn off the desire, so I could live my life without this gaping hole. Repair my marriage and truly move on.

The little boy crawled to his mom, and I lifted my coffee to my lips, reminding myself that I was a whole person without a child. That I had a full and happy life, that this would pass. Surely, it was greedy to want more than all I had.

Mara nudged me, then nodded toward the babies. "Why don't you have one?"

The question—so simple, so complex—brought tears to my eyes. One of the babies began to cry, the high-whine wail of an infant. I could feel the sound deep inside me, like I was personally tethered to that tiny beating heart. And then the thought returned. If I could have just one. Some people had dozens of babies, more than they could care for, and all I wanted was one.

"Lexi?" Mara said, her hand on my arm, but I couldn't move. Like that baby was crying for me.

And then the mother lifted her sweater, brought the baby to her breast, and the spell broke. Another reminder of something my body couldn't do. Mara guided me up from the bench, and we walked in silence until we reached the far end of the park; there, she pulled the sleeve of her sweatshirt down over her hand and used it to wipe the tears from my face.

"You would be a great mom," she said.

"I can't."

None of the available words seemed sufficient. They lacked the weight I felt, the deep sorrow. So instead, I waved at my midsection and shook my head. Mara pulled me toward her, wrapping me in her arms. She was a few inches shorter, but her hug enveloped me.

"There are other ways," she said. "You don't have to give up your dream. You shouldn't give it up."

It was the kind of thing friends said to each other. Mara let it go that day, but over the following weeks, she drew the truth out of me— the failed IVFs, the sperm donor and the remaining embryos, frozen in a lab. Neither of us brought up the idea of her being a surrogate that day. It didn't occur to me until a few days later, and it took several weeks to gather my courage to ask—and much longer for Mara to get comfortable with the idea—but four months after that day in the park,

Mara was newly pregnant with my child, and I had never felt so grateful, so optimistic, so full of joy. Mara had sensed my pain and urged me to share it. In doing that, she offered to give me the one thing I wanted most.

When the airline pushes our departure back another forty-five minutes, I start to pace the long corridors, wondering what Mara is doing at this very moment. If she can feel Goose moving inside her, stretching elbows and knees. Fighting back the very real fear that maybe Goose isn't inside her anymore.

I left a note on the kitchen table, just in case.

Mara,
I'm so worried about you. Please call me!

I added my cell phone number, the same number that was programmed into the phone she left behind. And then, to remind her that everything can still be okay between us: I love you. Pinky swear, Lexi.

I palm my phone, willing it to ring even as I remind myself that her phone is sitting in a drawer in the coach house. As I'm about to pocket it again, the phone does ring. It's Nolan, checking on me.

"Are you doing okay?"

I can't respond. I don't want to cry, and I don't have an answer either way.

"I'm sure she and Goose are fine," Nolan says. "She was really excited about the baby the other night." He speaks with the same calming tone as his dad, the unshakable certainty about the way the world works. Nothing bad has ever happened to any of them. "I wanted to thank you for dinner the other night. I'm sorry I won't get to say goodbye, but I'll definitely fly home soon, okay?"

"Of course," I say. "It was so good to see you." There's an awkward quiet on the phone. He's heading back to Chicago tomorrow, and I feel guilty for my inability to focus on the conversation, but all I can think of is Mara. I've always had an easy relationship with Henry's kids. Even with Henry living in an apartment these days, I still talk to them to check in and catch up, albeit less often than before. The dinner two nights ago feels like ancient history, the details blurred by the tidal wave that followed.

"I can't wait to meet her," Nolan tells me. "And I know everything's going to be okay."

I store this to share with Henry, to remind him how wonderful his sons are, before acknowledging that I likely won't tell him. Nor will I think more about it, not while Mara and Goose are missing. I feel another wave of guilt, the same one I used to experience at the end of a long day of parental duties—shuttling to games, making meals, washing uniforms and helping with homework—when I considered trying to engage the boys in a game but couldn't summon the energy. "Thank you, Nolan. Let us know when you're home safe. I love you."

"Love you, too, Lexi," he says, and ends the call.

An announcement informs us that our plane is on the ground and soon we'll finally be on our way to Philadelphia with an updated arrival time of eight p.m.

There is a collective groan and eruption of complaints about the delay, so I go sit at the gate across the wide aisle, on the far side of the moving walkways. As I watch people pass, many of them solo travelers, the loneliness of the airport strikes me, making me long for home. For the time when Henry and I were first married and Nolan and Kyle were in seventh and fifth grades. I miss the boys. Henry, too, though Goose has complicated things between us. I wonder if we can ever be whole—if there is some way to meld our two families into one. If that's even what I want.

For our first wedding anniversary, Henry took us to Hawaii. The boys were fourteen and twelve, Nolan long and lean like his dad but Kyle still small, even for his age. At the end of the trip, the boys, worn out from a week of planned activities—snorkeling and boat trips and hikes— spent the morning burying each other in the sand. A little girl, maybe three or four, came over after a bit and asked if she could play, too.

Her mother sat only a few feet away, clearly exhausted and overwhelmed with a newborn in her arms. Her husband was golfing, she explained, grateful for the way Nolan and Kyle included her daughter.

As the girl and Nolan hauled buckets of water up the beach to fill in the moat around the impressive castle, an older couple stopped to watch. The woman turned to me and said, "What a beautiful family. Cherish every moment."

As they walked away, some piece that had always floated inside me clicked into place. A truth became obvious and, in its wake, I felt both deep despair and rising fear. Despite the boys I loved, the sweet scene, I knew, with a fierce certainty, that I wanted a child of my own.

Ten years later, I am so close.

Or I was, until yesterday.

Finally, we board the plane. The reticence normally expected from strangers on a plane has eroded after so many hours, giving everyone permission to be unnaturally friendly.

For a moment, I feel a surge of doubt that Mara is actually headed to Philadelphia. I fight the urgent desire to get off the plane, fearing this is some sort of wild-goose chase. But what choice do I have? I don't have any other leads. The only other person in the world who knows Mara is her brother. As the flight attendants announce the safety guidelines, I Google Caleb Vannatta and find his Facebook page and a LinkedIn profile. I already know his Facebook profile is private, so I click on LinkedIn. His profile offers little information—he graduated from Indiana University, which means he'd transferred schools after I left for Washington. Under "employment" is a short list of director/manager jobs at a handful of companies whose names are either acronyms or totally unfamiliar. Below those listings, a website offers his current address and phone number for $29.95. As the flight attendant instructs us to put our devices in airplane mode, I enter my credit card details. The site is slow, the spinning wheel making my breath shallow. Remembering yesterday's panic attack, I press a palm to my chest and count my breaths. And then the screen displays Caleb's information. A phone number.

The plane jerks as it backs away from the gate, so I copy the number and type out a hasty text.

> Caleb, hope this is you. It's Lexi McNeil—Lexi Overly, from Shaker Heights. I'm on a flight to Philadelphia but need to talk to you. It's about Mara—I'm trying to reach her. Can you confirm this is your number? And if it's okay to call you first thing tomorrow?

I reread the words and wonder what he'll make of the message. If he'll think something bad has happened to his sister. *Has* something bad happened to her?

The flight attendant stops in our aisle and points to the phone. "Airplane mode?"

"Yes," I lie, hitting the send button.

I don't put the phone in airplane mode but set it next to me on the seat, eyeing the message, waiting as the blue line crawls across the top of the screen until it shows it's been delivered. When the flight attendant comes by again, I accept a pair of headphones and plug them into a classical station, hoping to mute the noise of the man next to me, already snoring loudly, and the woman in the window seat lost in a game of *Candy Crush*, the volume on max. The flight attendant must notice my misery because she offers me extra snacks and a mini bottle of vodka with my soda water. I stick the vodka in my backpack for later. As much as the numbness of alcohol appeals, I can't be anything less than my sharpest self right now.

When we land, I skip baggage claim and catch a taxi, directing the driver to the address of the hotel I booked. I've packed clothes for three days, a toothbrush and toothpaste, and an envelope of cash from the safe at the house, which contains about $2,000. In the entryway, I'd held the pack on my shoulder and looked around, certain I was missing something crucial. But whatever it is, I'll buy it or do without. The only crucial thing now is Goose.

As we drive away from the airport, I wonder when I'll return to Denver. Whether I'll have Baby Goose with me.

I'm not going home without her.

# CHAPTER
# 12

*2 days before due date*

THE DOWNTOWN PHILADELPHIA bus station is open twenty-four hours, but aside from the dim halogen lights and a scattering of people who may or may not be living here, nothing much is happening at five a.m. There are machines to buy tickets and a large screen mounted overhead listing arrival and departure times, as well as the numbered lanes where the buses park.

The bus I'm assuming Mara took is scheduled to arrive this morning at 5:30. The idea of staying awake for another thirty minutes seems like a Sisyphean task, and though there are benches along the arrival lanes, I barely slept last night and I don't dare sit down. Instead, I walk the length of the station, keeping a close eye on the monitors as I pass.

I find a rhythm in the movement, letting my mind wander. Counting people. Counting buses. Henry was traveling all day yesterday, not checking email or texts, but he finally responded last night to tell me he'd requested the background report on Mara and would forward it when the investigator sent it. I miss him, wish I had an excuse to touch base, but it's too early.

For months, I've been growing independent from Henry, and now

suddenly I feel the opposite, like I need him more than ever. Acknowledging this spikes an uncharitable stab of frustration at my husband.
When I met Henry, his decisiveness was a drug. I loved the way he taught
Nolan and Kyle to be self-sufficient. The boys learned to make decisions
on their own, while I simply leaned into the choices he made for the two
of us. Though we have lived separately for more than six months, Henry
continues to make decisions for me. Ordering me the Caesar salad at our
lunch last weekend without asking, buying my car out of its lease so I
wouldn't have to deal with shopping for a new one with an infant.

But that isn't fair to Henry. Despite not wanting to be my baby's
father, he has continued to be my partner in all the ways that matter.
At the sperm bank, I went through hundreds of donor profiles before
selecting one who seemed the most like Henry in the hope that we
would continue to be a family. He was the man I loved, the father I
wanted for my baby, despite the fact that he had no interest in raising
more children. And it's not just Henry I want in my baby's life—
I want her to have brothers in Nolan and Kyle as well.

The week after my second IVF, I came out of my bedroom to find
Kyle watching me from across the hall.

"Lexi, you don't look so good," he'd said. "Are you sick?"

He was just starting his final semester of high school, his older
brother away at college in Ohio, and Henry and I had agreed not to tell
them about my IVF.

"I'm trying to have a baby," I admitted. "But it's not going well."

Immediately, I regretted the words, worrying Henry would be
upset. But Kyle had surprised me, pulling me into a hug. "A baby would
be amazing, Lexi," he told me. "Don't give up."

When Kyle walked away, I noticed Henry in the doorway of the office, a kind smile on his face. We watched each other for a beat before he
beckoned me forward and opened his arms, holding me while I cried.
That day, he rubbed my back and feet, drew me a bath and made chicken
soup for dinner. Though we didn't discuss babies or parenthood—it was
a conversation we'd already exhausted—Henry's actions reminded me
that, children or no, I was loved.

Though there were still embryos left after that, I was too tired to go through the process again. At nearly thirty-four, I tried to accept that my time had passed, though I knew women had babies much older than that. Summer came and went and Kyle started junior college. The house was empty. By then, I had stopped talking about it—maybe that's why Henry blames Mara for my desire to be a mother. But Mara wasn't the source of that desire; her arrival in Denver only offered a fresh spark of hope.

A beeping sound comes from behind me as a driver navigates a cart through the station, which is growing busier now. I step aside to let him by, passing a young boy, maybe three or four, with a stuffed blue dog in one hand, dangling by its ear. The thumb of his free hand is in his mouth and his mother cups his shoulder to hold him close as they navigate the station.

That's the kind of mother I want to be to Goose, if I get the chance. To kiss her sweet round cheeks, inhale the smell of baby shampoo and the salt of her tears, the fuzz of hair coming loose from her tiny braids. Dress her in pink until she announces that she hates pink, that she will only wear blue or orange. Only now does it occur to me that Mara won't give birth, as we'd planned, at Rose Medical Center. I won't be fastening Goose into the car seat Mara and I bought—the pink one with the leopard print—or snapping it into the back seat of my Honda CR-V to drive us all home. The birthing plan we so carefully designed—whether or not to do an epidural, how to handle a C-section if the need arose, how Mara would stop breastfeeding after the initial colostrum so I could transition Goose to formula—all of it, moot.

I check my watch to see Mara's bus is due in five minutes, so I make my way to the lane and wait. The scheduled arrival time comes and goes. Another half dozen buses arrive, none from Norristown. I check online for an update and find only the word *delayed*.

Thirty-five minutes later, the Norristown bus pulls in, and I'm flooded with relief. I stand as close to the door as I can, remembering the summer after junior year when Cate and I had waited at Mara's house for her to return from a family reunion in Michigan. How giddy we'd been, shrieking when the red Dodge Caravan came into view, Mr. Vannatta at the wheel. How Mara had tumbled from the car and into our arms and how Cate and I had surreptitiously eyed Caleb as he sauntered past, shaking his head at us. Cate and I had caught each other's eye and giggled at the attention—or lack of it. How long just two weeks had felt without our third. Seeing Mara, hugging and being held by my two best friends, made me feel like some integral piece of me had been returned.

Now, I wait as people file off the bus, gathering bags from the storage area underneath. I scan for Mara, clocking every face that appears, none of them hers. Hugely pregnant, she is likely going to be one of the last off. The disembarking passengers are disheveled, half asleep. A woman with a walker takes an eternity to descend the bus's narrow steps and, through the windshield, I see that behind her, the bus is empty.

Mara is not here.

I'm breathless and stunned and, after a beat, furious at myself. As I stand, staring at the empty bus, the absurdity of my assumption soaks in. All I had was a single piece of paper with a bus schedule, dropped behind the printer, and I assumed it was Mara's plan.

Defeated, I sink onto a bench and stare at the strangers as they pass. If she wasn't on that bus, where is she? Where has she been? Fighting off the building panic, I draw deep breaths and catalog the nearby smells. Diesel fumes, cigarette smoke, hot dogs, and a faint whiff of burned coffee. On the next bench, a woman smokes with intense focus. Her frosted hair is teased high, her lips stained red, her black tracksuit dingy from wear. Beside her is a girl in a similar tracksuit, the word PINK up one leg, eating a hot dog with the same concentration as her mother's smoking. When the woman looks over, her expression pinches in a way that suggests maybe *I'm* the one looking particularly rough this morning.

Standing from the bench, I'm heading toward the station exit when a phone call comes in from an unknown number. I can't help the little jolt of relief, expecting Mara's voice, as I answer. "Hello?"

Even after seventeen years, Caleb's voice is instantly familiar. "Lexicon," he says, distance echoing across the line. "How are you?"

I laugh at the nickname, a giddy rush as the ancient crush flares again. "Thank you for calling me back. Where are you? You sound like you're on Mars."

"Ugh. Making my way home from Singapore. I was there for work. Have to say, I was surprised to hear from you."

"Well, I don't know if you knew, but Mara has been living with me."

"I didn't." His tone shifts. "Has something happened?"

"No," I say. "I mean, I don't think so. She left the house a couple of days ago and I don't know where she went. I'm worried about her. Any idea where she might go?"

"No," he admits. "We don't really talk. I had to track her down when our dad died, six years ago now. She was living in Philadelphia."

I think about Lance and wonder how much of her life Mara shared with her brother. "Was she already married then?"

"Not sure, to be honest." He blows out his breath in a long hiss. "She never came home for the funeral, though she called pretty often for a while. Anxious to get her hands on money from the sale of the house, not that she helped clear it out." He sighs. "We haven't been close since high school, and she pretty much stopped talking to me after I laid into her about the twenty-five grand my dad spent to save her ass in that shitshow with the cruise ship job."

It takes a beat to process what he's said. They're not close anymore. Pressing her brother for money. And the cruise job. Mara told me about working on the ship, but in her version, getting fired was a humorous anecdote, not a story of how her dad had to bail her out. Twenty-five grand would have been a fortune to them. I take hold of the last bit, trying to make sense of what he's telling me. "Why did her getting fired cost twenty-five grand?"

"The wife threatened to sue."

I remember the story—the old couple caught screwing in a closet. "How could she have sued Mara?"

"Mara signed a contract that she wouldn't get involved with the guests."

What is he talking about? "Involved?"

"Of course, she had to fuck the richest asshole on the damn boat on day three of a two-week cruise," Caleb goes on. "His wife caught them in their stateroom when he thought she was getting a massage. Turned out it was a couples massage—in their room. The massage therapist saw it all. Mara hadn't even gotten her first paycheck, so she was totally broke. Dad paid for her flight home and hired an attorney to keep her out of jail." A deep sigh fills the line. "Mara is toxic, Lexi."

*Toxic.* The word vibrates in my head until it no longer sounds like a word at all.

My gaze lands on an overhead screen, words ticking across as though the letters are being typed one at a time. *Please keep track of your belongings. Greyhound is not responsible for lost or stolen items.*

"Look at all the Cate shit," Caleb says.

"What do you mean—what Cate shit?"

When he doesn't answer, I think momentarily that the connection was lost. "Caleb? You mean the hot tub? The accident?"

"Yeah, the accident," he repeats. "But where the hell was Mara? I mean, what kind of person lets her best friend die in her hot tub?" His anger surprises me.

"Mara didn't let Cate die," I say defensively. "That's awful, Caleb. She wasn't even there."

"They're calling my flight," Caleb says. "I should go, but it was good to hear from you. Hope everything works out with Mara."

And then Caleb is gone.

# CHAPTER

# 13

ONLY AFTER CALEB ends the call do I remember the reason Mara wasn't home when Cate died was because she'd had to go out to pick up Caleb. His words replay in my head. Is he saying that Mara *wasn't* picking him up when Cate died? That Mara was lying about where she was that day? But it's so much more than that. Despite what she told me, Mara doesn't know anything about her brother's life now; they've been estranged for years. More lies.

I want to fear *for* Mara, not fear Mara herself. Despite everything I've learned the past two days, shifting my perspective of Mara from best friend and confidante to liar and manipulator requires an emotional distance that I'm unable to achieve. But it's more than emotional distance. The leap also means accepting that the closest relationship of my young life—perhaps the closest relationship of my *entire* life—is a fraud. With my parents gone, with the way the pregnancy has created distance between me and Henry and his boys, Mara is my person. Not just a friend, but sister, therapist, and rock. Whether it's naivete or stubbornness, I was determined to believe that there must be a justifiable explanation for her disappearance.

Until now.

I have to face the fact that there's no way to reconcile what Mara has done with the best friend I thought I knew. Maybe I did know Mara once, but I certainly don't know her anymore. Mara arrived at my house a stranger, and she remains a stranger now.

The only difference is now she's a stranger with my child. I hold tight to my image of Goose—chubby little hands, tongue between her lips in concentration, as she learns to tie her shoelaces, making one bunny ear and then the other. I picture her tiny fingers, her furrowed brow, her elation when she pulls the ears and realizes her own triumph.

There is no tenable alternative to finding them, so I push the possibility from my mind.

Several blocks from the bus terminal, the smell of bacon stops me in front of a window. Inside, a long counter is visible, patrons eating from plates heaped with food. My hunger is an engine, revving. It feels wrong to be hungry at a time like this, when there is so much at stake, but I walk into the diner, and the hostess nods me toward a two-top surrounded by empty tables.

One of the few pleasures my dad enjoyed was a diner breakfast. He didn't have health problems, but he acted like eating greasy eggs and pork sausage was something he could only afford to do once or twice a year. The few times I was invited to join him, he was as close to gleeful as I ever saw him. We rarely spoke, he and I, and those breakfasts were no different, but he would make noises of appreciation as he inhaled the scent of the food, then little guttural groans as he tasted each bite. I knew better than to comment, so I'd sit across from him, savoring a stack of pancakes as big as my head as I absorbed his tiny slice of happiness, storing it to balance out the long days of silent brooding.

When the waitress comes by, she raises a pot and asks, "Coffee?"

"Please." I order eggs, toast, and bacon, just like my dad.

The food is out too quickly to have been cooked fresh but it tastes as good as it smells. I eat until I'm full, wrapping the second piece of toast in a napkin to eat later, and pay before walking back to the hotel. There's no word from Henry, and, unable to help myself, I call his cell.

The call goes straight to voicemail, and I leave an awkward message, asking whether there's been any response from the investigator about Mara's background report. I haven't actually told Henry that I'm in Philadelphia, and I still don't mention it. The feel of Henry's disappointed gaze when he discovered I hadn't executed a surrogacy contract with Mara still stings. Worse since he was obviously right. I'd never thought of Mara as a surrogate, not since the earliest days when she opened up to the idea of carrying my child. Womb Auntie, she called herself, a ridiculous name that somehow transformed into Goose Oven or Mother Goose. Surrogate, she argued, was too impersonal, too much like a hired outsider.

As the sun finally crests the buildings, I open the thick vinyl hotel curtains and watch dust mites cloud the air like a fresh swarm of gnats. I'm reminded of the long weekend the three of us spent on Lake Erie with Cate's family the summer before our junior year. For three days, we'd snuck the twins' fruit snacks and juice boxes and set ourselves up on the hidden side of a rock outcropping with our notebook.

A cloud of tiny bugs seemed to shroud us as we played hours upon hours of MASH, a game Mara had learned from an older cousin a year or so earlier. The choices for husbands were always movie stars—from Ashton Kutcher to Zac Efron and Johnny Depp—and the jobs all things none of us would ever have done—Astronaut, Runway Model. So determined to leave Cleveland, we never put our hometown as a choice in the game. As far as we were concerned, a shack in Timbuktu trumped any mansion within two hundred miles of where we grew up.

Despite strict limitations on where we'd live in the game, we'd always included outlandish numbers of offspring—five often being on the low end and sometimes listing as many as nine or ten. Ever the dreamer, Mara always managed to invent a story in which she'd be happy with her fate—even if it was to live in a shack, married to the high school janitor with twelve children. In Mara's story, the janitor would save the child of a wealthy family in some death-defying act of valor and be awarded a massive windfall and some high-paying job in Hawaii, so they could move into a mansion on the beach and she could afford three nannies for all those kids. "And a tummy tuck," she'd add.

Mara's ability to spin a positive outcome from any situation always seemed like a gift, but thinking back on the conversation with Caleb,

I wonder if the storytelling had always been a way of protecting herself from a reality she couldn't face.

What reality was she avoiding by coming to Denver?

The view outside my hotel window is of the top of the parking structure, a few dozen cars dotted among the spots. No sign of their drivers, or any people for that matter. In Denver, days can pass when I don't see people on the street, but here, in the density of a city, their absence feels almost apocalyptic.

The room could be a hotel anywhere, its mustard and maroon color scheme as memorable as a blank sheet of paper. Inside the bedside drawer is a wine-colored Bible, the King James version. Holding it in my hands, I sit on the unmade bed, feeling the book's weight, and my thoughts return to Cate. I wonder whether her god was with her when she died and how it would feel if the Bible's presence brought me peace. I let it fall open, the tissue-like pages fluttering as they land, but I can't focus on the words, feel the burn of frustrated tears and blink hard.

I am here. I have a room and a full stomach. By later today, I will almost certainly have the background report with more information about Mara. I've gotten myself here on my own. It's a low bar to set for someone my age, but I force aside the judgment and embrace a sliver of pride. Then I think of Mara—taking off at eighteen to travel alone through Europe—and wish I could recall the details of the postcards she sent. Had she really visited all those exotic places?

It's hard now not to question everything she's told me. And while Mara has always been impetuous, taking Goose feels different. The bus schedule, even the way the phone was returned to its factory settings, makes it feel calculated. Questions arrange themselves like a complex algebra problem as I frustratedly work to solve for X. Why would she go through the effort of carrying my child only to steal her? And why now?

The hours inch by. I have the bizarre desire to drop on the floor and do push-ups or sit-ups, something to move my blood, to pass the time. But the dark colors of the carpet, the subtle funk of moisture and sweat and old cigarette smoke, stops me even before I really consider it.

Instead, I refresh the mail app on my phone every few minutes, hoping for Henry's report. Today is April 6. Goose is due on the 8th. On top of everything else, the possibility that Mara might deliver early amplifies my terror. Though I'm always invited to join her ultrasounds, I don't go into the exam rooms, usually sitting in the waiting room until Mara comes out. Is it possible the doctor told her something in her last appointment, something she didn't share with me?

Somehow, ten o'clock finally arrives—eight a.m. in Denver—and I dial Dr. Lanier's office.

"This is Mara Vannatta," I say. "I was hoping to speak to one of the nurses."

The woman asks for my date of birth and I give her Mara's, holding my breath, half expecting her to call me out on the lie. Instead, she puts me on hold while she checks for an available nurse.

In moments like this, the shame of being unable to carry a pregnancy ignites, a thick smoke that fills me with self-loathing and doubt. Like I'd done something to deserve this fate; some higher power had decided I wasn't fit to be a mother. Could that be the reason Mara took the baby? Because she didn't think I would be a good mother to my child? The rational part of me knows the idea is absurd, but another part is less certain. When Mara agreed to be my surrogate, when she assured me that she was happy to do it, the burning shame was slowly snuffed out. But its heat crawls up under my ribs now, embers seeking oxygen as it blossoms to flames. If I could have carried a baby, this wouldn't be happening. Goose would be safe with me, inside me.

"Ms. Vannatta?"

"Yes," I answer, slamming the lid on my spinning thoughts.

"How can I help you?"

"The baby is due in a few days," I say. "I just wondered if the doctor could tell from my last exam how soon she might come."

The woman laughs lightly, a kind sound. "Oh, if I had a crystal ball in here . . . Honestly, from the chart, it looks like you were about one centimeter dilated at your last appointment." There's a pause. "We were supposed to see you yesterday?"

"Yes," I say. "I still need to reschedule, but I've got a bit of a cold so I'm hunkering down." The lie comes out of me like a cough.

"Sure," she says. "Are you having any contractions?"

"No." I say it with conviction, willing it to be true. Mara can't be in labor yet. I have to be with her, even if it's here instead of Denver, even if we have to surrender our birthing plan, even if we're in a damn elevator. My daughter cannot take her first breath without me.

"Okay, then," she says. "We wait."

"One centimeter," I repeat. "What does that mean?"

"It doesn't really tell us much. You could go into labor any time."

I let my head fall against the hard wood of the headboard, squeeze my eyes closed. "Or?"

"Or it could be another week. Every delivery is a little different."

"But I've heard that first babies are often late." I'm grasping at straws. Desperation spikes in my voice, as though the nurse has the power to give us more time.

"Yes," she agrees. "Statistically speaking, the first often comes after the due date. Did your first pregnancy end in a full-term delivery?"

Across the room, the word *Welcome* floats in slow motion across the television screen. "What do you mean?"

"I can see this is your second pregnancy. Your previous experience can tell us more about what this delivery might be like."

I turn to the side, put my feet on the floor, stand up, sink again.

No. Mara would have told me if she'd been pregnant before.

"Do I have that wrong?" the nurse asks. "Your chart says this is your second pregnancy. Did you carry that baby to term?"

A sound squeaks from my throat—half gasp, half sob. The nurse starts to say something, but I end the call and stare at the bouncing message on the television.

Suddenly, the equation is solved. Mara *is* a liar.

# CHAPTER

# 14

*April 2008*

Cate and Mara make excuses to leave their lunch table early—Cate says she left an AP Physics textbook in her soccer bag and Mara begs off to talk to Ms. Hall about her English paper. Lexi's reaction is the same low-grade suspicion she's carried since that night, and it's easy enough to dismiss. With graduation only eight weeks away, they all have crazy schedules, and the days of lazy lunches, stretched to the last minutes of the hour, are in the past. Cate and Mara agree to meet on the front steps of the school, out of view of the main hall and across campus from the parking lot where half the upperclassmen are coming or going from lunch.

Mara's already waiting for Cate, cross-legged on the concrete ledge, one foot bouncing nervously. "She knows."

Lexi. Of course she's talking about Lexi. The magnitude of the secret they're keeping from her, how hurt she would be, is another thing Cate does not want to think about. The way Lexi reprinted the rules of their notebook, the reminder that they promised to share everything. Pinky swears made when they were brand-new friends, giddy with the closeness of each other, naive about the ways life would drive them apart. Promise or not, they have no choice. "She doesn't know and we can't tell her," Cate says.

Mara's fingers play with the hem of her jean skirt, seemingly unable to stop her hands from moving. The motion is like her mother when she's trying to put off going to the garage to light another cigarette. "Every time I see his face, I want to kill him."

Cate studies her friend, searching for the right thing to say. She has no idea how to comfort her, if that's even what she's supposed to do. She'd love to kill him, too. But the practical side of her would prefer to simply reverse the weekend and do everything differently, as though this was an English paper and she could edit-undo the whole night. "Has he said anything?" she asks, the words slipping out unbidden. Hadn't they decided it was better to just forget the whole thing? So why would she ask?

"No," Mara says, swiping tears from her face.

Cate wraps an arm around her friend and sits in the silence. Eight weeks and they'll leave this town behind, never come back. That's what she has to focus on. Not that night. Her body vibrates with the need to get up and walk away.

Mara folds her arms across herself, but Cate doesn't let go. It was Mara who wanted to talk, and Cate feels like she owes her that. They only have each other. She tries to think what Lexi would say. All this time, Mara has seemed so much more worldly than she and Lexi, but it's Lexi who would steer them through this. Who would be able to support Mara the way she needs. Cate can't do that.

"Hey."

Cate starts at the voice, dropping her arm as Lexi emerges from the front door of the school. Cate has no idea how Lexi found them. Sure, Mara's commented that Lexi is watching them and Cate's felt her sidelong stares, but it's never felt so obvious as this.

She's eyeing them and scanning the street as though searching for the reason they're out here. The lie they told is in her eyes—she knows. Cate wants to grab hold of Mara, remind her that they've agreed not to talk about that night. That they're letting it go.

"What are you guys doing out here?" Lexi asks, crossing her arms as she stops in front of them.

Cate can feel the way Lexi is drawn into herself, the distance. The hurt is on her face and in her stance. Guilt and fear war within Cate, adding to the weight of Mara's tears and the notion that it's her job to console them both.

It's too fucking much.

"Mara just got a call from her mom—they're fighting again," Cate says, unable to look at Mara, knowing it's offsides to use Mara's parents as an excuse.

"Sure," Lexi says. "And you just happened to both show up out here at the same time." It's not a question, so Cate says nothing while Mara goes back to playing with the hem of her skirt.

Cate feels a rush of fury at Mara. It's her fault that they're hiding from Lexi. The desire to run reaches the base of her neck, and Cate jumps from the stairs, brushes off her jeans.

"Eight weeks and we'll be done," she says to both of them. "We can do anything for eight weeks. Right?"

With that, she forces a smile so hard her teeth graze her lips in a flash of pain and walks away, fighting the urge to sprint.

# CHAPTER
# 15

I WAKE TO the sound of ringing and scramble up in the bed. Stretching for my phone, I knock it off the table and onto the floor. It takes another ring before I have it in my hand and, without looking at the screen, I answer, breathless.

"Ms. McNeil?" a familiar male voice asks. "Ms. Alexandra McNeil?"

I recognize the detective's voice. Not Mara.

"This is she." I sit up, dread clawing its way up my spine.

"This is Detective Bentley, calling from the Denver Police Department."

His tone discloses nothing, and I lean onto the headboard as familiar panic hums through me. That my body still responds as it always has is oddly reassuring, a sign that everything will be okay. After all, it's always been okay before. Still, I am anticipating his words: Mara has been found. She never left Denver at all. She is dead and Goose is dead. I came out to Philadelphia and all along she's been in Denver, where she had some terrible accident.

"Yes," I say. "I'm here." I close my eyes and pull my knees to my chest, as ready as I can be to hear his news.

"Where?"

"What?" I say, confused.

"We were at your house today, hoping to speak with you, but you weren't home," he says. "We tried calling, and when we couldn't reach you, we spoke to your husband. He believes you might be in Philadelphia. Is that correct?"

Fury at Henry rises inside me, the sensation like cutting bone, pain in a place I'd thought impervious. Of course Henry would tell the police where I am. Law-abiding and deferential to authority, Henry is a wealthy white man, confident in his position. He has taken every precaution to make sure his life goes as planned, right down to refusing the child I wanted so much. While I resent him for it, I also envy his resolve.

"Ms. McNeil?" Bentley repeats.

"Yes," I say with false bravado. "I'm in Philadelphia, trying to locate my friend. Do you have news?"

"We do," says Bentley.

"You found Mara?" A crack breaks in my voice, threatening to split me in half.

"No," he says quickly, and the dizzying relief halts into sharp frustration. "There was a detective in town, looking for Ms. Vannatta. Detective Sullivan and I just learned that he contacted our department for assistance."

The remaining drops of relief evaporate completely. "A police officer?"

"Yes, ma'am. A detective from Philadelphia."

"What did he say? Why was he looking for Mara?"

"Have you had contact with Ms. Vannatta?" he asks in a tone that says he's done answering my questions.

"No. I haven't."

"Well, if you do find her, I suggest you call us. She's in quite a bit of trouble, your friend."

All the effort I've exerted clinging to the illusion of Mara I thought I knew is wasted. I clutch the bedsheet with my free hand, grasping for solid ground that doesn't exist. "What kind of trouble? Is she in danger?"

"I don't know the details, Ms. McNeil, but according to the Philadelphia officer, a warrant's been issued for her arrest."

At the word *arrest*, my fingers fist around the sheet.

"Wherever she's hiding out, the sooner we locate her and bring her into custody, the safer it is for both her and the baby. We'll be in touch, so keep your phone close." He ends the call.

*Mara is toxic.* Caleb's words. Such a brutal image, my baby swimming inside her, immersed in that toxicity. Even as the denials rise like hopeful flower buds—that Mara wouldn't take Goose from me, or leave without a note, or not contact me or lie—the reality rips them from the soil.

She's done all those things.

A memory comes back to me. One Sunday morning, a few months after Mara's sixteenth birthday, we were driving to the lake to watch a boy she'd met the weekend before at his crew race. Cate was at church and we were late, I can't remember why. A few blocks from the boathouse, a police siren blared behind us.

"Shit," Mara said. She pulled to the curb and gripped the wheel in both hands.

"It's okay," I told her, unsure what else to say, but Mara shook her head.

"Just don't say anything." She looked over at me, gaze as cold as steel. "Okay?"

"Sure," I whispered as the officer reached her window. He peered down, a man close to our dads' age, with a salt-and-pepper goatee.

Mara rolled the window down. "I'm so sorry."

"License and registration."

"Yes, Officer," she said, reaching for her purse in the back seat. To me, she said, "Can you get the registration? It's in the glove compartment."

She handed them to the officer. As soon as they were in his hand, she began to cry.

"My dad is going to kill me," she said. "He was a colonel in the Army for twenty years, and I'm late for his award ceremony." She sounded like she was choking on the words, but the officer looked up at her, expression softening. Mara's dad was a plumber; she had temporarily adopted Cate's as her own, and I was both impressed by how quickly she'd made up the story and also terrified that the officer would see right through the lie.

Mara peered at him, waving through the windshield. "We've been driving around for twenty minutes. It's supposed to be at the boathouse, wherever that is."

"I was Army," the officer said. "Not near as long as that. What award is he getting?"

Mara covered her mouth with one hand as her crying grew louder. "I don't even know," she admitted. "I'm such a terrible daughter. I had an AP English paper due this week, so I wasn't even paying attention. I should have gone with my family, but my friend wanted to come so I picked her up, and now I'm going to miss it."

Mara wasn't in AP English. English was her worst subject. A giggle rose in my throat as I watched in awe and terror to see if the officer would call her out.

The officer returned Mara's license and the registration. "You ladies follow me. When you see me point out the window, just turn left, and the boathouse is at the end of the street." He rose to full height, and all I could see was his finger when he added, pointing to Mara, "You slow down, though. Your dad might be angry that you're late, but he doesn't want to see you hurt. I guarantee that."

Mara clasped her hands together, thanking him and crying harder until the officer walked to his cruiser. Then she looked at me.

"Oh my God," I whispered as though the officer might hear us. "It worked."

"I can't believe it." She dropped her head onto the steering wheel, hands trembling in her lap. Tears continued to track down her cheeks and the redness in her nose deepened; the tightness in her expression made the emotion look real. "I've already got one speeding ticket," she said. "My parents had a massive fight over it. My dad actually left— walked straight out of the house." She exhaled with a little shiver. "He never does that." She wiped her face. "I panicked."

"It's okay now. They'll never know," I said, squeezing her arm. "You're brilliant."

She glanced over and exhaled, pushing damp bangs off her face. Her cheeks were flushed. I would have caved under a sideways glance, but Mara held her own. It was just like her to push the boundaries of what she could get away with. It wasn't like lying to the officer harmed anyone—not really—and her mischievousness was one of the things I'd always loved about her. If she could find a way to skirt the edge of the truth in pursuit of something we wanted, she'd gladly do it. In my mind, Mara had always been clever, but the other side of that coin was deceit.

And she was good at it.

What if she hadn't been able to talk her way out of an arrest warrant? Would she have run? I can't imagine—when we were young, she never got caught.

When I emerge from a shower, there are two missed calls and a text from Henry. I got a fraud notice from the bank, it says. Are you in Philadelphia?

Only now do I realize that it's after three o'clock in the afternoon. My body is so off-kilter from my early morning at the bus station, I slept through most of the day.

Another text appears. Lexi. Should I cancel the card?

My plane ticket and the deposit on the hotel are the only things I've charged since finding Mara gone, but since I never travel, it's not a surprise that the bank suspected fraud. The last thing I want to do is discuss my half-baked plan to find Mara, but Henry might cancel the card if I don't respond. Yes. In Philadelphia. Card charges are valid. I'll be in touch as soon as I have news. I wonder what Detective Bentley told Henry, whether he mentioned the arrest warrant, and add, Talked to the detective. All good.

A reply comes in right away. I just got the report on Mara. Sent it to your email.

The email stands out among the promotions and sales offers, the subject line in caps: MARA VANNATTA INITIAL REPORT. A pdf file is attached, the first page listing Mara's full name and date of birth. What follows is a standard credit report, beginning with known aliases. Anticipation momentarily edges out my panic as I search for her husband's name. The list includes Mara Renee Vannatta; Mara Renee;

Mara Vannatta; Renee Vannatta; MR Vannatta, and a handful of others, all misspellings of her last name.

There are no additional names.

My own credit report shows a mixture of my maiden and married names. I consider whether there's a difference in reports from state to state, but the top of the report says Experian, a national company. I skip down the page to a list of addresses, one of which is the house where Mara grew up in Cleveland. Two others are listed, both in Philadelphia. From the report, I can't tell which address is more recent, so I take pictures of both. I copy the investigator's email address and compose an email, introducing myself as Henry's wife and requesting additional information on Mara. I type my phone number and ask that he call or email, emphasizing the urgency, then send it off, hoping he'll get back to me quickly.

Returning to the email, I notice a second attachment, below the first. This one is titled *M. Vannatta, Public Records*. I open the document and see that the report barely fills half a page. The first line lists a bankruptcy from three years before Mara came to Denver. Vannatta is listed as her last name there as well. The second half of the page has a single line that reads *Recorded Marriages: 0. Recorded Divorces: 0.*

I replay the words Mara used when she'd first arrived in Denver— that she'd been married to a man named Lance, that he'd abused her. I skip over the fact that she isn't married. Maybe it was a civil ceremony. Of all the lies she's told, marriage seems the least of them. If he was hurting her, if he was dangerous, she had to escape no matter the nature of their relationship.

The problem is that the lie stings like a fresh cut on an old wound.

"His father was an alcoholic, and I knew he'd had it rough as a kid, but he was so good, so kind." The first thing she'd said about Lance that day, tears streaming down her face. "But he was struggling at work and things got tight. I worked as hard as I could, but it wasn't enough. He got angry, started drinking."

With what I know now, the cynical part of me wonders how long she'd spent spinning that story for me. Whether she'd specifically mentioned money because she saw how comfortable I was, how well

Henry did. Because money was something I could offer. Did she know how easily I would fall for it? Of course I would invite her to stay. And what was her plan from there? She couldn't have known about my infertility, my stubborn desire to be a mother.

But what luck. *She* could carry a baby. She'd done it before. Even if she'd had her concerns, Mara would have known that being my surrogate was the perfect way to ingratiate herself, to become indispensable. How readily I let go of my other friends, my stepchildren, my marriage.

She'd laid out her plan to conquer me like so many dominoes, then she nudged the first and watched them fall.

There was no abusive husband. There was no husband at all.

But I had *seen* Mara that day. Her unnaturally thin body, the bruises. Beneath the lies, there must have been some kernel of truth. If those injuries weren't from an intimate partner, then they were from someone just as dangerous—someone she'd made angry, by stealing or double-crossing, until she got caught and was forced to run. Colorado was pretty damn far from Philadelphia. Had she banked on the odds that no one would find her? After all, how unlikely was it that, after all these years, someone would link Mara to me?

I look at Mara's last known address on the screen. She had shown up, unannounced, at my house all those months ago. Now it's time for me to show up at hers.

# CHAPTER
## 16

THE CAB DROPS me in front of Mara's last known address. My first view is of the buildings across the street: several warehouses and what looks like a school, though there are no kids visible, just a red jungle gym, the paint chipped, behind a chain-link fence. My driver had looked wary when I told him we were going to Nicetown, but when we arrive, I don't have the sense that it's a dangerous place. Quite the opposite.

On the side of the street where Mara once lived, the block is a string of connected two-story brick houses. Each has a narrow raised porch a few steps off the sidewalk, surrounded by black iron rails, and on the street level, a small window down into a basement. Here and there, bikes are locked to the railings, and chairs—plastic mostly—sit empty on porches. I can imagine a warm summer day, kids on bikes, parents and grandparents talking and laughing, a community where children are raised not only by their own parents but by the collective neighborhood. It's the way I want to raise Goose—to give her a community of people, aunties and uncles and cousins, even if they're not blood. A community that I haven't yet formed, the one I imagine would grow from mothers' groups and, later, from school.

The opposite of my own childhood, trapped inside that beautiful dark house, never open to others, the exterior carefully manicured, the interior perfectly styled but devoid of joy. My parents each had siblings— my dad two older brothers and my mom a younger brother and sister— but they weren't close. I only met my cousins once, in middle school. My dad's brothers lived in California, and when they visited, they came as a team: my uncles, their wives, a gaggle of kids. Even in my own house, I was the outsider. There were rules I didn't know, a language I didn't speak.

I'd assumed Mara would be part of Goose's family. Her godmother, at the very least. I fold the thought away for now.

At Mara's old address, there is no sign of life. The attached two-story home is buttoned up. Drapes hang over the windows on the lower floor, still and lifeless. On the second floor, only darkened light fixtures are visible from the street. Undeterred, I climb the steps and ring the bell, listening for sounds from inside. On a Friday at four, people should be getting home from work, from school. There is no answer, so I ring again, as though I might conjure someone through persistence.

"She ain't home," comes a young man's voice, from close by.

I search for the source of the words, but the street is eerily quiet. "Hello?"

There's the sound of singing. No background music, just a baritone voice and a familiar tune. In an effort to locate where it's coming from, I turn in a slow circle on the porch, but the sound is too faint. I'm about to descend the stairs to the street when motion in the front window catches my eye. I could have sworn that window was closed before, but now the drapes rustle ever so slightly in the wind and I can make out the shape of a seated figure on the far side of the room.

"Excuse me," I call toward him. "I'm hoping you can help me find a friend of mine." When there's no response, I add, "It's important."

"What's important?"

This voice is different, so low it rumbles in my ribs.

I turn to see a man carrying a bike up the steps to the porch. There's no room to move around him, and my first thought is that we're standing very close. In his late twenties or early thirties, he's massive— maybe six five and close to three hundred pounds—with tattoos that cover his hands and neck, and a single cross below his right eye. I offer a nervous smile, thinking of the cab driver's response to Nicetown, the abandoned street. I hate myself for the fear that runs through me like ice water.

The shape in the window is gone, and a moment later, the door opens. A young man in a wheelchair fills the entry. He's younger than the other man by at least a few years—early twenties probably.

"Terrence. Guess it's spa time for the D-man," he says. The two men face each other and do a strange series of head motions—left left right down down up, then a double head bob.

"Yes, sir. Spa day," Terrence confirms. I realize that the man in the wheelchair is using his chin on a joystick to navigate the chair—the head motions are an intricate greeting, a customized handshake for a quadriplegic.

As Terrence enters the house, I remain on the porch, waiting. Down the block, an older couple emerges onto their porch. She opens a Dr Pepper and calls, "Damon? You have a good day?"

"Best one so far," the man in the wheelchair shouts back. "You got a Dr P for me?"

"Not 'til you've had dinner. Gladys would have my head," she says with a low laugh.

The inside of the house is bathed in amber light, highlighting the rich tones of old oak floors and banister railings, the balusters painted a white that has darkened to a yellow cream. Scents of lemon furniture polish and lilies drift through the air as Damon spins the chair toward me. He tilts his head. "Who'd you say you were looking for?"

"Mara Vannatta?"

"I know that name," he says. "Think she's one of Ms. Knight's ladies. You can come in."

"Thank you," I say with a rush of gratitude.

He reverses the chair so I can enter as a woman calls from inside. "Damon?"

"Out here, Ms. K. Terrence just arrived, and you got a visitor."

The woman who appears is barely five feet tall, with close-cut gray hair and watery green eyes. Her face is marked with deep wrinkles. She wears a long-sleeved dress with clogs and wipes her hands on the fabric as she enters the room.

"Hello," she says, tipping her head slightly as she studies me. "I'm Gladys Knight." She waves a hand. "Not *that* Gladys Knight, obviously."

"Alexandra McNeil," I say and offer a hand.

She grips it with surprising firmness. "And you met Damon?"

Damon offers a toothy smile.

"I did," I say. "He was kind enough to let me in."

Before I can continue, she raises a finger. "Let me get Damon and Terrence squared away, then we can chat." She motions to a living room. "Why don't you take a seat and give me about five minutes?"

"Sure. Thank you." A worn lavender velvet couch sits under the window, its arms decorated by yellowed doilies. Opposite are two up-holstered chairs, their fabric worn thin, the stuffing visible beneath more doilies, and, across the room, the fireplace has been filled in with bricks.

Behind me, Terrence lets out an exaggerated moan as he lifts Damon from his wheelchair.

"Best ride of the week," Damon says with a laugh.

"I think you're getting fat on me," Terrence complains as he carries Damon up the narrow stairwell, the old steps groaning noisily. Gladys Knight follows them at a distance, one palm stretched ahead of her as though she might catch Terrence if he slips.

I watch until all three are out of sight, then turn back to the room and approach the mantel to look at the photographs. A framed black-and-white features an older couple, probably Gladys's parents or even her grandparents. Beside that is a picture of a younger Gladys, with a boy of maybe twelve or thirteen. His dark hair hangs over one eye, and he glowers at the camera—beside him, Gladys beams proudly. A third picture features Gladys with an infant, and beyond that, a frame holding seven school photographs.

None of the faces in the school pictures resemble Terrence or Damon, or the child in the other photographs. They are arranged four across the top and three below, in no obvious order, and I lift the frame for a closer look. They are average high school students, well groomed with straight white teeth. Four girls, three boys, three Black, three white, one Asian. It makes me wonder whether Gladys runs a home of some sort—if that's why Damon lives here. How long has it been since this was Mara's address? I survey the room with the irrational hope that her image might be hanging on a wall. Turning back to replace the framed photograph of the seven kids, I notice something else on the mantel.

It's a plastic sleeve holding a newspaper article, only the headline visible. It reads, *Seven High School Seniors Killed in Charter School Shooting, Gunman Dead*. I study the faces of these young people, the seven lined up morbidly on the mantel, their smiling faces now haunting with the knowledge that they're all dead. Why would Gladys have these framed?

"Sorry about that," Gladys says, returning.

Before I can turn away, the plastic sleeve with the article slides off the mantel and drops to the floor. I stoop and quickly pick it up, returning it before facing Gladys. "Sorry. I just saw the picture—"

Gladys walks to join me at the mantel and straightens the frame. "My Charlie did that."

"Charlie?"

"My son," she says, motioning to the picture of her and the young man with the hair in his eyes. "He was a senior in high school when he shot those kids." Despite her stoic expression, her voice trembles a little. "I keep them here to remind me."

"I'm so sorry," I say, and it feels like offering a Band-Aid to the survivor of a plane wreck.

"Shot Damon, too," she says. "He was living with an aunt and uncle at the time. They couldn't manage his care, so he came here."

"In the wheelchair?" I ask because it's inconceivable—a paralyzed man, now living with the mother of his shooter.

"Bullet grazed his spinal cord," she says. "He was almost the eighth victim."

I glance at the smiling faces in the frame. Seniors in high school, all dead.

Just like Cate.

I think of their parents, of Cate's mother and father. How did they survive that grief? I imagine Goose, swimming inside the warmth of Mara's womb, picture the tiny arms that will stretch, the fingers that will uncurl when she emerges. The weight of her in my arms, the angry wail as she takes her first breath. What if I never see her face? Staring at the seven dead teenagers, I wonder if it's worse to lose a child you never knew or one you spent eighteen years loving. What does it matter? I would take one day with Goose over nothing. A week, a month, a year. I want her forever, but I will take what I can get.

Everywhere I look: evidence. Motherhood is an impossible job. Parenthood in general, but especially motherhood. No matter how hard you try, you will fail your child. And yet the desire to protect them trumps anything else. I have long seen myself as a willow tree, soft-limbed and bendable, more likely to agree than to stand up for what I want. But the desire for a child has changed me. I might have bent to Henry's will, enjoyed the limited ways I could mother Nolan and Kyle, but the draw of motherhood, the desire that took root in the deepest place inside me, hardened my limbs. The willow becoming an oak.

"Damon said you were asking after Mara," Gladys says.

"You know her?" A spark of hope.

"Yes. It was a long time ago, but women come and stay with me sometimes. When they're trying to get out of a bad spot and need a little help," she says, vague in her explanation. "Why are you looking for her?"

I study the faces on the mantel, taking in the shooter and victims side by side. Gladys is a mother who knows the grief of losing a child. I explain about Mara leaving her abusive marriage and staying with me. I don't mention Goose or the surrogacy, just that I'm concerned because she disappeared without a word.

"I think she's in trouble," I finish.

It's the truth. Just not the entire truth.

Gladys studies me, though her expression shows no surprise. Instead, she seems to be debating what to tell me, or possibly how much. "She visited about a year and a half ago," Gladys says. "But it was brief. It's been years since she lived here. That was the fall before Charlie's . . . incident." Her face goes momentarily pale, as though the memory of that day draws all the blood to her broken heart. "When she first settled back in the States after her travel, everything that happened finally caught up with her. She couldn't run anymore, and she was hurting. Couldn't forgive herself."

"What do you mean?" I ask. "Forgive herself for what?"

Her green eyes hold mine for a long minute, the wrinkles between her brow deepening. Then she answers, like it's the most obvious thing in the world.

"For Cate."

# CHAPTER
# 17

I SINK INTO Gladys's lavender couch, smoothing my fingers over the ridges of the macramé doily.

"Mara felt guilty about Cate? Why?"

Gladys moves around a chair and lowers herself slowly into it, like sitting is a rare indulgence. "You know what happened to Cate?"

"Mara, Cate, and I were best friends. Mara called me that day, right after she found her."

Gladys studies me a moment, as though gauging whether what I've said is the truth, or waiting for me to say more. She only says, "Well, then you can imagine why she felt guilty."

The comment surprises me. I can't imagine why Mara felt guilty about Cate's death. "Because it happened at her house?"

Gladys offers a small smile. I wait for her to say more, but she remains quiet. Mara never mentioned feeling guilt, but maybe that came later, after grief had released its claws. Is this something Mara had wanted to tell me, when Cate came up in conversation? Something I never gave her a chance to say?

"Mara and I were out of touch for a long time. Pretty much from high school graduation until January of last year when she came to

Denver," I admit. "She's lived with me for almost a year and a half, but she didn't talk much about her time here." I wait, hoping Gladys might fill in some gaps.

"We met through a friend of a friend when Mara was new to Philadelphia," Gladys says. "She was probably thirty by then, but in moments, she still seemed like a lost child. She struggled to find work and was in debt—to some local people and to her family, I think. She was dancing then." She raises a hand as though to ward off any comment. "I knew a lot of the dancers—there are women who love it—it makes them feel empowered and it pays well enough to live on their own, to make their own choices." She picks a piece of lint off her slacks. "But Mara didn't love it, and that forced her to make some hard choices. Staying here for a while helped, but it wasn't permanent."

"What kind of hard choices?"

Gladys settles those green eyes on me again. "If she lived with you for a year and a half, you probably know more than I."

It's easy to read between the lines. If Mara is my best friend, I shouldn't have to ask someone else about her life. "I think she's back in Philadelphia now," I say. "Do you know where she might go if she was here? Who she might turn to?"

"I couldn't begin to guess," Gladys says, which I take to mean she won't guess. Outside, it's growing dark as Gladys rises from her chair, a hint that it's time I leave. "If you need a ride, Terrence can take you."

I picture the bike locked to the porch railing. "I'm not sure we'll both fit on his bike," I say with a smile.

Gladys laughs lightly. "He takes my car some days," she explains. "Part of our trade." She shifts toward the door; I sense our conversation is ending and I long to keep her here.

Voices carry down the stairs, spiking a sense of urgency, so I lower my voice and tell her the rest of the truth. "She's carrying my baby. I couldn't get pregnant," I add, a whisper. A plea.

"That sounds like Mara," she says, and her words fill me with relief.

"Does it?" I don't want to admit how deep the doubt has burrowed.

"It really does."

"I don't feel like I know her. I thought I did, but then she left . . ."

Gladys holds my gaze. "She has a good heart, but she struggled. Got caught in something she couldn't get out of."

"Lance," I guess, but Gladys doesn't react to his name.

"It's been years since she and I really talked," is all she says.

"Is there anyone who might still know her? Someone she might go to."

"She brought a woman to the house a few times, four or five years ago. I can't recall her name, but Mara said they'd worked together."

"Do you know where that was? The place they worked?"

Gladys shook her head. "I don't think either of them said."

I want to sit her down and pepper her with questions, shake her until she remembers something useful.

"She spoke often about you three," Gladys says. "I don't think she had friends like that after high school."

"Me neither," I admit.

"When is your baby due?" she asks.

"Soon," I say, unable to admit just how soon.

She squeezes my hand as though she senses my panic. "Motherhood is the trickiest of gifts," she says. "Whether we dream about it for a decade or it happens accidentally, it changes us. It's irrevocable. And it is the very definition of joy and also the ultimate heartache—mother or child."

I try to read her face, to understand how she survived the loss of her son and the knowledge of what he'd done. "I am so sorry," I say, the most worthless words.

A soft smile curls her lips despite the sadness in her eyes. "Damon saved me." She exhales and her thin frame trembles, down to the hand that rests on mine. "People say that I saved him. That he'd have ended up in a group home or a hospital. My son is the reason he's in that chair, and he's the reason I'm alive." The stairs groan under the weight of someone descending. She holds my gaze. "No matter what happens, you find a purpose to go on."

I shake my head, terrified she's telling me that something has happened to Mara. That I won't find her and Goose.

"I have faith in our Mara," she says. "And I have something that may help you have faith, too," she adds as Terrence descends the stairs with Damon in his arms. Now clean-shaven, Damon wears a fresh shirt, a pinstriped polo, his short curls still damp.

"Now here's a man I'd like to dine with," Gladys says, leaning to kiss Damon's cheek. She turns to Terrence and thanks him, asks if he doesn't mind giving me a ride.

"Sure thing, Ms. K," Terrence says. "I'll be right back. Got to get my stuff."

Gladys excuses herself, too, and follows Terrence up the stairs, instructing Damon to keep me company.

Damon maneuvers the wheelchair between the couch and a chair and lets out a deep, satisfied sigh.

"She tell you the whole story?" he asks, nodding to the mantel.

"She did."

"It's pretty fucked up, but she's a good lady."

"She seems it," I say, then consider how long he's been here. "Did you ever meet Mara?"

"One time," he says. "It was right after I came here from the hospital. She came by with her rich friend."

"Rich friend?"

"Well, the lady married some rich older guy. Parked right out front in a brand-new Mercedes."

"Do you remember her name?"

Damon is quiet a moment and I hold my breath.

Gladys comes down the stairs, clasping a white envelope. "Mara gave this to me. She told me to keep it just in case."

My hand stills in midair. "When was this?"

"The last time I saw her—about a year and a half ago."

"I remember that, Ms. Knight. The time she brought the fancy lady. With the gold Mercedes," Damon says.

"I remember the friend, though I don't recall the Mercedes," Gladys agrees.

"Yeah, she had some weird name—Poppy or Bitty."

Damon is still talking when Terrence descends the stairs. "Car's out back," he says, and I rise to follow.

"They were heading to the Lucky," Damon goes on, talking to Gladys. "What was that lady's name?"

"Oh, Damon. I already said I can't remember," Gladys says, her tone a little impatient, and I feel like I'm the one being scolded.

I've taken up enough of their time. "Thank you again," I say, following Terrence through the kitchen and out the back door as Gladys tells Damon it's time for dinner.

Settled into the car, I consider waiting until I'm at the hotel to read Mara's letter, but by the time Terrence has taken the first turn, I'm ripping it open. It's a single page, but as I draw it out, something heavy falls into my lap.

A key. The top is squared off, the words *do not duplicate* stamped into the metal. Immediately, I think of the key-shaped impression on the cardstock behind Mara's picture frame. Is this a duplicate of that key?

The note is short, written in Mara's familiar handwriting.

*If something happens to me, check unit 2714. Don't tell anyone. He'll kill for it.*

My throat closes to form a scoff, but no sound emerges as my eye is drawn to the word *kill*. Mara has underlined the word with two hard lines and I trace them with a finger, feel the way the pen strokes almost cut through the paper. I can feel her fear in those lines, the plea to hear her. To believe.

It was real.

Farther down the page, she's written *Entrance Code* and an eight-digit number. When I flip the page over, the back is blank, save for a smudge of ink. There is no additional information. Nothing to explain who might kill and for what. Only the clear message that whoever she was running from, Mara was afraid. These words turn everything on its head again. I believe the fear in this note, but it doesn't change anything—the same questions burst to the surface. Why leave Denver? Why come here? Why not tell me?

"Everything okay?"

Terrence's voice startles me.

"Yes," I say quickly, skimming the page again. Unit 2714—where? I flip the key in my palm, but there is no logo on the metal. "Is there a storage facility near here?"

Terrence glances over. "Like, right near here?"

"I don't know," I admit. We hit a red light, and I show him the note and the key.

Terrence drums his fingers on the steering wheel as he waits for the light to change. "I know there are a bunch of them around town."

Surely Mara didn't mean for me to check every storage unit in Philadelphia. Maybe she left this for someone else, someone who would know which storage facility she used. Maybe 2714 isn't a storage unit at all—it could be a safe deposit box, or a locker somewhere. I tuck the key back inside and fold the envelope in half, then in half again, frustrated.

I pull out my phone to start a Google search for nearby storage centers when I remember that there was a second previous address listed on Mara's credit report. Finding the photo I took, I read off the address and ask Terrence if he knows where it is; he offers to take me.

Terrence, it turns out, is a very pleasant conversationalist. He explains that he's in nursing school, and Gladys arranged for him to get credit for coming to the house and helping Damon. In addition, she loans him her car so he can earn money driving for Lyft. I offer to pay him for this ride, but he firmly declines. While we drive, I check my email, but there's nothing. Where's the Philadelphia police detective who came to Denver to arrest Mara? It seems like an overreaction to send a detective to Denver instead of enlisting the help of the local police in Colorado. It implies that Mara's crimes warrant the extra caution, the added expense.

What the hell did she do?

When we reach our destination—an ugly concrete building with long dark streaks striping its exterior—Terrence insists on coming inside with me. I'm grateful for the company as we climb the stairs to what was apparently Mara's former apartment. The bare bulbs that light the stairwell are burned out on the first two floors, leaving only the glow from higher levels to illuminate the way. There are more stains on the stairs as we rise, and the scent of cigarette smoke and the sharp tang of liquor grow more pungent as well. Gladys said Mara was struggling, but it's hard to picture her here.

Half the hallway lights on the floor where Mara lived are also out, and at the end of the corridor, something darts in front of us. I tell myself it's a cat. No one answers at Mara's old unit, so we knock on the adjoining apartments as well. One is opened by a man about Terrence's age, who was obviously asleep. When I ask if he knows Mara, he says no and slams the door. We knock on a few other doors, but the residents are either not home, ignoring us, or have no idea who Mara is. And the numbers only go to 650. No unit 2714 here.

When we return to the car, I'm tired and hungry. And frustrated. A dead end.

"We could try to reach the super," Terrence says.

"That's okay."

"Where to now? Back to the hotel?"

"Sure," I say, reaching into my pants pocket for the hotel key. When I pull it out, a folded paper comes with it. It's the receipt I found in Mara's duffel, back in the coach house closet. "Wait," I say, squinting to read the details in the dark car. My pulse flares when I realize it's from a bar called the Lucky Dive. "Damon mentioned a place called the Lucky. Is that a bar?"

"Yeah," Terrence says as I lift the receipt in my hand.

"The Lucky Dive?"

"One and the same."

# CHAPTER
# 18

WHEN WE ARRIVE at the Lucky Dive, I force thirty dollars on Terrence, and he writes his phone number on the envelope with Mara's note, encouraging me to reach out if I need a ride. I thank him profusely as I emerge from the car and join a group heading inside. The sound of Bruce Springsteen and the roar of voices flood onto the street, trailed by the smell of alcohol and french fries and glow of amber lights. Groups of people stand in clusters, laughing and shouting over the music. From a back room, I can hear the snap of billiard balls striking one another.

It takes a few minutes to find an opening at the bar, where I slide in and order a beer, resting my elbows on the surface. The sticky wood is decorated by decades of initials and scratched messages, covered by a cloudy layer of plastic that renders the letters beneath almost illegible.

I lift the beer bottle to my lips and take a swallow, relishing the burn of carbonation as it slides down my throat. I work to digest what Gladys Knight said. Her faith in Mara, the little nudge that swings the pendulum back toward the Mara I was so sure I knew—the good-hearted Mara, the generous friend. The honest one, not the toxic one Caleb described. And yet, there's no denying that in the past few days,

Mara has done things that don't reconcile with that person. I sense someone approaching and turn to find a man standing too close. He's around my age with dark hair slicked back, bringing to mind Elvis in his early days, before the gyrating hips and swinging hair. But the similarities end at the man's narrowed angry eyes and the way he runs an index finger along the inside waistband of his jeans. His teeth are stained yellow and he reeks of cigarette smoke.

Before he can speak to me, I turn to the bar and slide a ten-dollar bill across to get the bartender's attention again.

"I was wondering if you know my friend?" I display a picture of Mara before he can ask me what I need. "She used to come here."

He stares at me an extra beat, like he's trying to place me, but says nothing, his attention shifting to the line of patrons at the bar. Two women huddle together, one cupping her hand over the other's ear as she shares some secret. Nearby, a man uses the thumb of his free hand to stroke the jaw of the woman beside him as she looks around, wearing a bored expression. No one meets my eye. When I turn back, the bartender stands at the far end of the bar. Head down, he makes a drink—something shaken, then strained and poured into two martini glasses. He takes a card for payment, his movements practiced and precise. A moment later, he ducks behind the bar, probably to pull something from a cooler. He's down there longer than the task should require, and when he stands up, he slides his phone into his pocket before setting two beers in front of another couple. I wait a full five minutes for him to make his way back to my end of the bar, but he never does. Even refuses to look in my direction.

He knows something. I can feel it.

I pocket the unclaimed ten and face the crowd, scanning. Was the bartender's strange behavior because I asked about Mara? Chances are his response has nothing to do with my question, but what was he doing on his phone? If Mara is wanted for some crime, maybe he thinks I'm with the police . . . though my appearance should make that seem highly unlikely: I'm wearing old jeans and a cotton shirt with a Colorado flag under a black windbreaker, and my hair, which hasn't been washed or brushed in two days, is fastened in a bun at the nape of my neck. A new group presses toward the bar to order, so I move away, standing awkwardly between a cluster of tables, all their seats occupied.

Determined not to give up, I take my almost-full bottle of beer farther into the bar. A line is queued for the bathroom—four women stand along the wall, each looking at her phone. I pull out my own, Mara's face on the screen. "Excuse me," I say. "Do any of you recognize this woman? She's gone missing and her family is really worried."

Down the line, the women shake their heads, murmur no. I use the restroom, ditching my beer on the counter, and wash my hands.

Mara was always the one who whistled and shouted, who stood in the sunroof of the limo at our junior prom, waving to passengers in other cars or people on the street. If she were here, she'd have talked to every person in the bar. Someone should know her—unless the receipt isn't a clue at all, just evidence that she was once inside this bar. Another dead end.

The woman beside me at the sinks is touching up her makeup when I ask, "Do you come here often?"

She laughs, twisting down the lipstick and returning it to her purse. "Usually, it's the guys who use that line."

I let out an awkward laugh. "No one recognizes my friend. I was just wondering if this is the kind of place where the same people come regularly or if it's more of a random crowd."

"I've only lived here about a year, but I come pretty often," she says, smacking her lips in the mirror.

"And do you usually recognize other people?"

"There are plenty of regulars."

She wishes me luck and leaves. I stand in the empty bathroom, the smell of beer and lemon cleanser and urine. Defeated, I decide to give up for the night. Tomorrow, I can look for Mara's storage unit, but it's too late for that now. I think back to nights spent on the living room couch, a movie playing while Mara and I watched in companionable silence. How I wish we were back there now, in our pajamas and socks, watching *Finding Nemo* for the nine hundredth time.

I zip my coat and exit the bathroom, pulling out my phone to call a Lyft. The battery shows one percent, so I hurry to open the app and request a ride to the hotel. The app says it's looking for a driver when the screen goes black. Damn it. I could ask the bartender to call me a cab, but he'd probably ignore me. Surely cabs must drive by. I'll just wait on the street.

The exhaustion of the day settles in as I step outside. Since marrying Henry, my life has been so contained. When I wasn't with Henry and the boys, I was mostly alone at the house, reading or baking or putting together a photo album from the hundreds of digital pictures Henry had taken and never printed. While he was at work and the boys were at school, on weekends when they would camp or go see baseball or hockey or soccer games as far as Arizona and Washington, I opted to stay home. One of the few habits I inherited from my parents is that I relish both silence and tidiness. In the first days that Mara lived with us, I remember worrying that I'd be overwhelmed or exhausted by her presence. But Mara seemed to understand, and gave me plenty of space.

And after what she'd been through, she likely needed the space as much as I did.

Maybe that's why I didn't pry into Mara's life after high school. I didn't want to hear about her hardships—I didn't want to open a painful conversation. The same reason I avoided the subject of children with the women in the flower shop or the friends I made in Denver. Even when all I wanted on earth was a baby of my own, it was so much easier to pretend that I was perfectly content to be a stepmom to Kyle and Nolan. I've long blamed my sensitive nature—my inclination to absorb the trauma of others as though it's my own. But really, it's an excuse to avoid the pain that comes with facing terror head-on. Some nights when Henry and the boys discussed some recent tragedy—a girl in the class below Kyle's who was hit in the school parking lot after a volleyball game by a distracted parent—I'd make up an excuse to leave the table, to pay a bill or fold laundry. Flimsy excuses to avoid hearing it. The same is likely true of whatever I might have sensed about Mara's past, her true motives. Rather than looking more closely, I kept my eyes stubbornly shut.

Outside, a man leans against the front of the building alone, smoking a cigarette. It's the same man from inside, the ugly Elvis. Without meeting his gaze, I push my hands into my pockets and quickly cross the street in the direction of the intersection where cars cross in a steady rhythm. Two cabs, roof lights on, signal their availability. A quick check confirms the smoking man isn't following. I shrug off the fear worming its way through me and return my gaze to the sidewalk. But when I do, a man stands directly in my path. He's huge, almost as large as Terrence, but white and blond. I let out an embarrassed laugh and shift to pass, but he moves with me.

I try a second time, and again, he blocks me.

An awkward smile pulls at my lips. "Sorry," I say, moving left.

He mirrors my movement, blocking me again.

There is no humor in his face.

He isn't going to let me pass. This isn't an awkward dance. The mistakes flash like a bright bulb—not asking the bartender to call me a cab, not waiting to walk out with someone else, a couple, a group. I step instinctively away, taking measure of how close I am to the street, the bar, the dark alley.

The man presses toward me.

I inhale sharply, air whistling a gasp through my throat, and dart toward the street. Too slow. I'm not even off the curb before he snatches my wrist and yanks me until I strike the hard surface of his chest. He twists me around, wraps his left arm across my throat.

In his right is a folding knife, blade open.

"You scream, you die."

My breaths come in shallow sips, my limbs soft and accommodating. I wonder if this man is Lance, if Lance even exists. It doesn't matter. I won't scream. I will do whatever he wants. I just want to hold my baby. *Please let me survive to hold Goose.*

I hear the rhythm of footsteps approaching. I close my eyes, pray someone will see us and help me. But the steps are too slow, too casual. Then, from behind us, another man says, "We got her."

It's Elvis, from outside the bar. Where the man who holds my throat is massive, Elvis is wiry and thin, limbs twitching even as he stands still. Like he's on something. A blue glare from a phone, pressed to his ear, casts a gruesome hue across his features. The men make no move to hide their faces. A statistic I once read swims to the surface of my brain—if they don't hide their faces, they're more likely to kill you.

"Please," I say, barely a croak. "What do you want?"

Neither one answers as I try to puzzle a way out. Two men versus me. No weapon.

"Mara's not with her," ugly Elvis says into the phone.

Mara. She wasn't lying about Lance. He's looking for her. She *is* in danger. So why the hell did she come back here?

The voice on the phone says something indiscernible.

"Shit," Elvis says. "What are we supposed to do for ten minutes?"

The voice responds in an angry tone. I think of the bar, how close we still are—surely someone will come outside soon. Someone will see us. I can scream.

"We can't wait here," the big guy says, his grip tightening as he starts to haul me toward the alley. I drag my feet, but he's too strong.

Images race through my mind: Goose's first birthday cake, little fingers digging into white frosting, her gummy smile, kindergarten, lacing up soccer cleats and running down the field, ponytails bouncing behind her, her first bike, her first horseback ride, her first drive—my life in fast-forward instead of flashing in reverse.

I do the only thing that comes to mind—let out a little moan and make my entire body go slack. The big man stumbles, the knife falling from his hand, as my deadweight pitches him forward.

"What the fuck?" Elvis shouts. "Mac wants her unharmed."

*Mac.* I fight my panic in an effort to appear lifeless.

"She fainted or something," answers Goliath. "Fuck, I dropped the knife. You see it?"

Their bodies shift around mine, the big man looking for the knife as the wiry one moves in, bouncing anxiously. I hold my breath, count to three. Then three again. I have one chance.

I picture Goose's little hand in mine and spring to my feet, sprinting toward the bar. "Help! Help me!"

"Shit," Elvis mutters.

Goliath rears up and grabs for me, scrambling to get a solid grip, but the thought of Goose gives me strength. I twist free and launch my left elbow backward. It lands with a satisfying crack, but I only make it two steps before his hands latch on to my shoulders.

"You're not going anywhere."

His fingers carve into my flesh as tears fill my eyes.

"We've got to get her out of sight," Elvis says, bouncing on his toes. "This way." He points toward the darkened end of the street, away from the bar, from the taxis.

I stub a toe, catching myself before I fall forward. As I do, I spot the knife in the sewer next to a beer bottle, only two feet from my foot. I pretend to trip, landing on all fours in the street. Bits of rock and asphalt dig into my palm.

"Christ," snaps Elvis. "Get her up."

I close my fingers around the handle of the knife, and when Goliath reaches for me, I scream and spin and slash the blade across his arm.

He howls, leaping back.

Before Elvis can react, I'm on my feet, creating space between me and the men, waving the blade. "Get back," I say. Tears stream down my face, and I put more space between us before I swipe my face with my free hand. The blade trembles, my legs jackhammer beneath me. The men freeze, predators watching for weakness, ready to pounce.

Goliath cups his left arm, steps forward.

"I mean it," I shout. "Get the fuck back."

Goliath takes another step to his left while Elvis moves to the right, the two spreading out, making it harder to keep an eye on both of them. All I need to do is get to the bar. Get inside. My daughter is depending on me. I bare my teeth and tighten my grip on the knife, ready to use it. I'm halfway across the street when a blast of music and voices spill out from the bar, at least three or four people judging from the noise. I check over my shoulder, the blade still out in front of me. Elvis shoves his hands in his pockets and pretends to be waiting for someone. Goliath slinks toward the dark alcove from which he emerged.

Without waiting any longer, I run, not slowing until I'm with the group outside the bar. They look up at me, collective shock rendering them speechless. The woman closest touches my arm, then sees the knife in my hand and jerks away.

"Oh my God. Are you okay?"

"I'm okay." My hand trembles as I struggle to retract the blade.

"Did that guy hurt you?" asks another woman. "We need to call the police."

"I'm okay," I repeat, folding down the blade.

I imagine sitting in a cold interrogation room and dismiss the idea. I once had my purse stolen in Seattle and spent four hours at the station filing a report. The officer dedicated more time staring at my cleavage than on the paperwork. I'd been out with a couple of girlfriends from work, so I was dressed up. The officer asked if I was single, if I'd ever consider dating a cop. *A girl alone in the city needs someone to keep her safe*, he'd said, then proceeded to tell me that he was off for the next few days and maybe we could grab a beer.

I don't want to talk to the police. I don't want to spend hours in a tiny room. I want the safety of the hotel, a room with a dead bolt and safety lock.

"I just need a cab," I tell the women.

"Are you sure? Your hands are bleeding—"

"I'm fine," I say, the words sharp. I want to lock myself in that room, regroup. "I just need a cab." I shove the knife into my pocket.

"You should really report—" the second woman starts to say, but her friend interrupts her. "I'll call a cab. We'll wait with you until it comes."

"Thank you," I say and check the street. The two men are gone.

My palms sting and my shoulder aches, but something else weaves through the pain—satisfaction. The blooming sense of progress, the blossoming of my own strength. Those men were going to take me, and I fought back. I escaped without help from anyone.

Whatever they wanted, whoever Mac is, they are looking for Mara. I tell myself it's good news, the fact that those men came after me.

Because it means they haven't found Mara . . . yet.

# CHAPTER

# 19

THE HOTEL ROOM is still, silent. To calm my nerves, I try to recall the trip with Henry and the boys to Hawaii, to return to that isolated beach, the warm breeze of that first night. With my eyes closed, I can almost feel the soft sand between my toes, the smell of jasmine from the lei that circled my neck. Seated in chairs overlooking the ocean, sipping a piña colada, I couldn't imagine a more perfect paradise.

Now, folded into the cotton sheets of the hotel bed, I reach for a sliver of that peace. The rush of adrenaline has ebbed, leaving behind a deep emptiness. Not calm but exhaustion. How I want to go home. I picture our house, the neutral furniture Henry has chosen, the rooms he decorated, the things I have added or changed along the way. Thinking of it now, the house feels less like mine than ever before.

My home will be Goose and wherever she and I end up. It will be colorful—rich jewel tones in blues and greens. A brightly striped comforter on my bed, where Goose and I will lounge and read books on Sunday mornings. A soft floral rug for her room, where she'll practice scooting across the floor.

After checking that the door's safety latch is secure, I strip off my clothes and climb into the shower, letting the water run over my skin.

My palms burn and I hold them loosely fisted as the fear hardens into anger—at those men and Mac, whoever he is. At the bartender, who must have fed me to them.

Mostly, I am angry at Mara for not telling me the truth—or not all of it. The attack has me spinning again in doubt. Is it possible that all her lies were a way of protecting me? But how does bringing my child back here, to the place where she's most in danger, protect me? A fresh flare of anger is washed cold by the memory of Mara's note, those frantic, fearful slashes under the word *kill*. Why didn't she talk to me? Fear or no, she owed me that. Didn't she?

Gently washing soap into my bloody palms, I imagine shampooing Goose's fine baby hair, feeling the thin silky strands, the delicate fuzz on her back and shoulders as I prop her up in her little plastic bathtub. Wrapping her like a burrito in a towel, burying my nose in the baby shampoo smell.

Dressed again, phone recharged, I find an Italian restaurant with decent ratings and order a spaghetti Bolognese to be delivered to the hotel. It arrives quickly and, when I go to the lobby to retrieve it, I purchase a couple of bottles of water in the sundry store and take it all to my room. While I eat, I flip through YouTube videos on my phone, a playlist of saved birthing films. I imagine Henry's expression—what a sight I am, eating Bolognese as I watch women give birth. He would tease me, occasionally leaning over, open-mouthed, for a bite. I try to picture him watching these videos. I'm quick to assume he'd be squeamish before I remind myself that he watched the births of both Nolan and Kyle and the videos no longer seem disturbing. To me, they are magical.

There was a period in high school where I was interested in medicine. I liked science class, the sight of the Bunsen burner flame as it transformed from orange to green to blue, the feel of the safety glasses snug on my face. While most of the girls in my class despised dissections, I found the insides of creatures endlessly fascinating. The fetal pig's tiny lungs, the frog's nickel-sized heart. I had an aptitude for science, but when I mentioned the interest in medicine to my parents, they shot down the idea like a party balloon.

"You may be good at science," my mother said, "but there's a lot more to being a doctor."

"It's true," my father agreed. "Doctors need to be fit to handle difficult situations with a cool head. Doctors need to be rational."

My parents conflated emotion with weakness; now I see how wrong they were. It isn't reason that makes us capable or strong. It's passion; it's caring for something enough to fight for it. The presence of strong emotion doesn't make me weaker—it fuels a desire to be better, to be stronger. A mother, lifting a car to release a child trapped beneath. In high school, I'd put medical school out of my head, but during Mara's pregnancy, the idea resurfaced. Maybe I should have pursued it. Maybe I still could.

I watch one of the C-section videos I've seen dozens of times before, filled with the same fresh awe at the nurses who bear down on the woman's belly and pull the baby from the opening. As the infant on the screen is set at his mother's breast, a text arrives from Henry.

I saw the latest charge. Heading out to a dinner, but is everything okay?

The only new charges I've made are the cab from the airport and my meal. All good, I say. At the Best Western. Eating in my room then going to sleep. xx

On-screen, the baby's mouth finds his mother's breast and begins to feed. I think about Gladys Knight and Damon, a man paralyzed by her own son. The way Gladys spoke about motherhood had projected a confident stoicism, but it's impossible to comprehend what she went through to get there. How did Damon react when Gladys offered to take him in? How did she survive the backlash from her son's actions—people who inevitably blamed her for raising a killer? Gladys turned an impossible situation into something meaningful, positive. I am terrified that I, too, will have to reinvent my life. Already, I cannot fathom a world without my Goose.

*Is everything okay?* Henry's words replay in my mind. It's almost like he knows what happened outside the Lucky Dive. But that's impossible. Henry is not prone to overreaction—the opposite, in fact. He's never been a husband who looks through my credit card charges or comments on what I buy, when or where. So why this? Obviously, with Mara gone, he's more concerned than normal.

Leaving YouTube, I navigate to our banking app. I see the charge for the plane ticket, the name of the airline and the dollar amount. I click the detail for the flight charge and see that it lists the departure and arrival cities. Denver to Philadelphia. Henry flies all the time. Why would a plane ticket trigger a fraud alert?

Then I recall our other credit card, the account we opened for emergencies. Mine lives in the top drawer of my bureau with my engagement ring.

The engagement ring I couldn't find.

I replay that morning in my head. I'd blown off the engagement ring as potentially misplaced, but I never thought to wonder about the credit card. I scan the list of charges and the last one pierces like a hook. It's from today, for almost two hundred dollars.

The payee line reads *Vybe Urgent Care, Philadelphia.*

# CHAPTER
# 20

*1 day before due date*

I WAKE, STILL thinking about the credit card charge at the urgent care. When I call, the receptionist informs me that they can't disclose any transactional information and won't pull surveillance footage without a warrant. It's frustrating but at least the charge proves Mara is in Philadelphia. Now I just have to find her. I regularly refresh the bank app, but there are no new charges. I have no emails or messages. If only she used the card for a hotel room—but she knew I'd see those charges and find her.

And she doesn't seem to want to be found. Hardly the behavior of a woman in trouble; more like the actions of a calculating thief. I sway between sympathy and fury. Once I find her, I'll make her tell me the truth of all of this. Right now, none of it matters as long as she and Goose are safe.

The receptionist at the urgent care did confirm that they don't deliver babies on-site, and there's some comfort in that, although it doesn't mean Mara hasn't given birth somewhere else.

Tomorrow is Goose's due date.

Months ago, Mara and I created our birthing plan. I had no expectations, but Mara said she would prefer a natural birth, if possible. She wanted me by her side. She'd read about false labor and was determined not to go to the hospital until she was fully in labor. Now I wonder if she was speaking from her own experience. What *was* her first delivery like?

Too amped to sit in the hotel room, I dress and, with Mara's note tucked into my pocket, head to the lobby for a bowl of cold cereal and bitter weak coffee.

The hotel desk clerk reminds me of Cate: the same blond wavy hair, the exact length it was in the framed photographs I gave her and Mara for Christmas our senior year—the one Mara kept for so long, now abandoned on the table in the coach house.

Each time a lock of hair obscures the young woman's face, I see my other best friend, the one who was as close to Mara as I was. The one person who might know what Mara was thinking, where she went. She reminds me of Gladys's comment—that Mara felt guilty about *Cate*.

Cate could sometimes be two different people; she'd fill the notebook with playful stories, like how the senior soccer players pantsed a freshman in front of the girls' team and how all the girls couldn't stop talking about how big he was. Or how one time, Madison, the younger of the twins, wouldn't leave Cate's room, so Cate stood in front of her mirror and pretended to trim her hair with a pair of nail scissors, telling her sister how good she'd look with bangs. "Then, no one would call you Hannah anymore," Cate had told her. "Hannah would *never* get bangs."

But then in person, she could be withdrawn. This was especially true in the months before her death. I'd assumed something was happening with her parents—maybe her dad was reenlisting and she was worried about moving. But she'd been accepted to both Kansas and Nebraska with good financial aid packages, so why would it matter where her parents went? Maybe she'd been worried about the money, or perhaps her parents had changed their minds and weren't going to let her go away to college, which was what she wanted more than anything.

While we shared most things, Cate was especially private about her family. Months would pass without a word about her home life, and then, like water boiling over, she would spew her fury at the way her mother spied on her or tried to trip her up as though working to catch Cate in a lie. But that spring, she didn't talk about her mother at all. Not even the excitement of prom could rouse Cate from her sullenness. Only the pull of getting out of Cleveland, of finally being free of her parents, seemed to spark Cate's fire. Mara and I had been excluded from whatever was happening in Cate's home life.

Or I was excluded. Maybe I'd just assumed Mara was, too.

Cate had been working at Mara's one afternoon, and Mara had gone out to pick up Caleb because they were sharing a car, leaving Cate alone at the house. According to Mara, she hadn't been gone long— twenty minutes, maybe a half hour. How could Mara have known something would happen? That her friend would decide to take a dip in the hot tub. That she'd slip and hit her head and drown. It's not like they'd been drinking; it was the middle of the week, a Tuesday. I would've joined, but we were way behind on the layout for the senior section of the yearbook, so I was stuck at school when they'd left.

Between Gladys Knight's mention of Cate, Caleb's comment, and Mara's lies—was there something about Cate's death that I'd missed? Has Mara been hiding something else from me all these years?

I pull out Mara's note again. Recently, when I've seen her hand-writing, it's been rushed, messy, but she's written these words slowly, lifting the pen between them. I try to imagine what she was thinking when she wrote it. I recall my own panic as I scribbled the note on the kitchen table, the unruly scrawl, begging Mara to call me. I reread each word, hoping for some clue about what the key opens, then study the key itself. One side is stamped *do not duplicate*, but it doesn't look like a safe deposit box key. The teeth look conventional, not like the anti-quated wide-spaced keys I associate with bank boxes. Plus, for most banks, I'd have to be on the account to access a safe deposit box.

No, it has to be to a storage unit, but where? I Google local storage facilities along with the eight-digit code and come up blank. Frustrated, I fold the letter again and move to return it to the envelope when I see the smudge on the back of the page. But it isn't a smudge. It's a crude drawing of an animal—a cat, I think. Then I notice the diagonal lines on the small face.

A tiger.

Cate's tigers. What is Mara trying to tell me? I hope like hell that it's related to the storage unit, so I do a fresh search of local storage centers on my phone, clicking on each link in search of something tiger-related. Most are nondescript names like Extra Space and Store More. And then I see Space Cat Rental Units, the face of a tiger at the center of its logo.

It's possible I'm wrong and the animal on the back is just a doodle, but it feels like something. And if the doodle is unrelated to the key, I have no idea where to go next, so I'm hoping that the drawing is a message. I catch a cab in front of the hotel and give the driver the address to Space Cat Rental Units.

Once we're on our way, I dial Detective Bentley's number and leave a voicemail to tell him that something has happened. I don't want to leave the details of last night's attack on a voicemail—nor do I want to say the words out loud in front of the cab driver—so I tell Bentley that I'd like to speak to someone in the Philadelphia Police Department, ideally whoever came out to Denver to arrest Mara.

The cab leaves behind the dense streets of the city for wide roads bordered by strip malls, nail salons, and liquor stores, a home improvement chain store.

Almost thirty minutes later, we turn off the two-lane highway and onto a road dotted with warehouse buildings and a massive RV dealership. At the end is an old building that looks like it was once a manufacturing plant. The brick facade is blackened with soot and age, the bulk of the building a stark contrast to a glassed-in vestibule and tall sleek lights positioned like columns at each corner of the structure. In the dim morning, the lights create bright white circles on the asphalt below. Several signs warn that the facility is protected by video surveillance and on-premise security. Through the building's original windows—narrow and deep, the glass reinforced by bars—the white interior lights glow like something extraterrestrial.

A half dozen cars are parked in the lot, the sun rising behind to stain their finishes with its orange glow. I consider asking the driver to stay, but I don't know how long I'll be.

Through the glass foyer is a solid steel door, a bulky lock above the knob. Beside it is a keypad, and I enter the eight-digit code from Mara's note, holding my breath until I hear the click of the mechanism's release.

I'm in.

The inside smells of steel and the damp musk of wet brick, and it's eerily quiet aside from the whirring hush of fans and the occasional moan of metal, which seems to come from the building itself. Around the corner is an ancient-looking elevator and a map. Unit 2714 is on the fourth floor.

As I step out of the elevator, the first units I pass have corrugated doors, like narrow garage bays, and most are secured by a padlock fastened to the latch. One stands open; inside, a dirty pink stroller for a baby doll is tipped on its side on the concrete floor. I imagine Goose navigating her baby doll in a stroller like this one, new and bright, her steps unsteady as she sings to her doll. At the grocery store at home, a small huddle of child-sized shopping carts sits beside the large ones and I can picture wavy-haired Goose pushing her miniature cart down the aisle, pausing to consider which Goldfish crackers will go best with lunch.

At the end of the corridor are rows of small lockboxes similar in size to bank safe deposit boxes. I follow the numbers up and down the rows until I locate 2714.

Box 2714 is so low to the ground that I have to crouch to put the key in the lock, but once it's in, it turns easily. I drop to my hands and knees to peer inside—curved along the walls of the small space is a single spiral notebook in a faded shade of green.

On the cover is a single word: *Physics.*

I know this book: It's the shared notebook the three of us kept in high school, the one that vanished after Cate died. Mara and I had traded theories about where the notebook had gone and decided it must've been left at Cate's. I'd always wondered whether Cate's parents had discovered it, our secrets cloaked behind the innocuous cover.

Had Mara had it all this time?

I feel the folds of Mara's letter in my pocket. *Don't tell anyone about this. He'll definitely kill for it.*

I page through the notebook for something that wasn't there when we were kids, something that would be worth killing over. But it's the same. I turn to the last page with the purple writing and catch a few stray words—*homework* and *exhausted* and *senior year*. The rest of the pages are blank. Impatient, I flip to the back of the notebook and notice a rectangular dent in the center of the last page, as though something had been pressed inside. A matching imprint on the notebook's cardboard backing.

This time, it's not a key shape at all.

Leaning down, I sweep around the inside of the box and feel a small piece of plastic. Approximately an inch wide and an inch and a half long and rounded on the sides, it's the cover for a thumb drive. I press the plastic into the page and see that it fits the indentation. I sweep my hand inside the box again, feeling the corners.

The thumb drive itself isn't here.

I open the front page of the notebook and see my own writing, skim the inane entry about the beauty of a fresh notebook—TABULA RASA written in all caps—and the anticipation of our senior year. Why on earth would Mara keep this all these years? Then I remind myself that she still had the old photograph of the three of us, too. Her way of holding on to what we'd had so unlike my own instinct, which would be to pitch anything that would remind me of the loss.

I turn the plastic cap over in my hand and wonder where the thumb drive is, check the locker again to ensure it's empty. Someone must've taken it, and I try to decide whether the fact that it's gone is good news or bad. With the notebook under my arm, I lock the box and slide the key and the cap to the drive safely into my jeans pocket. There's no cell reception until I reach the first floor. I order a Lyft, and a moment later, my phone rings from a 215-number—Philadelphia.

"Mrs. McNeil," says a man's low voice. "My name is Peter Maxwell. I'm an officer with the Philadelphia Police Department, in the Narcotics Division."

This must be the officer who came to Denver. I replay his words, taken aback, so all that comes out is, "Narcotics?"

"Yes," he confirms. "I received your message through Officer Bentley."

"Drugs? Mara would never."

"Before we get to that, Detective Bentley told me something happened last night—that you wanted to speak to me."

"I was assaulted," I answer, surprised by my own steadiness. I give him a brief summary of the attack. "But I'm fine. What I really want to understand is what Mara has done, why she's in trouble, and what it has to do with drugs. Mara didn't use drugs." When he doesn't reply right away, I continue, "As you probably know, she is the surrogate for my child, who is due—" I cough to get the word out. "Tomorrow."

"I did hear that," he says. "It might be best if we sit down in person. Would that be possible?"

"Yes. I'm in Philadelphia."

"We could meet somewhere close to you," he offers. "Unless you'd prefer to come down to the station."

"No," I answer, too fast and with an unintentional edge. I have nothing to hide, but I have zero interest in going to a police station. "I'm staying downtown," I say before he can speak again. "There's a diner a couple of blocks from my hotel called something like Tiny Star?" I try to picture the words on the front glass. "Yellow Star?"

"Blue Star Diner?"

"That's it." I check my watch and see it's ten o'clock. "We could meet there, maybe in an hour?"

"That works for me," he says, and the calm in his voice is reassuring. "I'll be in a brown canvas jacket and jeans."

"See you soon."

Through the window, I see my Lyft arrive and check the license plate before climbing into the car. The driver is a red-haired woman with a line of gray hair at her part. She's cheery and talkative, and I respond dutifully from the back seat, the notebook in my lap. I move to open it, but the reality of the detective's words stop me. Narcotics. Drugs. The words bounce against each other with hollow thuds. So much of what I've learned about Mara these past few days makes no sense, but none of it less than this. No detective was going to travel across the country to arrest someone on drug possession. Even with intent to sell. That made no sense. So what did they think she'd done? We never even smoked pot in high school, and now someone thinks Mara was, what, trafficking *drugs*?

I close my eyes and envision her on my doorstep—beaten and bruised, thin, without any money and in cheap worn clothes. Hardly a drug kingpin.

I check my watch, counting the minutes until I can sit down with this detective and find out what the hell is going on.

# CHAPTER
## 21

*May 2008*

*Destroy this page immediately—and do NOT let her see you reading it! Every time I see a scrap of paper from a spiral notebook, I feel horrible.*

*Maybe she should be a detective.*

*I didn't think we'd have to do this again. I thought all that hiding was over. What's crazy is that I never considered this possibility. My life's about to go to total shit and I keep thinking that this really doesn't count against the rules. Is she watching you like she's watching me? I swear, she follows me into the bathroom. She knows something is up. I can't decide if she thinks I did something or you did something. At least she doesn't ask directly.*

*Not that it matters at this point. I'll lie if I have to. You will, too.*

*I want to tell her. No, that's not true. I want her to know. Once it's all over and we can put it behind us, I want her to know. And she will, right? We will tell her after. But I can't imagine her reading this. I don't even want you to read it. I don't want anyone to read it. I DON'T WANT IT TO BE TRUE.*

*But it is.*

*You know what's crazy? I'm not even thinking about him. That it's his fault. I'm not thinking about what he did to me. It's like that part doesn't matter anymore even though it should. It should be the thing that matters most.*

*Even more batshit crazy is that I'm not thinking about me either. My future. Like this is about ANYONE other than me. It's all about me, but all I can think about is my parents. That this will be the last straw. That it'll wreck them. How they'll fight about it and my dad will try to keep cool but my mom will freak the fuck out. My dad will blame anyone but me—the school, the teachers, the neighbor kid, every single person who has ever said a word to me.*

*But not my mom.*

*She will blame me and only me.*

*Fuck. I'm going to be sick.*

# CHAPTER

# 22

*HE'LL DEFINITELY KILL for it.* The words from the note Mara had left with Gladys replay in my mind as the driver navigates back into the city. I try to imagine what was on that thumb drive and where the hell it is now. God, I hope this detective has some answers.

Blue Star Diner is busier than yesterday, but I find a booth and sit facing the entrance. There's a small jukebox controller on the table, and someone has put a piece of duct tape over the coin slot that reads, *Sorry. I'm retired.* It makes me feel old and a little nostalgic. So many afternoons the three of us passed in Mara's bedroom, listening to music on her CD player or the radio, our favorite station always a little staticky as Ryan Seacrest counted down the week's Top 20. The last time I drove the three of us to the mall, the month before Cate died, we played "Four Minutes" by Madonna over and over, singing at the top of our lungs in my blue Honda Accord.

Cate was shy about it, but she had a wonderful singing voice, and she generally enjoyed singing as long as it was just in front of us. She didn't sing that day. Seated in the passenger seat, she tapped along with one hand on the handle of the door. The movement looked stiff, slightly offbeat, like it was a performance for our benefit. I'd tried to catch Mara's eye in the rearview mirror, to get her to notice Cate's with-drawn behavior, but she'd been occupied by the song.

At the mall, we'd run into a few boys from our class. Some of the cliques had started to evaporate in those last months of senior year. No longer jocks and nerds, we were unified by the clock that counted off the days until we were all high school graduates. The boys were head-ing to the food court, which was where we normally went, too, but as we turned in that direction, Cate announced she had to pick something up for her sisters at JCPenney and she'd catch up. Two hours later, when Mara and I emerged, Cate was waiting by my car. Mara had acted like her absence was nothing noteworthy, so I didn't ask Cate where she'd been. I did notice that the only thing she carried was the small purse she'd gone in with. What had she been doing, and why didn't I ask her all those years ago?

My attention is drawn by the same gray-haired waitress from yes-terday. "Be right with you, hon," she says as she passes.

Before long, I spot a man in a brown jacket and jeans through the window, and when he ducks into the diner, I am certain this is Detective Peter Maxwell. I lift my hand and he strides toward me. Probably in his late thirties, the detective is tall and lean with dark brown hair and a neatly trimmed beard. The dark hair is a pleasant contrast to his light eyes; he is handsome. At the table, he reaches across and takes my hand, shakes. "Thank you for meeting me, Mrs. McNeil."

"Call me Alexandra."

"I'm Pete," he says. "I'm glad you called."

The waitress swings by the table to pour coffee and take our order before leaving us alone.

As Maxwell sips his coffee, I notice his gold wedding band. He sets the mug down and speaks as though we're about to start a card game. "Okay. Mara Vannatta."

I lift my own mug to my lips, a sort of shield against what might be coming.

"She's a good friend of yours?" he asks, his tone neutral.

"She is." I explain about our high school friendship, about losing track of one another and Mara arriving in Denver. I leave out Cate—

though she's closer to the front of my mind than she has been in years, especially after finding our notebook in Mara's locker.

Maxwell pulls a small black notebook from his pocket and flips it open. "I understand that when Mara arrived in Denver, she was leaving an abusive relationship."

"That's right," I say. "She'd left her husband."

"I haven't found any records of a domestic dispute."

I picture Mara on my doorstep, her gray pallor, her skeletal frame. "I don't know whether she reported him before she left."

"I also didn't find any record of the marriage," he says gently, as though suspecting this will be news to me.

"Right," I say. "She called him her husband, but maybe it wasn't an official marriage." I wait a beat, then ask what feels like the most obvious question. "Is it common for police to fly across the country to arrest someone?"

He lets out a little chuckle, a dimple appearing on his right cheek. "God, no. Our department barely springs for coffee."

"But you did it," I say.

"It took a lot of convincing to get my captain's sign-off." He is quiet a moment before continuing. "Mara has been linked to a man known as Clayton. Did she ever mention him?"

"I never heard her mention a Clayton, no. I believe her husband was Lance."

"Husband?"

"Or boyfriend," I say, frustrated at myself, at how Mara's version of the truth is so implanted in my head. "Whoever hit her."

The detective nods slowly as though he's going to comment on the boyfriend. Instead, he says, "I haven't heard of a Lance, but Clayton is the man who runs a quarter of a billion dollars' worth of fentanyl-laced shit through this town every year. We can attribute at least thirty deaths to the drugs he supplied in the past ninety days, most of them teenagers and college students."

Breathless, I say, "Mara can't have had anything to do with that." But the words have an inauthentic echo because, the truth is, I have no idea what Mara might be involved in. Only what I want so badly to believe. Badly enough that it's made me blind. I slide my palm against my stomach, assaulted by memories of her initial hesitation about being my surrogate. Surely if she was involved with a man like Clayton, she'd have told me. No. *I* would have told her if I'd known a man like Clayton. Cate would have told me. But Mara?

"Maybe not. But we think she knows his identity."

I don't want to believe she'd agree to carry Goose if she might potentially be in danger from a drug lord, someone who wanted her dead and had the resources to reach her anywhere. I try to recall exactly what she'd told me about Lance, about their fights. He was the one who hurt her—at least that's what she led me to believe. She never mentioned a Clayton. Maybe Lance worked for Clayton and Mara got dragged into their business? Or Clayton worried that Mara knew something she shouldn't. As Henry said the morning she disappeared, a guy who could track Mara across the country was powerful, not unemployed. *A guy like that has money and a lot of it.* Maybe it was Clayton who found her, and not Lance. Where the hell was Lance, then?

I work to wrangle my thoughts. "Even if she did know who this Clayton is, that can't be enough to arrest her, can it?" I hear the plea in my voice and clear my throat.

The detective's expression turns grave, the dimple gone, vertical lines burrowing between his eyes. "It's complicated, and I can't discuss the details of the case. I know that's frustrating," he says, raising a hand. "But if she comes forward, she can help us bring him down and help herself at the same time."

"Do you think that's why she ran?" I ask. "Because Clayton found her?"

The detective studies me a moment. "You have no idea where she is?"

The letter flashes through my mind—the missing thumb drive—but that tells me nothing. The truth is I don't. "No. I have no idea."

"We don't know if Clayton located her," he says. "But I do wonder about the attack on you last night. Whether they're still looking to find Mara, or if they're cleaning up the collateral damage."

"Cleaning up? You mean . . . ?" I know what he means. "No, he told the guy on the phone that Mara wasn't with me. They were looking for

Mara, which means they haven't found her." Or they hadn't found her as of last night.

He nods, his mouth set in a grim line.

"Why would she come back to Philadelphia?" I don't expect the detective to know what Mara was thinking, coming here, but it's the question I most want answered. If Mara was in trouble and afraid, why return to the source of the danger?

"Your guess is as good as mine," he says gently. From his tone, I imagine the Denver detectives have told him about the surrogacy, about Goose. "We don't even know how they located her in Denver."

"How did *you* find her?"

We're interrupted by the arrival of the food. When the waitress is gone, the detective makes no move to lift his silverware.

"We had a flag on her records. Means we get notified if anyone accesses them. About a week and a half ago, someone requested background information on her. After that, it was just a matter of following the trail."

Henry. I remember his confession that he'd hired an investigator. The timing is right. Maybe his request triggered all of this. I don't let myself consider whether Henry's report helped Clayton find Mara too, but bring my thoughts back to the days around Mara's disappearance. "Did you see her at my house? Was that you, coming in? My neighbor saw someone."

He takes a bite and wipes his mouth with a napkin. "Wasn't me. We sent a local narcotics agent to make contact. By the time I arrived in Denver Wednesday night, she was gone, and you were already on your way to Philly."

The man Molly saw skulking around was probably the local narcotics agent, then. My stomach is too knotted to eat; I lower the eggs from my fork and take a bite of toast, which sticks in my throat. I swallow water to force it down and run a finger through the condensation on my glass, feeling unsettled and antsy. "What can we do to find her?"

"She's been spotted here in Philadelphia in the last few days."

I drop the toast onto my plate. "Spotted where?"

"Near where she used to live," he says. "I've got a few images taken from CCTV, but we haven't been able to locate where she's staying."

"Can I see them?"

He hesitates a beat, then shrugs. "Sure. Maybe you'll notice something we've missed." He unlocks his phone and toggles it before passing it to me. "There are a half dozen images there. Swipe right to see the rest."

In the first picture, Mara walks alone on a sidewalk, face tilted toward the storefronts like she's avoiding a bitter wind. Or a camera. She wears a gray Gap sweatshirt, stretched taut over her belly and the maternity jeans she finally let me buy her a month and a half ago, when not even her sweatpants fit anymore. I yearn for her to turn toward the camera so I can search her face for some shred of evidence that she's been taken and held. But there's no one with her, no one nearby. Behind her, the windows are plastered with notices and ads, the glass so cloudy and streaked it's impossible to see inside.

I continue to scroll through the images—all of Mara, on what looks like the same street. In the second picture there is a pawnshop behind her—Abe's Pawn. In the next, a laundromat, the round sign broken in the center. Then another section of street, new storefronts and different signs, the windows slightly cleaner. Mara passes a liquor store and a bar with a faded neon-pink logo in the window. It looks like the rise of a wave; twists that might be willow stalks in the water create dancing shapes in the design. I swipe again, see a narrow entrance to an apartment building. Several windows on the second floor are lit up. In the last picture, Mara faces the camera, her belly in full relief. There's nothing harrowed in her expression, though she looks wary and tired. It's her belly that captures my attention. I want to run my finger across the screen, hold on to the image of Goose still inside her.

"When were these taken?" I ask Maxwell.

"Wednesday."

The day Mara left Denver. She must've flown after all. "Why would she be in this neighborhood? Do you know?"

"She worked at a strip club there," he says.

Gladys had mentioned Mara was a dancer, so I say nothing.

"You asked why Mara would come to Philadelphia," the detective says, using the side of his fork to cut through a sausage patty with extra vigor. "I'm more curious about why Mara would leave Denver before she's delivered your child."

I sit back in the chair, feel the hard wooden slat on my spine. There is more than one answer to this question. A week ago, I'd have answered easily: The only reason Mara would have left was because she'd been afraid of something or someone, and she had decided, right or wrong, that leaving was the only way to keep us all safe—me, her, and Goose. There are a dozen reasons to second-guess that answer now, although I can't come up with a better one.

If this Clayton was after her, why come here? Unless there was something crucial she'd left behind. Not our high school notebook, but maybe that thumb drive. If so, where is she now? What's her plan? Is she out there, trying to make things right, or has something awful already happened to her? I lay my fork on the plate. I can't imagine eating now.

The detective blows out a breath, stabs the sausage with his fork, and brings it to his mouth. For several minutes, he eats, and I sit in silence as a new emptiness opens inside of me, something scooping out my chest and stomach. The absence of a next step. I consider the key and Mara's note, its cryptic warning: *Don't tell anyone about this.*

"Why do *you* think she would leave?" I finally ask.

"I'd sure like to ask her," he says.

As I head back to the hotel, my thoughts return to the notebook. Why had Mara kept it locked up? Or maybe the notebook was random—the way she'd hung on to the picture of the three of us—and the thing she'd said he would kill over was the thumb drive. Had Mara retrieved it, or did someone else get to it first?

I let myself into the hotel room and hesitate at the threshold, thinking I've entered the wrong room. Until I recognize my Colorado T-shirt draped over the desk chair.

Someone has torn the room apart.

The bed is stripped of its sheets. The drawers hang open and my few belongings are strewn across the floor. Something silky falls on my face like a spider and I startle, leaping into the hallway and swiping furiously before realizing it's my own hair. My heart batters on the bones of its cage like an animal desperate for escape.

There's a momentary sense that if I turn around and come back, the mess might be gone, the scene before me an invention of my own mind. But the drawer still hangs from the dresser like a tongue. Only then do I think of the notebook. I thrust my hand behind the mattress and feel the metal rings, twisting my arm to pull it free. It's still there.

Maxwell's number is at the top of my recent calls.

"Don't go back in," he says as soon as I explain what's happened. "Can you wait in the lobby? I'll get an officer over right now and I'll be there soon. You said the Best Western? On Vine Street?"

"Yes."

"We'll pull the hotel's video footage, see if we can catch him on film," he says, taking charge. "I'm going to hang up and call my dispatcher. Sit tight and I'll be there soon. I'll text you the name of my officer, so you'll know who to look for."

Then he is gone. I consider taking the notebook with me, but it's too big to hide inside my coat, so I check that Mara's letter is still inside and slide it into my backpack, burying it beneath a few items of clothing. Then, I return to the lobby where the front desk clerk is busy with a line of people.

Though it's warm, I'm chilled by the idea that, if the timing had been a little different, I might've been inside that room when the intruder entered. Did they break in to look for something? Or were they trying to find me? I have to leave this hotel. I certainly can't sleep here.

"Ma'am. I'm Officer Bernard. Stephanie Bernard. Detective Maxwell sent me."

The voice startles me, but when I check my texts, the name matches.

She asks for the key and explains that she's going to make sure the room is clear. Then she is gone. There is fear, but another, deeper emotion rises to the surface as well. Tectonic plates shifting against each other, the brewing of an earthquake that splits me at the core.

I am, I realize, furious.

Furious with myself for missing the signs, for not heeding the warnings, for not standing up to Mara, my parents, to anyone. For taking the easy way, for being so agreeable.

"The room is clear." The officer is back. She points to the chair beside me and asks if she can sit, ask some questions.

My mouth is dry, parched as though I've run a race without water. I wonder if this officer sees the anger rising in me. I unclench my hands at my sides, pain rushing into the fingers as the blood returns. I lay them in my lap, watch them turn from white to pink.

The officer's questions are benign, routine, frustrating. Tamping down impatience, I explain my movements this morning, mentioning that I ran an errand outside the city rather than explaining the trip to the storage center.

When she's done, Bernard snaps her notebook closed. "Detective Maxwell should be here soon, and a crime scene technician is coming to print the room. Hotels are hard—so many people in and out," she explains, preparing me for disappointment. "But we'll check the knobs and the light switches. Maybe we'll get lucky. And once the tech is done, we'll ask you to look through the room and tell us if anything is missing. Can I get you some coffee? Water?"

I decline and thank her. I am anxious to gather my things and leave this place. Detective Maxwell strides into the lobby, surveying the space. If he identifies anything suspicious, anyone who doesn't belong, it doesn't show on his face.

"Are you okay?" he asks, and though I know he means to be kind, the question is irritating, like a cloying perfume sprayed too close to my face. I wave a hand. As a kid, all I wanted was for one of my parents to ask me that. Not offhandedly, as they occasionally did, but in earnest. Ask me if I was actually okay. Hearing it from the officer and the detective now makes me feel like a child. Powerless. Who cares how I *feel*? Of course I'm not okay.

"I'll be okay when I have some answers," I tell him instead. "In the meantime, I'd like to get out of here."

"Soon, I promise," he says.

When the crime scene technician arrives, the four of us go upstairs together. I'm instructed not to touch anything. My only job is to identify what, if anything, is missing. The technician stops outside my room to print the door handle, even though I've already touched it. It's not a quick process and I am antsy, ready to move on from this. I doubt the intruder left prints. I want to see my things, have them all with me.

As the professionals discuss possible locations for trace evidence from the intruder, I take in the room.

My underwear is in the corner, on the floor. The pair I wore the day before yesterday from Denver to Philadelphia. Was that really only a day and a half ago? I snatch them in one fist. My backpack is on the floor, too, by the chair. Maxwell gives me the go-ahead, and I lift it up. The notebook slides around the base, but the pack feels light as I recall the envelope of cash zipped inside. I had a bundle of clothes in there, too, and now I see a pair of pants flung behind the bed, a T-shirt beside them. My sleep shirt is under the desk.

I pile the clothes on the bed, unzip the inside pocket of the pack, and remove the envelope of cash. I skim the bills, confirming it all seems to be there, and find my driver's license and Amex still there as well.

Maxwell makes a thoughtful noise. "He didn't take the money?"

"No."

"So he didn't take anything that you can see?"

"No," I repeat.

Unlike last night, this wasn't an attack on me personally. They were looking for something—maybe Mara herself, or maybe the thumb drive.

I don't mention the drive. I tell myself the reason is because I don't actually know if it exists. The only evidence I have is the small plastic cap that was in the locker, the one that looks like it fits a thumb drive, but I'm also afraid that whatever is on there might be damning for Mara.

The detective says he's going to talk to hotel security about possible camera footage. Once it's just me in the room, I shake out the sheets and check under and behind the bed, then fold my things neatly, moving quickly, pushing away the thought of a stranger's hands on them. I could leave everything behind, but it's not practical.

It's not efficient. There's no time for shopping. I will need a new hotel, but that is a problem for later. For now, I will keep my things with me. There is reassurance in having everything I own in this city on my back.

In the lobby, Maxwell stands at the front desk. "I'm about to meet with the hotel's head of security to look at the camera footage," he explains.

I don't back away. "I'm coming with you."

He hesitates, scanning my expression. He must see something determined there, or maybe he just pities me. Whatever the reason, he agrees, and we're ushered down a short hallway and into a room with a wall of screens. The head of security is a gray-haired man in an ill-fitting gray suit.

"I've asked Mrs. McNeil to join us in case she recognizes the person who was in her room," Maxwell explains with a sweep in my direction.

"Absolutely," the man says as he lowers himself into a chair and strikes a few keys. A screen flashes black, then fills with the view of an empty hallway. Small twitches in the lighting, like tiny explosions, make it clear that we're watching the footage on fast-forward. A woman races awkwardly down the hallway, her speed unnatural. A moment later, another figure appears, back to the camera, a hood pulled over their head. Beneath the hood, a baseball cap covers the eyes and the top half of the nose. There is a collective pause as the hooded figure stops at my room.

"That's our guy," Maxwell says.

The intruder grips the knob with a gloved hand and pushes inside.

"Enters at 11:08 a.m.," the man says, pointing to a time stamp in the corner of the screen.

Maxwell looks at me. "We met at what—eleven?"

It sounds right, but I wasn't paying attention to the time. Time has become another enemy, one that intimidates me with its single-minded determination to push forward without pause, hurling me, unprepared, toward Goose's due date. I press my crossed forearms into the hollow below my rib cage, try to imagine my daughter safe inside Mara.

I shift in my seat as the hotel's security officer toggles through camera feeds. In each one, the figure keeps their head down, the hood drawn tight. No profile shot, no view of the eyes or nose, not even a glimpse of hair.

When I stand up, the only thing I can say for certain is that whoever broke into my room isn't nine months pregnant. With that, I shoulder my pack and leave the hotel.

# CHAPTER
## 23

ON THE STREET outside, I hail a cab before the detective and his crew exit the hotel. The time with them feels like a waste, and every lost moment is itchy now, like I've been unknowingly trampling through poison ivy. As I climb into the cab, my mind is on the pictures the detective showed me of Mara on the street, the businesses behind her. It's the only visual record of her since she arrived in Philadelphia. I can only hope she might go back there.

"Abe's Pawn Shop," I tell the driver, searching Google for the address where Mara was last seen.

I watch our progress on the map, occasionally glancing backward to see if we're being followed, but there is a different vehicle behind us each time, and I try to reassure myself that no one is after me. About two blocks before we reach the pawnshop, I see a familiar design on a pink neon sign mounted in a dark window when the cab is stopped at a red light.

"I'll get out here," I say, pushing a twenty-dollar bill through the slot in the plexiglass. "Keep the change."

I stand in front of the window, eyeing the logo I recognize from the detective's photo. But also from somewhere else.

The shape I mistook for a wave is actually a full circle, the neon pink in one section burned out. The circle creates the outline of a flower, narrow leaves twisting from its center—but what looked at first like petals are actually women dancing, long thin shapes created by the stretch of their arms in the air.

Mara must know this place well, because the tattoo on her ankle is a blurred copy of this exact logo.

*Lotus Lounge.* The words are embossed in chipped gold lettering, the front glass shaded by a curtain in deep purple velvet, the vibrant color dulled by years in the sun. When I pass through the doors, the darkness inside makes me think the place is closed, but then a shadow shifts beside me: a bouncer propped on a barstool, lost in his phone, ignoring me. The sound of Prince crooning encourages me to step farther into the darkness.

Shapes slowly reveal themselves as my eyes adjust to the dark. In the farthest corner, a woman on a raised stage holds one leg in the air, her arm wrapped around a gold pole that stretches from the ceiling above. Cupping her calf in one hand, she brings the leg to her face while the other stretches out long, then slides down the pole to the floor, and she rolls herself into the splits. She rocks from side to side, grinding into the floor, her small breasts bouncing as she moves to the sound of Prince's lyrics.

Maxwell said Mara worked at a strip club. This has to be it.

There are only eight or ten patrons, all men, mostly slumped in chairs at the edge of the stage. Whether they're half asleep or very drunk, it's hard to tell. A muscular bartender wears a tuxedo vest with nothing beneath it, showing off well-sculpted arms as he wipes down glasses and lines them up on shelves below racks of liquor, set against a mirrored backdrop.

I climb onto a barstool and the man slides a black cocktail napkin in front of me.

"What can I get you?"

"I'm trying to locate a friend who used to work here," I explain, tilting my phone to show a photo of Mara.

He shakes his head, wearing a bored expression. "Sorry. You want a drink?"

I press on. "Sorry you can't tell me or sorry you don't know her?"

"Don't know 'er. Give a shout if you need that drink." He raps his knuckles on the wood, then throws the rag over his shoulder and moves down the bar, away from me.

I climb off my seat and follow, skirting a man asleep on the bar, his stool pushed so far out, he looks ready to slide onto the floor. Prince's voice fades out as the song ends, and my voice echoes in the empty space.

"Is there someone else I could ask? She's a friend and she's gone missing."

He crouches behind the bar, reminding me of the bartender at the Lucky Dive, and I feel a zing of fear at the memory of the assault, my tossed hotel room. "Black Widow" by Iggy Azalea pumps from the speaker as a new dancer struts onto the stage in hot-pink bell bottoms and a matching zippered top, her long red hair a fiery mane trailing behind like a cape. I lean across the bar. "Please."

"I don't know her. We get lots of people in and out, but I don't think I've seen her before," he clarifies, still crouched on the floor.

"I'm pretty sure she used to work here," I repeat. "Her name is Mara Vannatta? Maybe you've heard the name?"

He shrugs, pulling plastic jugs from the refrigerator and setting them on the counter above him. "I haven't."

He doesn't seem to be lying, though I don't want to believe him. Mara lived in Philadelphia for almost a decade. Still, it's entirely possible that she hasn't worked here in years. Or that the tattoo is some bizarre coincidence.

The bartender adjusts the line of jugs.

"This woman is carrying my baby," I explain, giving it one last shot. "And she's missing."

Today is the last day my baby is safe inside Mara. I'm aware that the due date is only an estimate. A best guess. Goose may not come for another week. Or, I consider, the thought rising like acid in my throat, she might already be born.

I slap my palm on the bar, rousing the sleeping man and gaining the bartender's full attention. I soften my tone, plead. "She worked here. Someone has to know her."

The bartender's expression remains disinterested as he glances down the length of the empty bar. "No one here but me, and I don't know her," he replies calmly. "Either order a drink or get out of here."

Beneath his bored tone is a warning. He's done with my bullshit. When I turn around, the bouncer stands halfway between the bar and the entrance, arms crossed, but he's distracted by a group coming through the front door. Seven or eight young women, one in a veil—some sort of bachelorette party. Grateful for the distraction, I follow the signs to the bathroom, angry at myself for being emotional, for letting my fear show and losing control.

Every dead end edges me closer to breaking.

I close myself into a stall and hang my pack, dropping my head in my hands. It's broad daylight, but in this place, it could be midnight. I am sick of the fear, the hopelessness. I'm sick of feeling like I'm not okay alone, that I can't do it on my own. It makes me realize that not only have I been depending on others to make my decisions, I've depended on them for my own sense of self. As a teenager, Mara and Cate made me feel safe, that despite having no siblings and parents who seemed disinterested in my existence, I wasn't alone. That I was safe because I had them. And after them, I relied on Henry to protect me, to take care of me, and in doing that, I internalized the belief that I *needed* someone else.

Physical safety is one thing. As a woman, I'm smaller, more vulnerable, dependent on quick wits and scrappiness to get out of dangerous situations, like the one outside the Lucky Dive. I don't know a single woman who hasn't imagined how she would escape a situation if confronted by a dangerous man. But there's more at stake than physical safety—so much more. It's the emotional safety of knowing that I can provide everything I need for myself, for my child.

Even after Mara agreed to be my surrogate, I almost changed my mind about the whole thing. If Henry didn't want to have another child, it would mean doing it alone. But once Mara knew how much I wanted a child, she wouldn't allow me to back out. We talked for hours about the resources I would have to raise Goose, her included. Maybe Henry, too, but it didn't matter, she said. I didn't *need* anyone. I could raise my daughter on my own, I was capable. But I'm alone now. No Henry or Mara or anyone to protect me. Sure, Detective Maxwell would probably answer the phone if I called for help, but his goals do not necessarily align with mine. He wants to arrest Mara, and I . . . I don't know what I want for Mara, what I believe she's done or knows, so I tell myself it doesn't matter. That, at this moment, I don't need to know.

I'm still in the stall when I hear the women enter. As they laugh and talk around me, I wash my hands, press wet palms to my cheeks, and emerge from the bathroom, exiting the club without a word to anyone.

The air outside is refreshing. With no real plan, I start down the street in the direction of Abe's Pawn. Across the sidewalk, I spot a pregnant woman walking a corgi. Her due date must be a few months from now; her belly is smaller and she doesn't walk with the late-pregnancy waddle that women seem to adopt in the final month.

The sight of her reminds me of Mara, days we spent walking and sharing thoughts. In some ways, Mara and I were like a long-married couple, talking nonstop for hours but also at ease with quiet between us. And while she was open and forthright about so many things, she was also guarded about what had happened to her. Once her external injuries had healed, she minimized the abuse, refusing to tell me exactly how long it had gone on. How many times he hurt her. "The stress of everything finally got to him," she'd said. "But I was right to leave. I'm good now." She'd squeeze my hand or touch my arm, a little moment to emphasize the conversation was done. Mara had always been that way—easily able to brush off things that would have worried at my mind for weeks. Her parents, for instance.

What little I knew about their relationship I learned not from Mara herself but from being in the house when they were fighting, which they did often and at high volume. Occasionally, Mara's mom made comments in front of me and Cate—barbs about infidelity or how men were impossible and to save ourselves the trouble. Mara had a tendency to say that they'd always been that way, and she swore they fought so they could make up. But that can't have been easy. As unaffectionate as my parents were to me, they were the same with each other, and they never fought. What I lacked in tenderness, I always had in stability. Now I wonder how Mara could possibly have healed from the trauma of her abuse—whether it was at the hands of Lance or someone else. As far as I know, she never talked about it with anyone.

And yet she did seem to heal. Or maybe that's just what I wanted to believe because, to my eyes, she looked better—stronger, her complexion rosy, her eyes bright. She was different than the eighteen-year-old I'd known, but we were adults now. Plus, after all that happened our senior year, who wouldn't be more reticent?

But what had I missed? By not pressing her to talk to me or getting her professional help, what parts of that pain had she kept bottled up, stuffed too deep to access? And when she offered to be my surrogate, I never considered what it might trigger for her. Here, I thought I was this rock for her, but she'd been the rock for me. She was the one who gave me what I wanted most in the world: a baby.

And in return, what had I given her? I want to believe that I tried to get her to talk to me about the pain of what had happened to her, how she felt about the future. But had I really? Or did I reframe her future to fit what I wanted—for her to be in Denver, close to me and the baby?

Now I reach the pawnshop, where a velvet display is laid out with engagement rings. Some look similar to mine—a gold setting with a single diamond solitaire is about as basic as you can get. The only distinguishing mark on mine is a small dent on one side where my hand once got caught in a slamming door, the metal saving my finger.

I could go inside, ask to look at them, but I don't care about the ring. Instead, I wonder if Mara has used my credit card again, if I've heard from the investigator Henry used, suddenly anxious for news. When I reach for my phone to check for messages, my pockets are empty. No phone.

Frozen on the street, I retrace my steps. I had the phone in the club, took it into the bathroom, hung my pack on the hook. Had I set the phone down there? Or left it on the bar? Damn it.

The trip back to the club is only a few blocks, and the bouncer gives me a raised brow as I enter but says nothing. My phone isn't in the bathroom stall. Nor any of the other stalls and not on the counter. I swing my pack off and check the pockets, though I'm positive I didn't put it there. I return to the stall, ducking to look into the toilet paper dispenser and the trash bin before checking the other stalls, the counter, peeking into the large trash can.

It isn't here.

Then I recall the group of women and turn toward the tables, but they are gone. Oh God. At the bar, I scan the empty surface. "Did you see a phone?"

The bartender glances up. "Nope."

The bouncer leaves his post at the door and approaches. "Can I help you?"

"I left my phone," I explain. That phone has everything—access to my email, the reports Henry ran, the detective's number. Henry. "Maybe someone turned it in?"

"I'll check," the bouncer says and walks to the far end of the bar, taking his time before returning. "No luck, I'm afraid."

I motion to the stage. "There were some women here, a bridal party. Do you know where they went?"

The bouncer glances toward the stage. "I don't. They weren't here long."

"Could I use a phone? Try to call it?"

"Sure." The bouncer hands me a cordless phone from behind the bar, and I dial my own phone number, stirring the memory of dialing Mara's number Wednesday morning. I hold my breath, waiting for the ringing tone, but the call goes straight to voicemail. My own cheery voice, asking me to leave a message. I hang up and set the phone on the bar and jog for the door.

One of those women must have taken it. If I find them, maybe I can get it back. I emerge on the street and scan the sidewalk in both directions. No sign of them. I walk several blocks, staring into restaurants and bars, looking back in the other direction and praying the group will emerge.

An hour later, winded and cold, I give up.

My phone is gone. It's only a phone, I tell myself, but it feels so much bigger than that. Like the phone is the last connection to the life I thought I was building. One where I would soon hold my newborn child, bring her home and raise her.

It's like everything, and not just the phone, is lost.

# CHAPTER

# 24

AT A CONVENIENCE store, I buy an inexpensive burner phone with texting capabilities. I place a call to the police department to leave a message for Detective Maxwell with my new number, then I text Henry, whose number I thankfully know by heart, to tell him how he can reach me. I long to talk to him, but he's still at the conference in New York, and from experience, I know he'll be booked solid every day. I want to ask if by some chance he's heard from Mara, but I don't want to worry him. More than that, I don't want to admit that I still don't know where she is. I could also ask him to send the background report on Mara to this phone, but I would have no idea how to view it or if that's even possible. I'll have to find a public computer tomorrow to access my email.

My new hotel room smells like cigarettes, dust, and cat piss. The sign for Penn Inn & Suites is only half lit, leaving the letters *Pen I S es* illuminated. Henry would take one look at this place and steer us far, far away. But Henry is not here, and it is the only hotel I could find in the vicinity of Lotus. After the failed visit today and losing my phone, I doubt that I'll gain anything from a second visit, but Mara's presence in this area and the matching tattoo are all I have. My best guess is that she was looking for someone, so tonight I plan to try to talk to some of the women who work there. I'm hoping the dancers might be more sympathetic than the bartender and bouncer.

If that doesn't work . . .

No. It has to.

I look around the hotel room. Despite the smells, it's decently clean and feels safe enough. With two fingers, I yank the ugly brown spread off the bed, trying not to think about what fluids might remain in the fabric, and let it drop to the floor. As far as getting one of the dancers to talk, my best bet is probably to catch them heading home after their shift. The club closes in eight hours so, still in my jeans and shirt, I climb between the sheets.

Our high school notebook in my lap, I flip toward the end and stop on a page where Mara has scribbled: *Lexi: University of Washington. Cate: University of Nebraska, Lincoln.* Below that, *24 hours, 1,666 miles. Or, Cate: University of Kansas, 27 hours, 1,861 miles.* She must have been mapping out the drive between the two schools or just considering how far apart we would all be. At the bottom of the page, in all caps, it says, *MARA VANNATTA, LOST AT SEA.* It feels almost like a premonition, sending shivers down my spine.

The next page is a chart that reads Ultimate MASH in my own, younger handwriting. At first glance, it looks nearly identical to the dozens of games we played. The winners are circled—Heath Ledger as the husband. House and Houston are circled, as is career as an oil woman. Under children, the number six is circled in a thick blue marker. But someone has scratched a giant $X$ across the game in dull pencil. A new row of options has been added, reading: *homeless, unmarried, no future!!!* And then there's a final word that has been scratched out with so much vigor that the page is torn.

I've never seen this before, so Cate must've done it in the weeks before her death when the notebook went missing, but I can't make sense of it. Of all of us, Cate was the most focused on the future and getting out of Cleveland. She'd been accepted to two colleges with close to a full ride at each, so there was no reason to fear she'd end up without a future.

I flip back to check that the writing scrawled beside the MASH game is in fact Cate's. It is. Maybe the entries simply point to the reality that we were all feeling unsure of our futures. These were just words written with the same fear we each felt that spring. About how much was unknown.

I turn the page and find another chart in Cate's handwriting, two columns labeled *pros* and *cons*. What I expect to follow is a list of differences between Nebraska and Kansas, the two schools that were her top choices. Instead, the left side reads only *God*.

The *con* side is empty.

In my mind, a disturbing picture starts clicking into place.

Both Cate and Mara had been strange that spring, secretive and distant. Cate was disinterested in the things she used to love, and the dreamer quality in Mara also eroded in the last months of high school. Her parents were always fighting, and more often than not, we ended up staying at my house instead of hers. Just the fact of being at my house always muted the energy between us.

Through the back side of the paper, I trace my fingers over the scratched-out word from the MASH game, feeling the indentation of the letters. It takes me a moment to reverse them and make out the word, a tiny portion of the *a* missing. *RAPE*.

My first reaction is that it can't be right. If one of my best friends had been raped, I'd have known. They would have told me. But there's no other reason for that to be written in our shared notebook, for it to be so violently scratched out. No other explanation for the desperation in Cate's words: *homeless, unmarried, no future!!!*

Below the chart, someone has written down a phone number with a 216 area code. Cleveland. Without thinking, I dial the number. An automated voice message says, "Thank you for calling Planned Parenthood of Greater Ohio."

Sometime in our senior year, Cate had been raped. And she'd gotten pregnant.

# CHAPTER
## 25

*G*od. It's the only thing she's written on the *pro* side of her list.

Surely, there are other pros for having a baby, for not getting herself to a clinic and ending this nightmare, but she can't come up with a single one.

There's a knock at her door. With the word *God* etched in her brain like the flash of a bulb, Cate snaps the notebook closed and tucks it under the stack of schoolbooks on her bed. "Come in."

Her mother enters and perches on the edge of the bed, reaching out to rub Cate's arm. "Catie, it's your senior prom."

"I'm not going," Cate says again, pulling the covers up around her waist. She does want to go to prom. Or she did. But not now. The idea that prom was ever important is ridiculous now.

More than anything, Cate wants this nightmare to be over, but in this moment, she wishes her mother would go away. The sensation of her hand up and down Cate's arm is making her insane. She can't remember the last time her mother actually touched her other than to grab her arm in a flash of anger.

The twins made her parents affectionate all of a sudden. The younger twin—by four minutes—is like a puppy. If Cate is in the living room watching TV, it's like Madison can smell her, and within minutes, she's in Cate's lap. The whole family now does all this touching—hugs before they leave the house, hugs when they come home, before bed.

Cate wishes everyone would stop touching her.

"Matt," her mother calls out to her father, who appears quickly enough that it's obvious he was waiting outside the door. "Your daughter doesn't want to go to her senior prom."

Unlike her mother, her dad at least keeps his distance. "Why not?"

Cate looks up at him. "Are you saying I have to go?"

"I'm not," he answers as her mother says, "It's your senior prom!"

Her parents stare at each other for a beat before her dad crosses the room. "Why don't we go do our errands?" he says to Cate's mom. "There's plenty of time before the dance."

Boys don't understand anything. She doesn't have a dress or shoes or a date, even though Mara and Lexi have been hounding her to go and offering to find her something to wear.

"That's not exactly true," Cate's mother says.

"She's almost an adult," he says. "Think it's time we let her decide if she wants to go to a dance."

Before her mother can speak, Cate blows out a breath. "Thank you. I'm glad someone understands."

Her dad levels a warning look, and Cate closes her mouth.

Accepting defeat, at least momentarily, her mother removes her hand and rises from Cate's bed. "Fine. We'll be gone a few hours." From the doorway, Cate's mother studies her for a long few seconds before walking away.

Cate imagines how the evening will go: her parents insisting she join the family if she's not going to prom. Probably a pizza dinner, which is fine, although she's already looking chubby in her clothes. And then some stupid Disney movie. Maybe prom isn't a terrible idea. She could dress up and pretend she's going, then go hide out somewhere until it's over. She wants to be anywhere other than under her mother's watchful eye. Each time she enters the house, each time her mother glances up at Cate from the kitchen table or they pass in the hall, her heart stops. Her mother has to know something is off.

These days, after school, Cate crawls into bed and falls asleep, some novel for AP English on the bed in case her mother checks in. Cate used to love reading for English, but these days, she can barely keep her eyes open. She's mostly quit writing in the stupid notebook, too. It feels so useless, and she's terrified to leave the words on a page her parents might see. Ripping the pages out isn't enough anymore—she planned to burn Wednesday's entry while her mom was out on Thursday with the twins, buying new dance shoes, but by the time she got up the guts to do it, they were home again. Cate is never alone. If she burned the pages, they'd smell it, so instead she tore them into little pieces and tried to drown them in a glass of water, like they might melt. What an idiotic idea.

All she did was make a soggy mess. She flushed some, but on the second try, the toilet started to back up, so she took the rest into the kitchen and ran them down the disposal until it started to make an awful noise. The remaining confetti-sized scraps, she wrapped in a paper towel and hid in a pocket of her backpack to dispose of at school. But Monday feels so far away. Her dad pulled a tiny scrap out of the kitchen sink while Cate was drying the pans after dinner last night, and she almost barfed all over the counter. He muttered something about the twins and the disposal while Cate said nothing, her tongue like sand.

Finally, they're gone again, supposedly for a couple of hours, so Cate opens the notebook and writes down all the questions that fill her head.

> *What's going to happen to me?*
>
> *What should I do?*
>
> *If I tell my parents I'm pregnant, they'll kick me out now. If I don't, they'll kick me out as soon as they find out. Do I try to graduate and just blow off college? You guys, I'm having these vivid dreams. Nightmares where my dad's dragging me to the street like a bag of trash while my mother shouts* Slut! Whore! *And the twins cry. Will they cry? Or maybe my mom will just turn her back on me, without a word, leave me to my dad who will drive me to a nunnery where they'll lock me up until the baby comes. He won't say a word, just drop me at the door, and turn and leave me. No longer his child.*
>
> *If I don't show up for school one day, at least you'll know I'm*

*probably on all fours scrubbing some cold stone floor, wearing a thin
cotton nightgown and freezing my ass off.*

She rips out the page. It's too dark, too terrifying. She flashes back
to that night, to the minutes when she imagined her future, college and
soccer, a boyfriend who would kiss her for hours and never pressure her
to do more. Who would hold her hand and walk across campus with
her. She lets herself imagine this boy—his sandy brown hair, his thin
build. Maybe another soccer player. She recalls how the goalie on the
boys' varsity team flirted with her last fall, even had the courage to ask
her to a movie. She politely declined, deciding he was too young. What
an idiot she is. A year younger than her, he would have been that boyfriend. The good one, the kind one.

Leaving the pro/con list to finish later, she takes the crumpled page
to the backyard and adds it to the remainder of Wednesday's shredded
entry in the metal coffee can her dad uses for random screws and bolts
in the garage. She lights the fire on the concrete patio, then, when it's
all burned, she rinses out the ashes and dumps the sooty water in a
bush at the far fence line.

She's heading back to the house when she hears her name.

Mara peers over the fence. There's a small concrete retaining wall
at the edge of the house that makes it possible to see over. It's not the
first time Mara's used it.

"Jesus," Cate snaps. "You scared me to death."

"We rang the bell," Mara says, whipping a plastic-wrapped garment
over the fence.

Cate studies the teal green through the plastic.

"We found you a dre—"

Cate's gaze returns to Mara, but her friend is not looking at Cate's
face.

Cate follows Mara's gaze down her body. In the rush to get rid of
the pages, she'd run outside in a sports bra and leggings. She hasn't
studied her body in weeks, has refused to glance sideways in the mirror,
but now she sees what Mara does. How Cate's breasts fill the bra, and
then some. And below that: a small but obvious bump.

Mara's voice is a whisper.

"Oh, Cate."

"Is she here?" It's Lexi's voice.

Cate shakes her head, holds her hands together in prayer and mouths, "Please."

Mara pulls the bag back over the fence. "No," she calls over her shoulder. "She must've gone out."

"I thought her mom said she'd be here," Lexi says. "And her car's here."

Mara gives Cate a last pitying look before dropping out of sight. "Let's try the doorbell again. Maybe she's in the shower."

Cate takes a moment to breathe before hurrying through the back door and ducking into the kitchen where she's out of sight from both the front door and the fence line.

Then, she waits as the doorbell rings and someone—Lexi probably—knocks again. Finally, mercifully, it's quiet.

Cate lowers her head to the kitchen table and closes her eyes. She sees Mara's face, hears the sorrow in her friend's voice when she says, "Oh, Cate."

And Cate begins to cry.

There's no hiding it from Lexi now. Not this. It's too big. She needs them both to know because she's going to need them both. And truthfully, maybe she even needs Lexi more than Mara. She can lean on Lexi the way she can't on Mara.

This is no longer about a bad night.

This is the rest of her life.

# CHAPTER

# 26

UNABLE TO SLEEP, I shower and watch reruns of *Seinfeld* until it's time to head to Lotus. I carry only a wad of cash and a single credit card zipped into my coat pocket alongside the hotel key. As a last-minute addition, I tuck the knife acquired from the man outside the Lucky Dive into my pocket. The weight of it is comforting as I approach the truck-sized man seated out front of the club. It isn't the same bouncer from earlier, so I ask him about my lost phone, but it still hasn't shown up. I'm not surprised, but I feel a pang of disappointment as I walk away.

Intending to catch the dancers when they emerge after the show, I circle around the outside of the club, turning at the corner and walking down a back alley to get a feel for the area. A large parking lot, surrounded by a high fence, is filled with cars, the chain-link gate propped open. No sign of anyone manning the lot, so I continue, following the loud music until I spot the club's rear entry. The same logo, Mara's tattoo, is spray-painted in purple on the black building, and another bouncer, as large as the first, is stationed by a back door.

Leaned against the building, I recall a night a few months ago when Mara and I decided to get pizza and watch a movie. I'd suggested

*Hustlers*, the Jennifer Lopez movie about strippers, but Mara had cringed. *God, no. I don't want to watch strippers.* As long as I'd known her, Mara had never been prudish. I'd assumed she'd been reacting to the thought of seeing thin, muscular bodies when she was so pregnant.

Now I wonder.

I settle in against the cold concrete wall of the adjacent building to wait when I hear a woman shout from behind me. "You can tell Angel to fuck off! I'll be back tomorrow for my last check, and he better not short me, fucking prick!"

There is a muffled response from a male voice before the woman yells back.

"Fuck you, too, then. Fuck all of you!"

The clack and scratch of hard-soled shoes on the pitted asphalt grows louder as a woman in a yellow dress and a pair of hot-pink stiletto heels emerges from the rear door of Lotus and marches toward me, a black satchel slung over her shoulder as she texts using only her red-nailed thumbs. She can't be taller than five two, her limbs tawny and slim as she stomps down the alley. Still leaning against the building, I shift to watch her in my peripheral vision. A few feet from me, she stops to adjust a bra strap, and to avoid looking like I'm ogling her, I pretend to be occupied by my own phone. The gray screen reflects nothing, and the device's inability to provide even a realistic alibi makes me want to throw it at a brick wall.

"Excuse me," I finally say. "Do you work at Lotus?"

She whirls toward me, dark hair swinging like a raven's wing.

"What the hell do you want?" she barks, sidestepping to put distance between us.

"Sorry. I didn't mean to scare you. I was just hoping you might—"

She puts a palm out, holding it to block my face. "Nope. I don't do girls."

My cheeks glow with heat. "That's not—I just want to talk."

"Uh-uh. I don't do kink either," she says, walking on. The muscles of her calves are chiseled stone.

"Seriously," I call after her. "I want to ask about the club, about your experience there."

She glances over her shoulder and scoffs. "No way Angel would hire you. You're too old, for one."

She marches across the street without checking for cars. I follow.

"Please. Just ten minutes. Just talk. I'll pay for your time."

My voice spikes to a painful peak. On the far side of the street, she steps onto the curb and pulls her phone back out. Touching the screen, she halts. "Shit."

I catch up to her. "Is everything okay?"

Her fake lashes are so long that it looks like her large brown irises are locked behind bars as she spends a long moment studying me. Then she softens, shrugging. "It's my kid."

"You have a kid?"

"Sam. He's two." She eyes her phone again. "My ex is watching him until eleven."

I picture Goose at age two, pigtails in her hair as she turns the pages of a picture book, saying nonsense words as she pretends to read a story she's heard a hundred times.

"What time is it now?"

She scowls at me. "Not even nine thirty."

"You don't want to run into your ex," I guess.

"God, no."

"Then you've got an hour and a half to kill," I say. "Let me buy you a meal. Anything you want."

The tiniest hitch in her step. It's barely a glimmer, but I chase it like gold.

"Any place you choose," I tell her. "Just one hour of your time. That's all. Nothing strange, nothing . . . kinky." The word is sour in my mouth.

"What if I want a steak?"

"Absolutely," I say. "A steak sounds great."

"And red wine? A bottle?" she adds, chewing on her lower lip.

There is something childlike about the negotiation. She has no idea how far I'll go. "Sure. Steak and wine."

She adjusts the satchel on her narrow shoulder.

"And that's it. Just dinner and—"

"Talk," I finish for her. "That's right. Anywhere you'd like to go."

She lifts a finger, telling me to wait, and makes a call. "Is Callie there?"

Down the block, an old woman in a canvas jacket and worn cargo pants talks to herself in an animated voice, stopping momentarily to swing her fist at an invisible opponent. A group of young men walking in the other direction dissipate to give her space before reconvening with whispered words and laughter.

"Hey, girl," she says, her back to me as though the conversation is a secret. "Asshole fired me." She makes a murmur of agreement. "But someone wants to buy me a nice dinner tonight. Can you get the two of us in? Say, twenty minutes?"

Her mouth dips into the exaggerated frown of a disappointed child. I don't know her name, whether she's been at Lotus for a day or five years, whether she has any idea who Mara is or where she might be, but the thought that she could leave before I can even ask feels unbearable.

"Fine," she says with a huff. "As long as it's not a forever wait, you know? See you soon." She ends the call and starts down the sidewalk. It seems almost an afterthought when she turns to me and asks, "You have a car?"

"No."

"We'll get a cab," she says, aiming a finger at me. "But you're paying."

"Sure," I agree. "No problem."

Then she's off, strutting down the street in impossibly high heels, and I follow, praying this isn't going to be a massive waste of time.

# CHAPTER
# 27

DEBRA SUCKS DOWN two drinks before our table is ready, both ordered off the specialty cocktail list, at twenty-two dollars each. Where she puts the liquor is a mystery, because she seems barely affected. The din of the restaurant makes conversation hard, especially by the bar, but I sit close and try to engage her, asking about her son. His birthday, December 12. His favorite things—trucks and trains and baby ducks. He's obsessed with ducks, she says. It's the longest answer she's given. To questions about where she grew up, she offers two or three words, her gaze never meeting mine.

I imagine, a few years from now, how I might describe Goose. What she will love—trucks or dolls? Will she run after the ducks in the park? Will she have my wavy hair? My hazel eyes? My two baby teeth that never fell out, because there were no adult ones beneath? I picture Goose with a round face, drool glistening on reddened cheeks as she mouths anything within reach. I will be the mother who carries photographs, shows them to anyone who asks and probably some who don't. I feel a rush of envy toward this woman, with her perfect little boy.

A young man with a bun approaches us, and Debra launches herself into his arms. He laughs and swings her side to side like a rag doll.

"Callie said you were coming," he says. "I've got your table ready."

Debra tips her glass to her lips, draining the remaining liquid before setting it on the bar. She links her arm through his as we cross the restaurant where he seats us at a small table. Debra slides into the plush bench seat against the wall, leaving me with a low, hard chair. Her friend gives her a kiss on the cheek. Debra shakes out the starched white napkin and smooths it across her lap.

"Debra," I start, "I'd like to ask some questions about Lotus."

"After we order," she says, lifting the menu between us and blocking any opportunity for conversation.

Though I know due dates aren't an exact science, the approach of midnight feels like watching a lit fuse. Time is precious, and I have so little of it.

When the waiter arrives, Debra orders grilled brussels sprouts, a Caesar salad, and a steak called the Tomahawk. I wait until she's done, not even glancing at the menu. I don't care about food. Can't even imagine eating. When the waiter asks, I request a Caesar salad with chicken.

"Debra," I say, deciding my best bet is to be totally straightforward. "Mara Vannatta is carrying my baby—she's my surrogate."

Debra says nothing, but her gaze flashes down my form—as though looking for a reason I didn't carry my own pregnancy. "I couldn't get pregnant," I tell her, which is easier than explaining the whole truth. "The baby is a girl . . . and she is due tomorrow." I choke on the last word.

For the first time, Debra's focus is fully in one place—on me. "Tomorrow?"

"Yes." I blink back tears. "And I can't find Mara . . . or the baby."

Debra falls back against her seat and lets out an audible sigh. "I can't imagine. You must be worried sick."

"I am."

Across the table, Debra says nothing. Her gaze slides to the plate in front of her, and she takes a sip of water and shakes her head as though fighting off a dizzy spell.

"Do you know her? Mara?" I ask.

"Not really. She hasn't worked at Lotus in a few years," Debra says.

"But you've met her?"

"Not exactly," she says quickly. "But I saw her at the club one night."

"Recently?"

"No." She takes another sip of water and scans the restaurant, her expression unreadable. "It was a year ago, maybe a little more."

Right before she came to Denver. "Was she injured?"

She gives me a strange look. "No."

It feels like there's something here, so I keep pushing. "Do you know what she was doing there? Why she came to the club?"

Debra ignores the question. "She danced for a while under the stage name Kitty Cat."

Kitty Cat, a nod to Cate surely. Our conversation halts as the server sets two large wineglasses on our table.

"Did she seem like she was afraid—" The question is cut off by a wave of Debra's hand and the reappearance of our waiter with a bottle of red wine. He lifts it like a piece of art and tilts it in his arms, displaying the label to Debra. She clasps her hands together gleefully.

"Perfect."

The waiter grins, flashing big white teeth, and pulls a corkscrew from the pocket of his apron, wielding it expertly. He pours Debra's wine first, and she grips the glass by its stem, lifts it to the light, then swirls it so the liquid paints crimson circles against the glass before bringing it to her mouth. The waiter tips the bottle to my glass, and I stop him mid-pour.

"That's plenty for me. Thank you."

"Certainly, madame." His thin lips pinch into a tight circle, tiny lines springing out like the spines of an anemone as he smiles. He fills Debra's glass almost to the rim. As soon as he is gone, I lean across the table.

"Debra, did she seem afraid? Or did anyone talk about someone hurting her?"

"You talk like it was a damn book club," she says with a shake of her head and lifts her glass toward the center of the table. I grab mine, a little too quickly, slopping wine over the lip, and reach across to touch it to hers. "Cheers," she says and takes a long sip. For several moments, she holds the wine in her mouth, letting it saturate her taste buds. After she swallows, she smiles brightly. "That is so good."

I take a sip as well, but the taste doesn't register.

"I'm sure it was a hard job, Debra. And dangerous. I just need to know who she might have talked to, who her friends were."

She swirls the wine in her glass. "We didn't talk about the men at home. There wasn't a girl in there who hadn't been scared and hurt. She was no different."

"Do you recognize the name Lance? He was her husband."

"No idea." Debra no longer meets my eye. The veneer of empathy—or perhaps it was pity—has vanished, and she looks bored again.

"But surely you guys all talked. She must've come up. Maybe you heard something?"

She shrugs and lifts the wineglass as the waiter arrives and sets a silver bucket on a stand beside the table. As soon as Debra lowers the glass from her lips, he refills it. "Food should be here any minute."

"Thank you," I say with a tone meant to encourage him to get lost. He does.

Thinking of Mara's arrival in Denver last January, I change tactics. "You said she came to the club about a year and a half ago. Can you be more specific? Was it winter? Close to the holidays?"

"Actually, yes." There is a flash of fear on her face as she scans the crowd. Rather than looking for something more interesting than the conversation she's having, Debra now seems to be searching for a threat . . . or an exit.

"After Christmas, the year before last?"

Debra stares at me, unblinking. "Before Christmas. Just before."

The waiter returns with the brussels sprouts and Debra's salad, refilling her glass once more. Debra digs into the food while I hold my tongue, running theories in my mind. Was the man who hurt Mara involved with Lotus? The old manager, maybe? Or did she go to Lotus for help?

Debra drains her wineglass and sets it down as the waiter lowers another plate in front of her. A massive oval dish with a wood handle emerging from the center. Not a handle—a bone.

"The Tomahawk," the waiter announces. It is a monolith of meat. I can't imagine how Debra could possibly eat it. The waiter fills her glass again, shaking the empty bottle. "Would you like to order—"

"We'll take another," Debra says with a wave, and his big white teeth flash. He lowers the salad in front of me with a frown that might be pity or disdain. "But let's hold off a few minutes. I'll wave you down when we're ready."

As soon as he's gone, I lean forward. "What happened when she came to Lotus? Why was she there?"

"She tried to warn Angel, but it was too late."

I grip the edge of the table and lean in. "Warn Angel about what?"

There is a shift in Debra's mood, darkening. The woman who had simply been enjoying an expensive meal on someone else's dime vanishes, like a rabbit catching the scent of a predator. She keeps her mouth busy on a piece of meat. She does not answer. Though only a few minutes have passed, Debra lifts a hand and motions to the waiter for the second bottle of wine. As though she needs it to continue.

"Warn him about what?" I press.

She shakes her head. "I shouldn't have said anything. I don't even know why they did it. They never pressed charges. The dancers were back at work two days later." She stabs at a piece of meat, and I reach across the table to grab her hand, holding it still and rattling the glassware in the process.

Debra starts.

I tighten my grip. "Debra, tell me what you're talking about."

She looks up. "It was like three days before Christmas. Maybe ten o'clock or a little later, and the club was quiet. We were in the dressing room, and one of the girls came back from her set and said Mara was out front, arguing with Angel about getting us all out of there, about how we were in danger. I wasn't paying attention, I had a set coming up, but then Angel dragged Mara backstage. He was furious—telling her to keep it down, that she was going to run out all his customers. The two of them fought—he kept telling her to leave, but she was crying and begging him to believe her. Ten minutes later, the club is stormed by a half dozen guys, like a SWAT team. Black jumpsuits and helmets with goggles, all carrying these automatics."

I picture Mara with these men. Goose with these men. What would they do with a pregnant woman? With a baby?

"All the patrons were cleared out and the dancers rounded up in the dressing room." Debra lets go of the fork and I release her hand. She's trembling. "They made us face the wall, down on our knees, hands on our heads—Mara, too, even though she didn't work there." She swipes a hand across her face. "The dancer beside me, Kimmy, had just finished her set. She was in her thong and one of the men reached around and groped her, pressed his crotch into her face while she cried. We were all so scared."

I'm not breathing.

"In the end, they arrested four dancers for solicitation. Mara first and then three other older dancers, ones who were there long before I got there."

"Do you remember their names? The other dancers?"

"No."

I don't believe her.

"Mara yelled at them the whole time. Hands cuffed behind her back, she actually spit at one of them. I didn't see it, but I could hear her. She told the guy he didn't scare her. He didn't say a word, but from the corner of my eye, I watched how she shut up when he stepped closer. She was terrified."

I try to picture the man under that helmet. Lance? "Did their gear say *police* anywhere?"

She pauses as though taking herself back to that moment, then shakes her head. "I can't remember. I don't even know if I really saw them. It was all just a blur and then we were on our knees, facing the wall."

"What happened then?"

"They took the four women and let the rest of us go. One guy told us he hoped we were smarter than those others—that we remembered who was in charge."

"What did that mean? Who was in charge?"

Debra sniffles and lifts her fork as she cuts angrily into the remaining steak. After a beat, she eyes the piece as though deciding whether there's still space in her stomach. In the end, she slides the fork into her mouth and begins to chew.

"Were they police?" I ask again.

She shakes her head. "I don't think so. The main guy was scary as fuck—warning Mara that she'd get what she had coming."

The room is suddenly too loud, too small. "What? What would she get? If the men weren't police or FBI or something, who were they?"

She shrugs.

I press my hands into my lap, fighting off the trembling in my body, imagining Mara now. A man screaming at her, hurting her. And Goose. "What happened?"

Debra chews and swallows. "Angel closed up, told us to forget it—not to talk about it to anyone—and sent us all home with pay for the night." She shakes her head. "We were out tips, though, and none of us was living on what he paid us. After that, no one talked about it, and Mara never came back."

"Did anyone know the men? Any of them?"

She shook her head. "Kimmy wanted to file a complaint against the police, but Angel told her he'd fire her if she did. Told her to let it go. No charges were filed, and those other dancers came back, acted like it was a big misunderstanding. They tried to pretend it was no big deal, but those women were scared. We all knew it."

"Someone must know who those men were," I say. "I need to know. I think it's possible they have Mara and my baby. They're in danger."

"The dancers aren't going to talk to you," she says, lifting her napkin to blot her mouth.

"I need you to ask. Tell the others that Mara is in trouble? Please."

"You don't understand," she says. "*Mara* was trouble. Whoever those guys were, they came because of her. It's the only thing that makes sense—the way she yelled at the one guy, the fact that she got arrested along with her friends and the rest of us were left alone. Angel promised us she'd never be back. Like that was supposed to make us feel safe, but it's never happened since. Mara's gone and so are those men."

Before I can ask anything more, Debra slides off the bench. "I need to use the restroom. I'll be right back."

As she slips past me, I grab her arm. A frantic fear floods me, and I don't want her out of my sight until I've gotten answers. "I really need your help, Debra. That was our agreement."

She pulls her arm from my grip. "I'm just going to the bathroom," she says, rolling her eyes.

I tighten my hold, not letting her pass. "You must've heard whispers from the other dancers. I need that man's name, the one she spit on."

She scans the room, and I feel the rapid clip of her pulse under my fingers. She knows.

"What is his name?" I repeat.

She huffs out a frustrated breath. "There was someone called Mark, I think. But I never heard a last name."

"Mac?" I ask, and there's a flash of fear in her eyes.

"Yeah, that's it," she confirms, and slips past.

Alone at the table, I seesaw between rage and despair. Mac again. Who is he? His men almost found me at the Lucky Dive, tried to take me. It must be eleven by now, Goose's due date approaching like a freight train. I look for the waiter and signal for the check. Within minutes, he slides the bill on the table, and I pull the credit card from my pocket, slipping it into the leather folio without looking.

Even if some of the dancers think Mara was trouble, someone besides me must be worried about her. Gladys Knight was fond of Mara. Surely she had other friends in this city.

The waiter returns to the table, and I lift the page to scan the itemized receipt, notice a charge for a second bottle of wine.

"We only had one bottle."

The server glances at the empty wine bucket, three lines cleaving the space between his brow. "No . . . a server came out with the second."

"It never arrived at the table," I tell him, one eye on the dining room as I wait for Debra to reappear.

He pinches his lips, forming the displeased little anemone. "One moment." He turns and catches a server by the arm, pulling him to the table. "There was a second bottle of wine."

The server is a tall, skinny kid with rosy cheeks and a nervous manner.

"I ran into the other lady, by the bathroom," he says nervously. "She took it. She insisted."

"She took it?" I repeat.

The server looks terrified. "Yes."

I stand. "Where is the bathroom?"

I dart around the tables, through the bar crowd, until I reach a dimly lit hallway. The women's restroom is at the end and I shove the door open hard enough to slam it into the far wall. An older woman applying dark red lipstick at the sink startles and spins around.

"Sorry," I mutter, passing her to reach the stalls and push open the first. Empty. It suddenly feels harder to breathe. My vision wavers as I sidestep to the second. Also empty. There is only one more stall, and it's not latched. I open it anyway. Empty.

Debra is gone.

# CHAPTER
# 28

BACK AT THE table, I cling to the final threads of hope that Debra will return as I settle the bill. Images of women half naked and on their knees, hands raised and terrified, swirl in my head. Mara had gone to warn them. Then, she'd been arrested for solicitation along with three other dancers. Older dancers, Debra said. Like Mara. Were those men police? What else could they be?

Kimmy wanted to file a complaint, and Angel told her he'd fire her for calling. That they should forget it.

I think about the man Peter Maxwell called Clayton. A drug dealer whose identity Mara might know and the reason the detective was trying to locate her. Arrest her. That's what the detective in Denver had said, and Maxwell didn't contradict him. The fact that there's a warrant for Mara's arrest means I still don't know the whole story.

If the events of that night at Lotus were never reported, did Maxwell know that those men had held women at gunpoint? Was Clayton the man Mara had been arguing with?

I shift around the table to face the room, cast a long look around. The conversation has left me jumpy. I meet the glance of a man a few tables away. He offers a soft smile, and it strikes like ice. I hold his stare until he looks back at his companions—two other men, all dressed in suits—and laughs at something one of them said.

Is someone following me? Have I put Debra in danger? While I should be grateful she told me anything that could be potentially useful, I have a thousand more questions. It's surprising she even agreed to dinner once I'd asked about Mara. I wonder if some part of her wanted to tell the story.

Clearly she regretted it after. She was afraid, and now I'm afraid, too.

The terrifying story shines a stark new light on Mara's reasons for coming to Denver—men in black jumpsuits with guns. How would she ever feel safe after that? But while it made sense that she'd leave Philadelphia, coming back remains completely illogical other than the fact of that thumb drive. Returning only makes sense if something on that drive could protect her. But if that was the case, why hadn't she turned it in back then? Had she been worried about how it would look for her? Or was she protecting someone else? The assault took place almost a year and a half ago. I can't imagine Detective Maxwell hasn't already heard about it, but I'll call him tomorrow to be sure.

But right now? What do I do right now? I need to leave, but I don't know where to go. What to do. A frantic energy festers—an uncomfortable humming that escalates.

The busboy stops at the table and gestures to the untouched Caesar salad. "May I take your plate?"

The restaurant is full, and surely they're anxious to turn over the table. "Sure." As he lifts the plate, I think of the call Debra made, the woman she spoke with to get the last-minute reservation.

Callie.

"Wait."

He freezes, a single crouton spilling onto the table. He starts to lower the salad again, but I wave a hand. "I don't want it. I need to talk to Callie."

He studies the bill I haven't signed. I set the pen down and fold my hands in my lap, defiant. "I'll sign it and leave as soon as she comes here to talk to me."

Spots of red appear down his neck. "Let me see what I can do."

The wait is both quick and interminable, like the moment in a doctor's office before a needle pierces skin. Just the thought of a needle brings back memories of IVF, the skin of my stomach pockmarked with tiny bruises and tender from the injections.

"I'm Callie."

She's a young brunette with large blue eyes and bangs cut level to her brows. Seated at the table, I'm short and awkward, so I rise. My breathing is ragged—as though I've been running instead of sitting— and I smooth my pants, wiping my damp palms. Unable to stand still, unable to calm down. This is not the fog of panic but something else entirely. "I came with Debra."

Callie scans the room, but before she can ask, I continue. "She's gone. Took an unopened bottle of very expensive wine and left me with the bill."

She blinks, eyes closed an extra moment as though calculating the damage. "There's nothing I can—"

"I don't care," I interrupt. "I'll pay for it."

"Thanks," she says, clearly relieved. "And I'm sorry about that."

I grab her arm as she turns away, pulling with a jerk. She falls back toward me with a little gasp. I release her and lower my voice, talking through my teeth. Fear sharpens to anger. "I'm trying to find my friend, Mara Vannatta. It's urgent."

Her eyebrows pull together, shifting her bangs like a curtain above them. "I don't know her."

"She used to work at Lotus."

"Listen." She takes a step away even as she lowers her voice to a whisper. "I was there for like three weeks before I quit. I don't know Mara. I keep in touch with Debra and that's it. I don't even know *why*," she adds, an afterthought.

"Debra mentioned someone named Mac. Do you know him?"

"No."

It feels like the truth. "Mara has a tattoo of the Lotus logo," I say. "Do you know anything about that?"

"Yeah, there were a few of them who got those when Tom was there," she says, pulling herself free. "That's all I can tell you. I have to go."

Tom. She's half a table away when I grab for her, fingers catching a belt loop on her black slacks, and there's a wisp of fabric tearing.

She spins. "What the—"

I close the space between us as nearby diners shift to watch. "Who's Tom?"

"Jesus," she hisses, twisting to see the damage to her pants.

"Who is Tom?" I ask again.

"He was the manager of Lotus before Angel."

"How can I find him?" I demand, then soften my voice. "Please."

She exhales, exasperated. "Last I heard, he was managing Top Hat."

"Top Hat," I repeat.

"Another club, a shitty one where some of the older dancers go when they get dropped at Lotus." She puts a hand on my arm and gives a little push. "Now, leave me alone."

I let her go, watching as she slides through the crowd. My stomach growls, another reminder of the meal I didn't eat. The young server catches my eye as I sign the bill, reading until I find the time printed at the bottom. 11:11. Cate used to call them angel numbers. She said that seeing a clock when all the digits are the same means an angel is watching over you.

Outside, the asphalt is wet from rain that has already stopped, and a cab is waiting at the curb as though there *is* an angel watching over me. The thought of Cate taps the old well of grief. I wish I believed she was watching me, that she might guide me. I climb into the cab and ask the driver to take me to Top Hat.

None of the areas we drive through are especially nice, but the one we land in is noticeably rough. The driver pulls to the curb in front of a solid brick wall painted a flat black. Hooded lights are mounted on the exterior, only half of them functioning.

"This is it," he says, pointing to the building. He hesitates. "I can take you somewhere else?"

"No," I say, a hitch in my throat. "Thanks." I check my pocket for the burner phone, feeling the weight of the knife there, too.

Inside, the club is a sea of bright blue. A bouncer waves me in without a word—I consider asking for Tom but decide against it. This has to go better than the visit to Lotus, so I fight the urge to ask questions too soon.

Get inside. Buy a drink.

Despite the location and unassuming entrance, the club is more than half full. The music is unfamiliar, so loud the percussion vibrates my ribs. A group of young men occupies a half dozen tables along the edge of the stage, where two women are taking turns swinging on a pole, dancing close enough that the men can slip bills under their G-strings. I head to the bar, take a seat between two empty stools. Despite their lackluster environment, the bartenders work with an efficient grace, men who have done this job a long time. One of them sets a cocktail napkin on the bar in front of me. He's the oldest of the three, gray-haired, his face tan, with a hint of orange that seems unnatural.

"Drink?" he says.

"Bud Light, please." I slide a twenty across the bar.

He's back in fifteen seconds, setting down the bottle, whisking away the twenty and making quick change. Right now Debra is probably home with her son, giving him a good-night kiss. I imagine leaning over a crib of my own, pressing my lips to Goose's soft cheek, her skin sticky with sleep and sweat.

Beer in hand, I face the stage, surveying the room for someone who looks like he might be in charge. Probably there's an office somewhere—upstairs or in back. The stage is round and takes up most of the main area. Two doors mark the far corners of the room, and I weigh the odds.

A young bartender taps the bar in front of me. "All good here?"

I try to look casual. "I'm looking for Tom."

He scans the room. "He's around here somewhere."

The group of young men is growing rowdy. One stands, stretching widespread arms toward the woman on stage—the dancer pivots, spinning out of reach with an ease that suggests she does it all too often. The man tries to climb onto the stage, thwarted by his own drunken clumsiness, as several of his friends tug him back into his chair. A moment later, a man emerges from the left side of the club; he speaks to the group of men, gesturing to the drunk one.

I am certain this is Tom.

Several of the drunk man's friends nod solicitously, promising to keep him in check. Tom points to his watch, and I study his face, wondering how best to approach him. Before I can decide, he starts toward the door—his strides are long, quick, and I have to jog to catch up. Lunging after him, I don't look back as I slip into the dark hallway.

It's empty.

"Tom?" I call out. "Tom?" When there's no answer, I turn right, walking toward a lit room down the hall.

"Who are you?" The voice comes from behind me.

Tom is older than he looks from a distance, hard lines on his face and hands. His skin is weathered and tan, like the tennis pro at Henry's club. "You're not supposed to be in here."

"I'm looking for Mara Vannatta."

He barks a laugh, waves toward the exit. "I haven't seen her in years. Go on and let yourself out."

"I've got to find her. Just answer a couple of questions and I'll leave."

"That bitch is out of my life. You ain't dragging her in again." He marches toward the rear exit, expecting me to follow.

There's something in his tone. "You were together."

"We were *never* together. We were business partners . . . until she fucked me over." Fury burns in his eyes when he turns. His hand lashes out, grabbing hold of my arm, and he yanks. "Back door. Now."

A red exit sign casts a bloody shadow on us as the screen of his watch lights up. A message floats by, words I can't read, and then numbers fill the darkened screen.

12:01.

It's here. Goose's due date.

I pull at him, the contents of my pocket bouncing on my hip. "Please," I beg.

He yanks away and I hit the wall where there is a large dent in the

Sheetrock, maybe from the last person he threw out. Damp, cold air strikes my face, the smell of rain and dirt in my nose as he shoves. I unzip my pocket, pull out the knife, then duck and double back under his arm, refusing to be cast out.

"Jesus Christ," he says.

He reaches for me again, but I spin away, fingers trembling as I release the blade. He grabs my shoulder and spins me to push me into the night. I fist the front of his shirt with my left hand and drag him with me. We stumble into the alley and I twist toward the dumpster, catching him off guard.

He slams into the metal. "What the fuck?"

Goose is due today. She will be in the world, if she isn't already. There is no being patient or slow. There is only this now—rage and fury, the ugly children of fear. I press the knife to the buttons of his shirt.

"Get down," I say. "Slowly."

"You're fucking crazy." He starts to push me, but I drag the knife across his chest, feeling the blade slice through his shirt and into his skin. He jumps, striking the dumpster.

"Okay," he says. "Okay, okay." He lowers himself until he's in a squat, one shoulder against the dumpster. "What do you want? I don't have any money on me. I don't even have my phone."

"Hands on your head and get down on your knees."

I am shocked when he obeys. The hatred in his eyes is terrifying.

"Turn around. Face the dumpster."

He eyes the knife, but I clench it harder, pressing the blade to his neck. With a grunt, he walks an awkward half circle on his knees, muttering about the wet ground. I'm grateful when I can no longer see his face.

"I'm going to ask a few questions, then you can go. But if you fight me, I'll fucking slice you apart."

The words come from my lips, but it's the voice of a stranger. A woman pushed too far.

"Someone's going to come out here any minute," he says. "You want to go to prison for this?"

"Mara has something of mine," I say, voice trembling. "I don't want to hurt you, but I need your help. Where would she go if she was in trouble?"

"I haven't seen her in years. Most peaceful years—" He shifts.

"Don't move," I repeat. Flashes of the C-section videos I've watched over the past months come to mind, the ease of a scalpel cutting through skin.

"Why do you need to find her so bad?" he asks, leaning against the dumpster.

"I told you, she has something of mine."

"Whatever she's got, she's hocked it, sold it, rented it out, or broken it, I promise you that. I knew her almost ten years, and she cared more about money than humans. She'd have sold my last kidney if I let her."

I don't like him—the look of him, the way he talks about my oldest friend. But is he telling the truth? I replay Debra's story—the men at Lotus, that they came because of her. That Angel swore they'd be safe because Mara would never be back. The nurse's mention of Mara's earlier pregnancy—I wonder if that baby was Tom's. He says they weren't together, but maybe a one-night stand. If the baby was his, did he know? Is that why he's so angry?

"Tell me everything you know about her. Where did she work? Who were her friends?"

"She didn't have friends, lady. I was supposed to be her damn business partner and *I* didn't even know her."

His words echo, familiar. Like what Henry said. *How well do you really know her, Lexi?* But she did have friends. I'm her friend. Cate was her friend. We were best friends; that counts for more than the words of this asshole.

Doesn't it?

Collect the facts. "How long was she at Lotus?"

He scoffs. "A year, maybe. She only danced for five or six months. She was always fighting with the clients, telling off the handsy ones."

I fight not to react—to be proud of her. Then I remember Caleb's story about the cruise ship, how Mara had gotten involved with a married man, gotten fired and then sued. Her dad had to bail her out and pay her legal bills. A tangled mess of questions surround Mara in my head. I grip the knife more tightly, focus. "Where else did she work?"

"She had a dozen jobs, probably more. Never stayed in one place for long. Mostly she tended bar." He motions down the darkened alley, toward the street. "You walk into any of these joints, Mara worked there one time or another. Last I heard, she was out on parole, slinging drinks at Jimmy B's."

"Parole." The word is sharp in my throat. "She went to jail?"

The man's laugh is hard and cruel, a blade on my own skin. "I'm sure not just the once, either."

"No. You're wrong," I say, willing it to be true. "She doesn't have an arrest record." Henry's report would have shown it.

"Like hell she doesn't. I was there when they took her away in cuffs."

I'm jerked forward suddenly, and Tom is on his feet, my hand in his, the knife aimed away from us. He snaps my wrist toward my forearm in a hard, fast motion. A flood of heat and pain follow. Crying out, I drop the blade, my mouth filling with vomit. I spit as Tom grabs the knife off the asphalt and swirls toward me. I hit the dumpster and slide down, the earth wet below me. I try not to imagine it: Henry learning that I died from a knife wound in an alley.

"I thought she was good people, but I was wrong." He towers over me as he speaks. "Mara was a con woman. A thief and a liar and a bitch. She took advantage of everyone—me, my brother, Paul and Molly. Got caught and tried to convince people I was the problem." He barks the same harsh laugh. "She didn't care if they couldn't afford to help her, if they might lose their jobs or their homes. If Mara wanted something, Mara got it."

I track the knife as he paces in front of me.

"Hell, she charged five grand on a credit card in my name before it was all done."

I'm trying to focus on his words, on the names he mentions. Paul and Molly, Tom's brother. Even as he waves the knife, he's helping me. One of them must know something.

"When I finally kicked her out for good," Tom continues, "she managed to weasel an invitation to stay with Dottie Rosen in that fancy place of hers."

"Who is Dottie Rosen?" I ask in a whisper.

"Another stripper who managed to dupe some Wall Street guy into marriage." He wipes a palm across his mouth, mopping up the spit around his lips. "Who knows how much Mara stole from him."

"Where is Dottie now?"

"Dead, probably. She had cancer or a stroke or something. Knowing Mara, she probably helped her to the grave."

I sink against the hard, cold metal of the dumpster. "What about the others?"

"Jesus. Don't you get it!" he exclaims, leaning in as though I'm deaf or stupid. "You're not getting it back, whatever it is. That bitch stole it and she's sold it. It's gone forever."

Spittle flies from his lips, landing on my cheek. For a second it looks like he might leave, but then he swings around, swiping the knife at my chest. He comes so close that I lurch away, slamming my head into the dumpster as he grabs hold of my arm and yanks me to the asphalt.

Before I have time to draw a breath, the hard toe of his shoe strikes my kidney, bringing on a fresh wave of nausea.

"Get the fuck out of here," he says. The words are followed by the clatter of something on the ground, then after a beat, a thud as he disappears into the building.

For several moments, I don't move. My wrist has its own pulse, and so does the small of my back, where his shoe struck. I need to get up in case he returns. All I can manage is a shallow inhale as I struggle to sit, my spine protesting, chest tight and painful. Something warm is trickling from my shirt—when I touch my jacket, my fingers come away red. Bloody.

I use my left hand to unzip the jacket to assess the damage, but all I can see is a visible stripe of skin, six or seven inches long, and a line of dark red soaking into my cotton shirt. I stand, wishing I hadn't unzipped the coat. I snatch the bloodied knife off the ground and dart behind the dumpster. In the pale light above the club's rear exit, I study the blade, the dark stain on the steel. The blade wiped clean on my jeans, I close the knife and return it to my pocket. Part of me wants to curl into a ball right here; instead, I hurry to the end of the alley, trying to form a plan.

I probably need medical attention. I should go to a hospital. But a doctor would ask questions I can't answer. As would the police. I only hope Tom doesn't report the assault. Getting thrown in jail isn't a risk I can afford when Goose's arrival in the world is so imminent. I don't have time—to visit a hospital or explain myself to anyone.

While the wound on my chest and my wrist are physical discomforts, losing Goose would actually kill me. A slow shift between fear and hope, the fear expanding to a racing river as the trickle of hope runs dry. I have to keep searching. Finding Goose is the only way I know how to survive.

Blood trickles down my front, and I can feel it damp against my bra. I need a pharmacy, some supplies to clean myself up. Once I get back to my room, I'll see what I can find out about Dottie Rosen.

I have no idea where I am in relation to the hotel. I imagine dialing Henry's number, telling him what happened. The thought of his panicked response keeps me walking forward, a slow steady pace to prevent jostling my wrist. I try moving it, small motions. Maybe not broken, definitely sprained. I wonder how much blood I've lost.

Several blocks down, I spot a busy street and make my way toward the safety of cars and traffic. Passing a closed convenience store, I enter the closest bar and walk straight to the counter. Thankfully, the bartender is a woman, about my age, and her eyes widen momentarily at the sight of me.

"I need a cab. Can you call me one?"

She eyes me. "Just a cab?"

"You have a first-aid kit?"

She digs for a red zippered case. "Bathroom's at the end of the bar. You want a drink? Ice?"

I feel a warm splash of relief. "Ice would be great," I say.

With ice and the first-aid kit in hand, I lock myself in the bathroom. The room smells of cigarettes and beer. Blood has saturated my shirt, so I unzip the jacket and let it fall to the floor, hands trembling as I tenderly pull the shirt free of my skin. It catches on the drying blood, and I take several long, slow breaths before I move again. Leaning forward to prevent the shirt from touching the wound, I open the first-aid kit awkwardly, my left hand not nearly as adept as my injured right.

Inside are a dozen small plastic pouches with everything from Band-Aids to ACE bandages, tweezers, and a small set of scissors. Pinning the kit to the counter with my elbow to avoid using my right hand, I pull the scissors free and work to wield them on the shirt. I want to cut out the part that touches the wound, but the scissors are too dull and my left hand is incapable. Defeated, I wet a stack of paper towels and press them to the cut in an effort to clean off the dried blood. I don't rub, terrified the wound will reopen and bleed more. Once most of the blood is gone, I smear on antibiotic ointment before placing squares of gauze overtop, then tug the shirt up my right arm and wrap an ACE bandage around my wrist before putting my jacket back on. The kit is simple—no medication—but I take two more packets of triple antibiotic ointment as well as the gauze squares and a roll of medical tape, zip them into my coat pocket. As I wash my left hand, avoiding my right to keep the bandage dry, I dare a peek in the mirror.

The woman reflected back has my features—my hazel eyes and dark hair, my nose with its thick bridge, my arched eyebrows, which for so many years I tended with the care of a gardener with her rosebushes. But this woman is different. Her eyes are narrowed, blood smeared on her chin and throat.

The last time I was in a physical altercation was in the fourth grade, a fight with a girl named Valerie. We were sharing a tub of art supplies—colored pencils, safety scissors. Valerie kept pulling the container to her side of the table, as though it belonged to her alone, and I kept jerking it back to the center. "Leave it where we can both reach it."

She flushed, anger in her eyes. Ignoring her, I dug through the container for a pair of scissors before noticing she had both pairs in front of her. "Can you pass me some scissors?"

She slashed them at me, cutting edge first. They were hardly sharp, but the metal caught my forearm and sliced the skin. Valerie and I were both sent to the principal's office, our mothers called. Valerie's mother arrived first and emerged from the office holding her tearstained daughter by the hand and issuing me a hateful scowl. My mother eventually arrived, too. On the ride home, she lectured me about being a polite girl, not a barbarian. It was the first time I remember thinking: I am nothing like my mother.

If Valerie were here now, I would snap one of her little fingers.

I stare at the barbarian in the mirror, blinking away what happened in the alley. Injuries aside, I got a name that might lead me to Mara.

Dottie Rosen.

There's a knock, and I zip the jacket.

Back at the bar, the bartender pulls down a shot glass, fills it with an amber liquid.

"I didn't order—"

"It's on me and it'll help. Cab's out front. She'll take care of you."

"Thank you," I say, tears burning my eyes. "Here, let me—" I reach for my pocket to pay her, but as I do, she stops me.

"We're square," she says as she returns the first-aid kit to its spot behind the bar. Then she is gone and I'm alone with my pocket of supplies, the pain beating a pulse in my wrist, my back, the skin on my sternum. I lift the shot glass to my lips and drain it. It burns my nose even before I've swallowed, like drinking fire. On the street is a yellow cab, window down. The driver raises a hand, and I wonder briefly how the bartender described me. Beaten, bloodied.

Gray-haired and stout, the driver could be someone's grandmother.

Instinctively, I reach to open the door with my right hand. Biting back a cry, I switch to my left and climb into the taxi.

With some effort, she shifts to see me through the thick plexiglass. "I can get you medical help, no questions asked."

"I'm okay," I say. "I just need to get to my hotel."

"Tell me where, baby," she says, facing forward.

How lovely it would be to surrender to these injuries, to let someone fix me—put a cast on my wrist, check the knife wound, prescribe real pain medication. But all that matters now is finding Dottie Rosen. On the ride to the hotel, I think about the email I sent to Henry's investigator about getting more information about Mara and wonder whether he ever answered. If only I'd thought to write his name down somewhere so I could contact him without my phone. Tomorrow I'll go to a library and check my email, do a search for Dottie.

If I'm lucky, she's still alive and living in Philadelphia. And damn if I'm not due a little luck.

# CHAPTER
## 29

*May 2008*

*I've still got the notebook! I know, I know, I'm giving it back. Just need to survive the next twelve hours . . . Less than that. My appointment is at 9:15 a.m.–it's four a.m. right now. I gave up on the idea of sleep hours ago.*

*Lexi, I hope you'll forgive me for not telling you. At first, I just wanted to forget it. And then, it was too much. But by the time you read this, it'll be OVER!*

*I'm so sick about this, but I have to do it. I can't have a baby. And now this can't happen soon enough. A few more days and everyone was going to know.*

*Case in point: I threw up at soccer practice yesterday–in the middle of a one-on-one breakout drill where I was paired against a sophomore. A sophomore! I was dribbling and suddenly the granola bar I'd eaten was at the back of my throat. You know the feeling? I knew it was coming up and I sprinted like hell to make it to the bathroom but I was halfway across the field and it was too far. I ended up hurling behind the bleachers. I'm sure the whole damn team heard me, and then Coach was there, asking if I was okay. If I needed to TELL HER ANYTHING?!*

*I almost vomited again, but I lied and said I'd had a fever the night before and it must've been the flu. But clearly she knows, right?*

*Then I got home and my whole family was waiting in the kitchen–Dad, too. Home from work two hours early. I've never been so freaked out. I was ready to confess to all of it right then. Thank God Madison can't keep her mouth shut, so she starts shouting at me to blow out the candles . . . wtf. But sure enough, there are two cupcakes on the table, one blue and one red, little half-burned birthday candles on top. (God forbid my mom splurge on new birthday candles to celebrate my acceptance to college.)*

*Yep. I got into both schools. Big-ass envelopes from Kansas and Nebraska. Money's better at Nebraska, but I can swing either.*

*So, if I can somehow get unpregnant–that's how I'm looking at it now–then I get to go to college.*

Cate shoves the notebook under her mattress and closes her eyes, exhausted even though she still has three more hours before her alarm will go off.

It still feels like a miracle that she escaped the family celebration. But Madison pounced on Cate for a hug—and a promise of more cupcake because she knew their mom had bought extras—and announced that Cate smelled like feet, so she was able to excuse herself for a shower. Once she was clean, she climbed into bed, pulled the covers over her head, and slept for two hours until her dad woke her for dinner.

"You deserved the nap," he said, perched on the edge of the bed. "You've been working so hard."

How she longed to tell him.

Nothing has been right since she saw those two blue lines. She got into two great colleges, with scholarships, too, and she can't even feel excited. She can't go to college pregnant. There are moments when the truth comes so close to bursting out of her—when Lexi and Mara are rambling on about homework or graduation and Cate can only wonder when this thing will be over. Lexi keeps asking about the notebook, and

Cate has twice lied and said she's misplaced it somewhere in her room, swearing she'll give it back. She could just rip out the page with the pro/con list and pretend nothing's wrong, but she wants to come clean with Lexi. And now that Mara knows, she's helping, so they'll need to tell Lexi, too.

Only she doesn't want to tell Lexi until it's done.

"You have to find the notebook soon," Lexi said yesterday as they were leaving school. "We only have a few more weeks to write it all down. And I've been saving all my stories from prom . . . Sarah G stuffed chicken cutlets in her bra and one of them was totally sticking out the whole night."

Cate isn't even sure she could hide it another week. The nausea is awful, and she's barely avoided throwing up where her mom might hear. Cate's bathroom backs her parents' bedroom, and twice, she's gotten sick in the trash by her desk, sneaking the can into the bathroom to clean it out when everyone else is downstairs.

School has been miserable. While Mara has finally stopped begging Cate to tell Lexi, her friends follow her through the halls like a second skin. Cate has always loved Mara's shampoo, which reminds her of sleepovers in better days, where they watched movies and gossiped and ate so many Smarties and Sour Patch Kids that she got sores on her tongue. Now, the smell of that shampoo makes Cate gag, worse even than the coffee brewing in the mornings, or her mom's chili. And the way Lexi studies her when she thinks Cate isn't looking, like she doesn't recognize her, like Lexi is trying to place her face. She obviously knows something is up. It's bad enough at home, Cate's mother always watching.

Last Monday during lunch, she went to the library to search the web for abortion clinics in Cleveland. She found warnings about the dangers of abortions, horror stories about how the baby feels everything, images of white paper dressing gowns streaked with blood. The worst were the photographs of dead fetuses at seven and eight weeks— their tiny human shapes. Cate does want children—she's never imagined not having them. But not now. Not like this.

That afternoon, when her mom took the twins to ballet, Cate used the kitchen phone, dialing *67 to hide the number, and made an appointment at the clinic under a fake name. She was both surprised and relieved that they could get her in so quickly.

Thank God Mara is coming with her. All she has to do now is get to the bus stop where Mara will pick her up, which feels hard enough. The nausea is worse than ever at breakfast, but she manages to eat half a piece of toast and pretends she's got to be at school early. Mara is already waiting at the bus stop and, when Cate gets in the car, Mara looks almost as nauseous as Cate feels. They're quiet on the drive, save for the few times when Mara lifts her hand off the gearshift and touches Cate's arm. "After today, this whole nightmare will be ancient history."

Cate only nods. It takes all her willpower not to vomit on the floor. She's only been to downtown Cleveland a handful of times, and always with her parents, but the directions are simple, and they arrive well before her appointment time.

They park in a lot a block from the clinic, and as she climbs out of the car, Cate swears she feels the baby move. She doesn't tell Mara. Doesn't say anything as the two of them, heads bowed, walk to the clinic. By the time she reaches the front desk, she's crying, telling herself it will be over soon. But then the woman asks for proof of her age.

Mara's hand grips her arm as Cate sputters. "What?"

"I need to confirm you're eighteen."

Cate isn't eighteen. She won't be eighteen for five more months. Mara's grip tightens as the woman says, "If you're not eighteen, you need a parent's consent."

Cate's eyes land on a pamphlet, the bold letters that decry *Your Body, Your Choice.*

But not for her. Her two choices are: find another way to end this pregnancy or tell her parents and get kicked out of her house.

Mara wraps an arm around her shoulders and turns her toward the door, steering her across a floor she can't see through her tears. "It's okay," Mara says, with a confidence Cate can't imagine feeling. "We'll find another way. It'll be okay."

Cate repeats the words in a whisper as she stumbles out the door of the clinic and into a bitter wind. *It'll be okay. We'll find another way.*

There has to be another way. Because Cate will do anything not to have to tell her parents.

# CHAPTER

# 30

*Due date*

I HAVE IMAGINED this day a thousand times. Crouching next to Mara in the delivery room, holding her hand and offering ice chips until it's time to push. Watching the crown of Goose's head come through the birth canal. Holding my child before they can clean her or wrap her, the closest I will ever come to experiencing pregnancy.

Instead, I wake to a pain that makes a full breath impossible. I've taken all the Advil I had, so I don't imagine I'll fall back asleep. From the corner, the radiator makes a ticking sound, and I pick up Cate's notebook again, revisiting the pro/con list. Mara told Gladys she felt guilty about Cate's death. Did Mara know Cate was pregnant? If Mara kept our notebook for all these years, then she had to have known about the baby. Is her guilt related to the pregnancy? To not being there for Cate when she needed a friend? Or was it something worse?

Cate's strange distance in those final months makes so much more sense now, and I wonder how I missed it. I can only imagine how scared she would have been. How her parents would have reacted to the news. She told a story once about a neighbor girl from their church who had gotten pregnant, and her parents had kicked her out of the house with nothing. I asked Cate about it one time, and she said she never knew where the girl ended up. Cate would surely have assumed her fate would be the same.

Had Mara been acting differently, too? Once Cate was gone, we never talked about the way she'd been before her death. It was too painful to shine light on questions we would never be able to answer.

If Mara had kept this secret from me for so long, what else didn't I know?

Once I've managed to sit upright in the hotel bed, the first thing I do is call the local hospitals to see if Mara has been admitted. If she has, she hasn't done it in her own name. I consider calling Maxwell to ask about Dottie Rosen, but I'm hesitant. He'll likely ask questions about where the information came from, and I don't want to admit anything about what happened last night with Tom. I decide to find a library, but I dread the idea of navigating this city on foot the way I feel now. I also want to talk to Gladys again. She and Mara clearly spoke about Cate; maybe she can make something of the notebook. I can't find a connection between Cate's notes and Mara's current situation, but maybe I'm overlooking something. I pray that I am.

I find Terrence's number where he wrote it on the envelope Gladys gave me and send a text, cringing at the time. It's barely seven thirty on a Sunday morning. hi terrence. It's Lexi from gladys' house. sorry to text so early. hoping for a ride today. need a library, and maybe a few other spots. insist on paying! It takes nearly a minute of hunting to figure out the exclamation point on the flip phone.

Then, I open Cate's notebook and move past the pro/con list. There are several blank pages, and for a moment I assume the writing is done before my fingers hit uneven texture. Turning the page, I see an entry written upside down in tiny, cramped lettering.

Cate.

> *I have to get out of here. I can't live another month under my mother's thumb. Why doesn't she understand that I don't want her life?? I don't want babies and a house with pillows that say HOME IS WHERE THE HEART IS. BARF. I want to play soccer for a college team and take random classes about shit that I might be good at. I want a*

*career—a power suit and a seat at a conference table where I'll show those men that I've got a brain in my head. I want my own apartment in a high rise building in Chicago or New York and I want to travel to Europe with my friends. I am NOT staying in Cleveland. Fuck that. I'm getting the hell out of here.*

It breaks my heart to read the words, knowing that Cate never got out. She never had her power suit or her seat at the table. Her trip to Europe. I wish I'd known, that I could have been there for Cate. There are so many things I want to ask Mara. Need to ask her.

By the time I'm showered, rebandaged, and dressed, a message from Terrence waits on my phone. Happy to help. Taking Damon to church at eight thirty. I can pick you up after, around 10. Just tell me where.

Plenty of time to find food, and more pain medication. And maybe a library.

will text when i know where. thx

I'm just done getting ready when the mobile phone rings. The strange tone is unfamiliar and makes me jump. I recognize the number and hesitate. I'm afraid the sound of Henry's voice might make me break, but I long to hear a familiar voice.

"Hi."

"Lexi." He says my name with audible relief. "Are you okay?"

My throat closes, and I shake my head as though he could see me. "Yes." The sound is barely a whisper.

"You haven't found her."

Shame fills me. "No."

"Okay." I can hear him processing this. "Are you safe?"

"Yes."

"What can I do?" he asks.

Henry means this literally. When something is wrong, he wants to fix it. There's so much he can't do, but there is one thing he can. "I reached out to that investigator who ran the initial report on Mara, to see if he could help locate her. But then I lost my phone."

"You want me to reach out to him?" I love that he understands without my needing to explain, a tiny weight lifted.

"Please," I say. "And will you also ask him to see if he can locate a woman named Dottie Rosen? Dorothy, I assume. She was a friend of Mara's, and I think they may be in touch."

"I'll do it now," he says. "Also, don't forget I'm in New York. Scheduled to be here until Monday afternoon, so I could be there in a couple hours. Three, tops," he offers.

As I'm thinking it through, he adds, "If you need me."

"I do," I answer quickly, and realize how true it is. I do need Henry. "But not here. Not yet. Just—"

"I'll get in touch with the investigator," he says, reading my mind. "Or find someone there. Put them on a rush job."

"Thank you."

"And I'm here. I'll keep my phone close. Call, okay? Please call if there's anything I can do."

"I will." And I will call him. In the time Mara lived with me, I shifted so much of my energy from Henry to her, but I need them both. I need a community to survive this, and Henry is at the center. I don't know how I lost track of that. There is a beat of silence between us— not strained silence, but the comfortable kind.

"I'm thinking about you today," he says, voice soft.

On her due date. But he doesn't say that. Instead, he offers, "I love you."

"Me too," I say, and tears stream down my face as I end the call. I quickly swipe them away and savor the knowledge that my husband will come if I ask. He doesn't suggest that I can't do it on my own, but if I want him to be here, he will come. For once, talking to him doesn't raise a dozen questions about what we are now, what we will be. Whatever happens to our marriage, he's my family.

Preparing to leave the hotel, I pull on my jacket and realize how obvious the slices in the fabric are in daylight. Not to mention the bloodstains. I toss the jacket in the tiny bathroom trash can and pull on a hoodie, grateful for the zipper.

The front desk clerk points me toward a pharmacy and a decent diner, both within a five-minute walk. After stopping by the pharmacy, I sit at the diner and order a big breakfast, which reminds me of dinner with Debra the night before. Though not even twelve hours have passed, that conversation feels like it happened days ago. As I eat, I try to imagine where Mara is right now. Where Goose is—if today will be her actual birthday or if it's still to come. I can't consider the other option. That she's already been born.

Mara, Cate, and I used to be able to communicate without words—a raised brow, a tiny twitch at the corner of a mouth. That changed when Cate died. At the time, I blamed it on grief, but it was more. After Cate was gone, some of that transparency in Mara also vanished, as though the magic required all three of us to work. Now, I long to sense Mara, would do anything to feel whether she is in labor.

After breakfast, I make my way outside and find a text from Terrence.

> You could use the library at the community college on Spring Street. Think they open at 8.

The words are a balm.

> public computers?

I long for the Google app on my iPhone. I don't expect an answer, since Terrence and Damon are in church, but a response comes through a minute later.

> First room on the left past the front desk. I'll meet you there unless I hear different.

The wind cuts through my sweatshirt, and I am grateful to climb into the warmth of a cab, which drops me in front of a white building with tall arched windows. The front desk is occupied by a student, so I follow Terrence's instructions without stopping. Inside the room are two long tables, computers spaced evenly along their surface. Two users occupy computers at opposite ends, so I take one in the center. I move the mouse and stare at a home page, its background an image of the Liberty Bell.

Search engine open, I try every combination. *Dorothy Dottie Rosen Lotus Lounge cancer married Wall Street obituary.* Dorothy Rosen is not an uncommon name, and there are dozens of marriage announcements and obituaries. None of the results mention the Lotus Lounge. The next page lists more obituaries and a growing number of links to cancer treatments and funeral homes. I'm trying to drum up a different set of words, thinking back to Tom's comment—that Dottie Rosen had lured a wealthy man into marriage. Entering a search for *Rosen, Financier, Wall Street, marriage to stripper, Philadelphia,* I get a hit.

*JP Morgan Vice President Marries Longtime Stripper.* The article details how Arthur Rosen married Dorothy Pratt in a small private ceremony. I use his full name in a search and find an obituary for Arthur, but none for Dorothy. A link offers up Dorothy's current address, behind a paywall, of course. I enter my credit card number and find two addresses for Dorothy listed: one in downtown Philadelphia, from two years ago, and a second in care of a Longview Retirement Center. A search tells me Longview is about five miles outside the city. I scramble for a piece of scrap paper and write out the name and both addresses as neatly as I can with my left hand before folding it carefully into my jeans pocket.

Terrence will be here soon, so I clear the browser history and send a short text to Henry to let him know I found Dottie Rosen myself.

# CHAPTER
# 31

AT A QUARTER to ten, I'm waiting outside the library for Terrence when the driver of a light blue minivan honks his horn in a quick double beep. A familiar voice calls out.

"Hey, Alexandra lady. You coming? Terrence and I ain't got all day."

Damon grins through the open window in the back seat, and I hurry over to climb in.

"How was church?"

"Godly," Damon says with an impish grin. "Damn godly."

Terrence turns in his seat to face me. "We're supposed to take Damon home, but he wants to come on the adventure."

"Sure," I say, noticing the deep frown lines carving between Terrence's brow as he eyes the ACE bandage on my arm.

"You okay?" he asks.

"Just a sprain."

Damon lets out a series of whoops. "Where are we going?"

The van's interior has been reconfigured so the wheelchair can be rolled through from the rear and locked in place behind the passenger seat.

"Where *are* we going?" Terrence asks, one eyebrow lifted.

"I think I found a friend of Mara's. Her name is Dottie Rosen."

"Yes!" Damon declares. "That's the lady she brought to Ms. Knight's place. In the Mercedes."

I look back at Damon, who is grinning. I want to squeeze his hand or hug him—confirmation that Dottie knew Mara is the closest I've gotten to a sense that I'm making real progress.

"Where's Dottie now?"

"I have an address," I say, handing over the folded page with the information on Longview Center.

"Wow," Terrence says. "This place is pricey."

I try to imagine how Dottie Pratt became Mrs. Arthur Rosen. The article in the paper didn't offer any details. Maybe he picked her up in the club, *Pretty Woman* style.

"Here we go," Damon sings as Terrence pulls away from the curb. While we drive, Damon provides commentary on church and people from the neighborhood. They are vignettes from his life, and even without knowing any of the characters, the stories are entertaining. The last is about the couple in the pew behind him. "Turns out Larry isn't Larry Jr's dad," he says with a whistle.

"Damon," Terrence warns. "You know what Ms. Knight says about eavesdropping."

"A man's got to have a hobby, Terrence," he says, and I swivel in my seat to see him, the expression on his face layered with joy and mischief. He raises his left eyebrow, then winks at me. "And I don't like golf."

"What do you like about listening to people's stories?" I ask Damon.

The goofy expression on his face shifts into thoughtfulness. "I like to imagine how other people live."

I think about how insular my own life has been—how rarely I pay attention to those outside my immediate circle, and I wonder if this experience will change that. "I need to do that more," I say, facing front again.

His voice is soft when he speaks again. "Well, it took a bullet to teach me."

I turn back, and Damon meets my eye. "I'm so sorry, Damon. I can't imagine what you went through."

"I was so angry. Hell, I was angry before I got shot. Angry that my parents were dead. That my aunt and uncle were hard on me. Felt like I'd been treated wrong since the day I was born."

Terrence shifts in the driver's seat, and I know he's listening as intently as I am.

"I've been plenty angry since that day—sometimes way angrier than I was before. But I'm also thankful, and I don't think I was ever thankful before." Damon's gaze shifts out the window and, as I turn back around, Terrence offers the smallest nod.

"Your Mara and I talked about gratitude—that day she came over to give Ms. Knight that letter."

I twist in the seat and grip the armrest. "What did she say?"

"Was after her friend Dottie left."

"The time she brought Dottie—that was the last time you saw her?"

"Yeah. She came by to talk to Ms. Knight. Dottie drove her, then came and picked her up later."

Mara was with Dottie right before she came to Denver, which makes it all the more likely that they're still in touch. I feel like I'm getting so close to finding her. "What did Mara say about gratitude?"

"She and Ms. Knight had been talking a while. I was in the kitchen, watching a game, but when it was over, Ms. Knight invited me to join them. Your Mara was talking about some work she was doing with the women Ms. Knight knew—ones who were in trouble."

"Working with them how?"

Here Damon shifts his head in a way that suggests a shrug. "Seems like helping them however she could. One lady was trying to fill out an application to school, and another just needed someone to talk to after splitting with her baby daddy." He smiles. "Terrence knows how Ms. Knight is—she's so proud of all her people. She was smiling at your Mara like she was the mother of Jesus herself."

Terrence makes an affirming sound, and I think about what Gladys Knight said about him, about how he trades hours helping with Damon toward credit for nursing school. I can imagine Mara leaning over another woman, talking through how to manage on her own.

How angry I've been at Mara. How easy it is to let go of the gratitude

I had and blame her for everything that is suddenly wrong in my life. But I don't know what her life has been like these past seventeen years any more than I can imagine what it's like to be Damon. I try to shift that focus to gratitude, to the incontrovertible fact that my child is about to be born into the world because of Mara.

Terrence merges onto the freeway, and Damon returns to recounting stories of fellow churchgoers. He's still talking when Terrence turns down a tree-lined road through what looks like a sizable estate. As we round a corner, a massive stone building comes into view. Its windows sparkle and topiaries sit in oversized terra-cotta pots on each stone step.

Damon whistles.

"Like I said," Terrence comments. "Pricey."

A dozen fears drop like hailstones. What if Dottie Rosen is dead? What if she doesn't live here anymore?

"You'll wait?" I ask Terrence and Damon.

"Heck yes," Damon says. "How will we know what happens next if we leave?"

Terrence shakes his head, but his affection for Damon is clear. "We'll be right here." He motions to his phone. "Call if you need anything."

"Thank you," I say, my voice cracking as I get out of the van. Before I can second-guess myself, I ring the bell and wait as the double doors swing slowly outward. I enter with my head high and shoulders back, trying to telegraph the message that I belong. An older man sits at a desk, a newspaper spread out on the table in front of him. His buzz cut says ex-military, the gut hints at retired police, and the disinterested expression suggests that nothing much happens in his current post. Not the kind of man who's going to help for the sake of helping. Maybe I should've called Detective Maxwell first.

"Here to see a resident?" the guard asks, not looking up.

"Yes," I say, then flat-out lie. "I'm here to see my friend Dottie Pratt—" I wave my hand. "Dottie Rosen. Or you probably have her listed as Dorothy." I lean over and lower my voice, like we're sharing a secret. "I'm here to surprise her."

"And what is your name?"

"Mara," I say. "Mara Vannatta."

"ID?" he asks.

"I lost my purse yesterday," I say, scrambling for an excuse as heat rises in my cheeks. I display the burner phone, as though it explains everything. "Had to buy this just to survive the weekend."

"I can't let you in without an ID."

"Isn't there another way?" I consider whether I could get in with my own license, whether it was a mistake to pretend to be Mara.

"I'm afraid not. To go in, you need a government-issued ID, and you've got to be on the resident's approved visitor list."

"Approved visitor list," I repeat. "Can you at least tell me if I'm on the list?"

The man grunts and sits up in his chair. "Spell the last name?"

I spell Mara's last name and hold my breath while he pecks at the screen of an iPad.

"No," he says and sinks back in his seat. "You're not on the list."

"How do I get on the list?" I ask, hearing the tremor in my voice.

"A resident, relative, or power of attorney has to add you." He takes a business card out of a Lucite holder. "You can call the office tomorrow."

A tiny curled fist flashes in my mind, each finger dimpled. I have to see Dottie. "I'm only in town for a few days, from Colorado. Isn't there any way to make an exception? Maybe ask Dottie if she'd like to see me?"

"I'm afraid not," he says. "We've had issues in the past, so we're very cautious now."

He returns to his paper, and I spin to the exit, breathless and panicked.

Back outside, I scan the building's facade, thinking for a brief wild moment that I could scale it and climb through a window. Bitter wind cuts through my clothes as I climb back into the van's warm interior.

"That was fast," Damon says.

As I tell them what happened, I blink back tears, pretending they're from the wind. "I'm going to call the detective, see if he can get us in." I can tell him about Dottie without mentioning what happened last night. Surely if Tom was going to report the assault, he'd have done it already.

"Stop that right now," Damon announces.

"Damon," Terrence says softly. "She needs answers."

"Terrence, pull this van in front of that building and unload me."

I turn in my seat, smiling at Damon's determination. "Thank you, Damon, but—"

"No buts," Damon says. "Terrence, man." He shifts his attention to his caregiver. "You let me out of this car before I report you for all those times you left me in the back seat."

Terrence lets out a wry laugh and glances at me. "Can't have him reporting all my abuses. Might lose my job."

"Wait," I say, clinging to the last crumbs of hope. "What are you going to do?"

"You'll see," Damon replies, cocking that same eyebrow high on his forehead.

Terrence reverses out of the parking space and pulls to the front of the building.

"This will be fun," Damon says.

"Damon," I say. "It's nice of you, but—"

Before I can finish the thought, Terrence is out of the van, unlocking Damon's chair. Damon hums to himself, rolling his head on his shoulders like a fighter preparing to enter the ring, as Terrence backs him onto a lift. Once Terrence climbs out, he straps the wheelchair to the platform and lowers it to the ground. Using his chin to move the joystick, Damon turns in a half circle and wheels himself along the curb in front of the building.

"Wait," I call, untangling myself from the seat belt. "I'll come."

With precise movements, Damon pivots the chair to face me.

"You two stay here. There's no use for you able-bodied folks where I'm going." And then he's moving toward the handicapped ramp. Terrence jogs toward the building and presses the same button I had minutes earlier. Damon rolls through the doors, hitching up his chin.

"We better park again," Terrence says, and I watch through the glass as Damon speaks to the man at the desk.

"What's he going to do? That guy's going to turn him right around."

But Terrence only chuckles. As we circle the lot for a space, I look back to see the guard through the window, but there is no sign of Damon.

"He's not there." I crane to look again. "How did he get inside?"

Terrence puts the van in park and shuts off the engine. "That is what I like to call D-man magic."

# CHAPTER
# 32

FIVE MINUTES PASS, then ten.

After fifteen minutes, a shiver of light reflects off the glass door as it opens. Terrence and I sit up, waiting for Damon to come down the ramp. Instead, an older woman bent over a walker appears, a nurse in purple scrubs following her down the path.

No Damon.

Terrence groans, and I clench my fists.

Another minute passes, vibrating with anxiety.

"Should we be worried?" I ask. "Should I go in there? Or maybe you could call him."

"He doesn't have a phone," Terrence says with an audible sigh. "Damn, Damon. Come on, man. You're killing me."

Finally, Damon emerges from the building, a grin stretched across his face. Terrence hops out of the van as Damon rolls down the ramp.

"What happened?"

Damon says nothing until his chair is parked behind the van, then he aims his chin at me.

"You," he says, "are going around the left side of the building. There's an entry there. It's unlocked—well, broken," he admits with a half smile. "Go through there, and Dottie's room is the second on the left. She's in there until they all go to lunch at twelve, so you got time."

"You found out where her room was?"

Damon tips his head back and laughs. "I found out a lot more than that. Ladies in these places love to chat with a handsome young man," he says with a wink.

"How did you get past the guard?" I ask.

"Asked to speak to whoever was in charge. Guard told me there aren't any administrators in on Sundays, and I said he better find someone since I wasn't leaving, and I thought my colostomy bag was getting a little full." He laughs. "He snatched up that phone like the place was on fire."

Glee shines in Damon's expression. I picture his days spent in Gladys's house, awaiting visits from Terrence or the hour when Gladys and the neighbors come home from work. The treat of a Dr Pepper after dinner, the little joys he looks forward to, all that he misses out on. For the first time, finding Mara is meaningful to someone other than me. I'm not alone in the hunt. Terrence and Damon are taking risks for me, a woman they hardly know. I am someone worth helping, worth knowing. I wish I could find the words to tell them how much this means.

"Didn't take three minutes before a lady came off the elevator. The resident manager," he says, giving the last words a snobbish inflection. "She said I should come back tomorrow."

"What did you do?" I ask, as hooked on his obvious joy as the story itself.

"Opened my mouth and started to drool, like this." He lets his lips go slack, and a thin strand of saliva leaks from one corner and trickles down his chin. Next, he starts to jostle his head in small rapid motions like he's seizing.

"Damon," I cry. "Stop it."

He laughs, ignoring the spittle on his chin. "That white woman got about four shades whiter. When I stopped trembling and told her I was sorry, it happens sometimes, she'd have given me her damn car. I mention my mom's need for memory care, and next thing you know I'm invited to coffee by a couple of old ladies. Treated me like a puppy," he says. "I said I'd love a tour since I don't drink coffee, and they showed me the whole place. The garden was my favorite, though." He motions his chin again, toward the left side of the building. Here, he grins. "I mighta run into that door a little. Wasn't latching quite right after, but those ladies told me not to worry about it. The manager tried to tell them I wasn't authorized to be back there, but when I explained about the bullet in my brain, migrating toward my cerebellum, and how I needed to get my mama sorted out before that bullet kills me . . ." His lips twist into a satisfied smile.

"There's no bullet in your brain," Terrence says, to my relief.

"And my mama's been dead since I was two," he adds. "Well, no old white lady can stand a sob story like that."

"And you found Dottie?" I ask.

"Yep. Met her neighbor, Mrs. Reynolds. Mrs. Reynolds is not a Dottie fan, I'll tell you that," Damon went on. "She lived in the same place downtown where Dottie and her old man did. According to her, Mr. Rosen married way below his station. Dottie liked to invite all sorts of sketchy types around."

"Recently?"

"No," he says, confirming my fears. "She says it's been real quiet here, since Dottie's mind is mostly gone. She had ovarian cancer after her husband died—was in remission and doing great 'til she had a stroke last year and moved out here. According to Mrs. Reynolds, Dottie hasn't had a visitor since last summer."

I wonder if that means she hasn't heard from Mara. "Nice work, Damon. You should be in the movies."

Damon grins. "I should, shouldn't I?" There is a shift in his expression, a flash of sadness or nostalgia. "Now get in there and find out what happened to Mara."

"We'll be right here," Terrence assures me.

Beyond a row of boxwood hedges is an open space with a path that curves through the grass like a snake's trail. Benches dot the landscape while large trees create shade in small patches. The entrance Damon mentioned is farther back than I expected, but when I reach it, the lock mechanism isn't latched. A moment later, I'm inside the hall. I pause, listening for any sign that someone is nearby, but the only noises are muffled voices in the distance and the whirring of the HVAC system.

I find Dottie's door and knock.

A small, raspy voice responds. "Hello?"

I peer inside. "Hello, Dottie. May I come in?"

Nervous to remain in the corridor where I might be spotted, I step into her room. It's surprisingly cozy—a braided rug fills the center of the floor, and in one corner is a bed with a small table and lamp. Dottie sits in an armchair in the corner, her feet propped on a matching ottoman. Her hair is still mostly brown, cut in a bob at her chin, the static electricity in the room giving her a halo. The left side of her face is slightly drooped, and she lowers an iPad to her lap and closes the cover before setting it on a table beside her. The process is slow. If she danced at Lotus while Mara was there, she can't be more than ten or fifteen years older than we are, which puts her somewhere around fifty, but she looks at least a decade past that. Her brown eyes are sunken, her lips curled into a frown.

"Jill?" she says hesitantly.

I take another step inside. "My name is Alexandra McNeil. I'm a friend of Mara Vannatta's."

Dottie lifts a hand to push a lock of hair behind her ear. "Who?"

"Mara Vannatta," I repeat, shifting forward.

Dottie frowns, carving deep creases between her eyebrows.

"I'd really love to chat, Dottie," I say, unable to disguise the tremor in my voice. "Would it be okay if I stayed a few minutes?"

Dottie's frown lifts slightly, and I take that as a yes. With only one chair in the room, I perch on an old trunk at the end of the bed.

"Your room is lovely," I tell her, looking around for personal items. There are no pictures, just a few magazines stacked on a stool beside her. "This is a beautiful rug."

"Arthur hated that rug."

The mention of her husband offers me hope. "Did you have this rug in your apartment in town?"

Dottie shifts in her chair and stares out the small window beside her. For several moments, she says nothing, and I waver between wanting to say more and giving her time to speak on her own. Henry's dad, whom I never met, had Alzheimer's. Henry often told stories about how his father battled his own brain, how his body stayed strong and healthy even as his mind grew fragmented and feeble. On more than one occasion, Henry told me he'd opt for euthanasia before living with Alzheimer's. We'd never discussed the impossibility of this request.

Voices in the hallway make me freeze, but they pass and the room is quiet again.

Suddenly, Dottie points to the ACE bandage on my hand, alarm in her gaze. "Mara, what happened this time?"

I straighten up at the sound of Mara's name and pull up the sleeve of my sweatshirt so the bandage is more visible. "It was just an accident," I improvise, trying to keep her talking.

"I told you to leave that man," she says, aiming a finger at me. "He'll kill you one of these days."

"What man?" I ask.

Dottie's focus shifts, and she goes quiet, lost again.

I lean forward. "I need to find someone, Dottie."

"I'd like to find my Arthur," she says with a sigh, her gaze shifting back toward me. "I loved him so much."

"How did you two meet?"

She doesn't acknowledge the question.

"Did you meet Arthur at Lotus?"

Her attention moves to the window, and I fight to stay still as the edge of the hard trunk digs into the backs of my thighs. I search the room for some detail to talk about, a way to break through the barriers of Dottie's mind. On the wall beside the door hangs a line drawing of a dancer in a narrow gold frame. She is on pointe, her arm raised, fingers fanned gently, her leg lifted behind her.

I wonder if Dottie had been a dancer as a girl, if she'd imagined a future in the ballet rather than a club. Studying it, I recall a similar black-and-white sketch that lived in Mara's parents' bedroom.

"That's a beautiful drawing," I say. "Is it you?"

Dottie continues to stare out the window, and I let out a long sigh. I'd been so confident that Mara and Dottie were in touch, that Dottie would know exactly where Mara is. And maybe the information is in Dottie's mind somewhere, but trying to access it is pointless. Dottie is another dead end. As I watch, Dottie's expression seems to open, its lines vanishing, and she looks, momentarily, like a child. I've never watched someone lose themselves like that.

Aside from losing Cate, I've never suffered any real hardship. Until this past Wednesday, my life was charmed. I wish Dottie could tell me what drove her to dance at the club, what it felt like to lose Arthur. Does she have children? Siblings? Did she know her parents? As much as I love Henry, and Kyle and Nolan, the loss of them in my everyday life feels like a dull pain, an emptiness, not the raw agony that comes with the thought of losing Goose.

A ringtone breaks me from my thoughts, and instinctively, I reach for my phone, before realizing my burner is on silent. Dottie pulls a phone from between her thigh and the edge of the chair, stares down at it, reading something, then returns it to the same spot.

I hadn't considered that Dottie would have a phone in here, but of course. On good days, she probably talks to friends or family. Maybe she even talks to Mara.

I lean forward and perch my elbows on my knees. "Dottie, could I give you my phone number?"

Her frown is back.

"I could just put my contact information into your phone," I add. "In case you ever want to talk."

Dottie says nothing. I stand, knees bent to avoid looking like a threat, and step toward her.

She watches me, eyes narrowed, hawkish. "I remember you."

I smile, the effort trembling in my cheeks. Does she still think I'm Mara?

Before I can ask, she waves a finger at me. Her gaze moves across my face as though trying to sort something out. "I saw you in a picture. She had it on her dressing table. Nobody kept much personal there. Sometimes a picture of a kid on the inside of a locker, but she had that picture. Three of you, just babies."

Can she be referring to the photograph of Mara, Cate, and me?

"Arthur was very strict about who came to the house," Dottie says without a segue. "Mara had a terrible breakup, and she was so distraught. The guy was an asshole, anyway. She knew how to pick 'em. Well, most of them are assholes, but not Arthur. Though he could be strict—his stupid rules. No ladies in the house. And he didn't mean ladies, just my friends. He was always hoping I'd make friends with the wives of his business partners, but I couldn't stand those snobby women."

She waves a hand as though swatting a fly.

"So, she stayed at Frank's." Dottie smooths her pants, running flat palms along her thighs. "It was easy enough to get down there, and she knew the code. Tony at the guard desk helped her get in. We came from the same neighborhood, Tony and me, and he even changed the code to Mara's birthday, so she'd never forget."

"Mara used to stay with someone named Frank?"

"Not *with* him." She laughs. "And only until Arthur passed. Then, she stayed in the guest room. Had her own key and everything, until she had to leave town."

I'm still processing the pieces, but what matters is that Mara used to stay at Dottie's old apartment, and it's possible she's there now. I stand up, excited. "Mara has a key to your condo?"

She presses a hand to her chest and emits a small squeak of alarm.

"Sorry. I didn't mean to startle you." Mara might be in that condo right now. "Do you mean Mara, Dottie? Mara stays at your old condo? The one downtown?"

Dottie blinks like she's woken up from a dream. Folding her hands in her lap, she turns to the window. I eye the phone beside her, debating how quickly I could grab it. If Mara is staying at Dottie's condo, there could be messages between them.

"What if I put my number in your phone, like I said? Can I do that, so we can talk another time?"

Dottie snatches up the phone. "Don't you touch my computer," she warns. She grips it tightly as someone enters behind me.

"Hello, Dot—" The woman's voice cuts off when she sees me. "I didn't know Dottie had a visitor."

"We were just catching up."

The woman plants her hands on her hips and steps into the room, which suddenly feels small. "And you are?"

"Mara Vannatta," I say, then without waiting for her response, turn to Dottie. "Thank you for such a nice chat, Dottie. You take care of yourself, and I'll see you soon."

I brush past the nurse and walk directly out the way I entered. When I glance over my shoulder, the nurse stands in the corridor, arms crossed, watching me. I jog along the building, wondering what they can charge me with for sneaking into an old folks' home. Thankfully, Terrence has the van idling at the curb.

"Well?" Damon cries once I'm in the passenger seat.

"I think Mara might be staying in Dottie's old condo," I say.

I locate the address I wrote down in the library this morning and read it to Terrence as he punches it into his navigation app. He's just pulling away when the security guard emerges from the front door, along with the nurse who came into Dottie's room. I duck down in my seat, but Terrence is already turning back down the tree-lined road.

Since I lost the detective's number when I lost my phone, I call the nonemergency line and request to be connected with Detective Maxwell. Without a key, there's no way I'll be able to get into Dottie's condo without him.

Finally, I'm connected with Maxwell.

"You have an address?" he asks once I've filled him in, and his voice holds something I haven't heard before—excitement. I repeat the address I gave Terrence.

"Got it," Maxwell says. "I'll have someone check it out ASAP."

I'm about to mention that Mara stayed in the building with someone named Frank when he cuts me off. "Thanks for the call."

I sense he's about to hang up, so I quickly say, "I'm heading to the building now. Should I meet you there?"

"Not a good idea," he replies. "Let me check it out first, and I'll call you as soon as I know anything."

"Actually—" I stop talking when I realize he's ended the call. What the hell? He hung up.

The man is insane if he thinks I'm staying away.

# CHAPTER

# 33

NO ONE SPEAKS on the drive to Dottie's old apartment. The jovial, excited energy we had on the way to the nursing home has flattened like day-old soda. How soon will Maxwell reach the building? My desire to see Mara in person, to be reassured by the rounded bulge of Goose inside her, is painfully intense.

Finally, we arrive. The stone-and-brick tower is Victorian in style, with tall rounded windows adorned by intricate carved designs and gold-accented columns at the corners. A gilded awning hangs over the imposing front door. It looks expensive.

There are no police cars at the curb, no sign of anything happening inside. "Maybe the detective isn't here yet," Terrence says, staring through the windshield.

"I'll go inside and find out."

"We'll be right here," Damon says.

Terrence catches his eye in the rearview mirror. "We will?"

"We can't leave now," he insists.

Terrence nods slowly, his gaze shifting to mine before he offers a little shrug. "You heard the D-man. We might have to make a pit stop, but we'll be close."

Just in case, I set a wad of cash on the console and leave before Terrence can argue.

The building is overwhelming. I'm reminded of walking into the doctor's office, prepared to hear what I already knew: that the second round of IVF had failed. The harsh punch of reality that I'd never have my own children. The fear now is the same—that I'm about to learn that Mara is dead and my chances of being a mother are gone. That my Goose is gone.

Inside, I stop at the front desk, wondering if the guard stationed here is the one Dottie mentioned. Tony. He looks the right age, but there isn't time to chat. "Is Detective Maxwell here?"

"He is," the guard says, sitting a little straighter. "He's up—"

I pivot for the elevator without waiting for permission.

"I'm not sure—"

"He's expecting me," I toss back over my shoulder. Inside the elevator, I jam the button for the seventh floor and wait in fear until the doors slide shut. There's a small jolt as the elevator begins to rise. I'm here. I'm in. I bunch my fists and pray. *Please be here, Mara. Please have Goose. Please.*

As the elevator doors open, I hear a slam and a muttered curse.

"Damn it."

Around the corner, Detective Maxwell stands in the stairwell. He's alone. I expected a team of people, at least as many as he brought to my hotel room after the break-in. Where are the others?

"What happened?" I ask. "Did you find her?"

A flash of surprise shows on his face before his expression turns grim.

"Someone was already here." He motions across the hall to the apartment, the jamb cracked, door hanging askew. The living room is visible, dishes on the coffee table. They're Mara's. I can tell by the way the plate is stacked on the mug, a small spoon that I can guess will be sticky with honey or sugar.

Maxwell turns his back and takes out his phone, so I walk into the condo, make my way down the hall. Recalling the scolding I'd gotten from the Denver detectives for touching things in the coach house, I push my way through the first door with the toe of my shoe. Then the next, a room with bright floral bedding.

On the floor is Mara's Rolling Stones sweatshirt.

The sight of it brings me to my knees. I lift it and inhale my favorite brand of laundry detergent, the rose conditioner I bought for her, a vague whiff of peppermint tea.

"She's here," I whisper, tears filling my eyes.

"Well, she's not here now," Maxwell says, appearing behind me. "I've cleared all the rooms. Gone down the rear stairs, too. I'm guessing she took the back-alley exit."

He's speaking as though he's the only officer in the building.

"You're here alone?" I ask.

He shakes his head. "I've got three units looking for her in the surrounding area."

We were so close. How can she be gone? If only I'd known she was here earlier. I hold the sweatshirt as I look around. There is no evidence of a baby—no diapers or onesies, no blankets. I rise and enter the bathroom, finding none of the large sanitary napkins that women use after birth. Nothing at all that implies Goose has been born.

"What do we do?" I ask Maxwell. "Do you think she'll come back?"

"No way to know," he says with a sigh, seeming much too calm for my liking. "Maybe we'll get lucky."

I can't count on luck anymore. I set the sweatshirt on the bed before going to the closet. Mara's things—the green sweater she loves, her gray sweatpants—are shoved onto the shelves, not folded but balled up, an empty duffel on the floor. I yank the clothes down, pick them up one at a time.

The Colorado Rockies shirt is in the second drawer. I press it to my nose, inhale the same smell—Mara.

Maxwell grabs my arm, his fingers painful on the skin. "What are you doing? You're messing with evidence."

I step away from him, surprised by the anger in his response.

"No baby clothes." It takes an extra moment to draw the next breath. "There's no sign of an infant here."

"She can't be far," Maxwell says. "We'll find out what happened, where she went. Okay?"

"Okay." The word is a whisper, weak.

"I'll be in touch the minute I hear anything," he continues. "You should go have something to eat, or get some rest, give us time to find her. We will find her. I promise."

I take a last look at the bedroom. Mara *is* staying here. It's the closest I've been to Goose since Tuesday night. I long to sit on the bed and wait for Mara to return. But she may not be coming back, and if there's a chance she's in the area, I'm looking, too.

I retrace my steps through the condo, noticing the decor for the first time. The heavy gold drapes, the ecru couch with gold-and-black accent pillows, the chandelier in the dining room with hundreds of teardrop crystals that spiral from the ceiling. The ornate walnut dining chairs are upholstered in gold brocade. It feels formal and outdated, and I can't picture Mara living in such a place. Or even Dottie, with her simple braided rug. What I can imagine is Mara, scarf wrapped around her neck as she sits proudly at the dining table, sipping whiskey from a teacup with one pinky finger stretched in the air. She would have loved pretending to be a wealthy woman. How that would make her laugh.

"What are you going to do about that?" I ask, pointing at the broken entry.

"I've got to go talk to security." The detective walks me out. "I'll be in touch."

I feel the echo of his grip on my arm and the sensation of something on my neck. I swipe at nothing as I step across the threshold, spot a red smear on the jamb. I stop in my tracks. "Is that blood?"

"We don't want to jump to any conclusions," Maxwell says calmly.

But my heartbeat is audible, a thumping in my ears. "She's hurt."

Maxwell sets a hand on my shoulder, and I fight the urge to shake it free. "We don't know that. Panicking isn't going to help anything."

The sense that something is wrong rises like steam from a kettle, about to shriek to a boil. A few feet away, another spot of blood mars the hallway's amber-toned carpet. I follow the blood to the stairwell.

"Whoa," Maxwell says. "Be careful, Alexandra."

His use of my first name heightens my unease. Through a fire door, the stairs are no longer carpeted, but concrete. Freckles of blood. The color is bright, not yet rusty. It's fresh. This has to be Mara's. I scan the floor, study the droplets and try to calculate how much she is bleeding. Farther down the stairs, the blotches are larger and closer together.

I arrived expecting a SWAT team. How did Maxwell clear the whole building by himself?

Maybe he didn't.

# CHAPTER

# 34

I DESCEND THE stairs in a rush, hoping at each landing for a sign that Mara exited the stairwell on another floor, that she hasn't left the building.

"Where are you going?" Maxwell calls.

"To find her."

His footsteps sound on the stairs behind me, the rat-tat-tat of dress shoes on concrete. "If Clayton has her, you're in danger, too, Alexandra. You need to let us handle this."

There is an edge to his voice.

"Did you call an ambulance?" I ask without stopping.

"We've got backup coming. Medical care, too."

I reach the ground floor, breathless, aching. Here, the blood drops are clustered, as though Mara paused, trying to decide what to do. Or maybe she was weak and needed to rest. There are two exits on the landing. The blood drops lead to the one that says *Street Exit*. I push it open and enter an empty alleyway with a large parking lot beyond. A dozen or so parked cars, but no people. She's not here.

"She either got a ride from here or managed to bandage herself up to stanch the bleeding," Maxwell says, startling me. I hadn't heard him reach the bottom of the stairs. He waves up at the building. "We've got a team pulling CCTV footage to figure out which way she went. Hopefully, we'll get a license plate."

Defeated, I sit at the bottom of the interior stairs, wrap my arms around my knees. The determination—the fury—that pushed me to Top Hat last night, that drove me to hold a knife to a man's throat, feels distant now, a raging fire reduced to ash. The cold of the concrete leaches through my clothes, reminding me of the day Mara and I visited Cate's grave after graduation. Standing in the grass, we'd huddled together against the cold wind. We didn't talk, just locked arms and stared at the seam cut into the grass where her coffin had been lowered. Her headstone had been placed only days before, and this was the first time we'd seen it. The marble gleamed in the afternoon sun. *Catherine Louise Murphy, October 3, 1991–May 12, 2008, Beloved Daughter and Sister.*

I sank onto a nearby gravestone while Mara squatted before Cate's and ran a finger over the word *sister.* We'd never used that word before— Mara and Cate and I—but that's what we were. Even after losing Cate and being out of touch for so many years, seeing Mara on my doorstep was like finding a piece of home.

As I stare at the concrete walls of the stairwell in Dottie's building, fear settles its shadowed cloak over me. Fear that I will lose Goose, but also that I will lose myself. All these months, my focus has been on the baby. And this week, I've been terrified of what it would mean to lose Goose. But losing Mara means losing the only person who truly knows me. Who would I be without her?

Maxwell's phone rings, and I am pulled back to the present as he answers it. There's a pause and he cusses, turning his back to me. He paces around the small space and as he moves, the second door goes in and out of view. Unlike the first, this appears to be an interior door. A placard on the wall reads *Superintendent F. Gomez* and below the name is a phone number, an office line maybe. I think of the man Dottie mentioned—Frank. She'd said Mara stayed at Frank's. Not Frank's house or Frank's apartment, but Frank's room.

I turn to Maxwell as he barks into the phone. "Get another team on it, then. How far could she get in ten minutes? Sweep the whole area and keep me posted," he says, and ends the call.

The first thing I notice is that the back of his collar is creased at a strange angle. I think of fixing it and stop as his words replay in my head.

"How did you know it was ten minutes?"

He faces me, looking confused. "Huh?"

"You said, 'how far could she get in ten minutes,'" I repeat.

"Oh, yeah," he says. "A patrol car saw her, but the officer lost track of her." Despite the words, I sense there's something he's not saying. He knows what happened to her.

I stand up and study him. "Detective, what happened? Do you know who hurt her?"

His beard has grown out since yesterday, and I notice a spot he missed with the razor. He's stressed about Mara, too. "She was in with some bad men, Alexandra." He's missed a button on his shirt. "That's why I have to find her."

As he takes a step closer, I smell cigarette smoke and stale beer, like I'm back outside the Lucky Dive. I think of the knife in my backpack, too far to reach. I imagine Frank's room somewhere inside this building. Mara could be there now, injured and bleeding, and I may never get to her.

There is a sound from above, footfalls on the stairs.

We both look up as a voice calls down. "Detective?" Over the railing, the guard from the front desk appears. "The residents on seven are asking to speak to you."

"Yeah," Maxwell calls back, raking a hand across his jaw. "I'm coming up now." To me, he says, "Sorry. This case has me running in circles, but you should go to the hotel. I'll let you know the second I find her." He lays a hand on my arm. "I promise."

*Pinky swear*, I think, hearing Mara's voice, but I can't bring myself to leave.

Maxwell climbs back up to the first floor and steps into the corridor with the guard. The moment they are out of view, I cross to the door.

The knob, when I test it, is locked. On the wall is a rectangular silver plate with a hinge, about the size of a light switch. Inside is a numbered keypad.

The code.

*Tony changed the code to her birthday so that she'd never forget.*

For a moment, I consider what this building must have been for Mara. A safe haven. A place where whoever threatened her, whatever she most feared, couldn't reach her. There's no way the code is the same, not after all this time. But with nothing to lose, I punch in 0719, the numbers that correspond with Mara's birthday.

The lock clicks and the knob turns. I open the door to a dimly lit hallway.

She has to be here, but I'm terrified to hope. And then, before I've taken a single step, I see it—blood.

"Mara?" I shout, starting down the hallway. The motion-sensor lights click on as I move. The blood on the floor stretches into a larger arc from side to side, like she was staggering as she moved through the room.

"Mara? Are you here?" I duck into a room, startling when the lights come on automatically.

Empty.

Down another corridor is a storage area for the building, two rows of wide grated lockers, everything inside them visible—plastic bins, bikes, skis.

"Mara?"

No answer. I run the length of the hall, past twenty or so caged units, scanning for any space large enough to hide a human.

"Mara!" I shout, continuing farther into the dark basement. There is a laundry space—four front-load washers and four dryers, high end, that look unused. "Mara?"

Nothing.

Did she come in here and leave? Then I spot a large dark stain on the ground. Push my toe into it, and see that it is wet, fresh. To my left is a steel door, a Lucite nameplate on the wall beside it.

*Frank Gomez.*

I shove my way inside. The room is an office—an old metal desk and chair just inside and across from them a file cabinet, its surface lined with dusty black binders. The space remains dark until I flip the switch. Halogen lights flicker on and off like dying fireflies. In the center of the floor are tall wire shelves filled with bankers' boxes, interspersed by open packages of what appear to be light fixtures and plumbing parts.

Behind them is Mara.

# CHAPTER

# 35

*May 2008*

*Today is the day!* She underlines it twice and closes the notebook. The next time she writes in the notebook it will all be over. It's almost two in the morning, but Cate can't sleep. This restlessness is different from the weeks after the pregnancy test—fitful nights where she fell asleep for a few hours and woke to enjoy a split second of amnesia. In those moments, she was just another high school senior, focused on finishing her thesis. Then she'd remembered, and in the next beat, her head was in a guillotine and she was preparing for the blade to drop. But the last week, she's been awake for a totally different reason: hope.

"I know how we can end it," Mara announced last week once the two of them were in Cate's room with the door closed. Cate blared "Just Dance" by Lady Gaga from the small speaker in case her mom was listening at the door. Which Cate would bet she was.

End it. The pregnancy.

Cate listened as Mara walked her through the plan. Once Mara had explained it all, she asked, "Is it safe?"

"She's fine now. Had two more babies after that."

Cate only wished that all of this had ended weeks ago, but she was grateful for Mara's help. What would she have done if Mara hadn't found out? Tried to find a place that would perform an abortion? Would she have been desperate enough to do something drastic? A coat hanger?

A week and a half passed before there was an evening where both of Mara's parents were out. Finally, it's time. Cate just wants her old life back. To finish high school and go to college, and remember how lucky she is to have her life and her friends. Once this was over and they'd gotten through graduation, Cate would confess everything to Lexi. She'd tell her who he was, when it happened, and save Lexi the terror of being in it with her. Let Mara gloat about coming to the rescue while Cate and Lexi shared the look that said it all. How Mara had come up with a crazy plan. How it had worked and now Cate would have a future because of Mara.

She can't wait until it's over and Lexi knows and they're high school graduates getting the hell out of Cleveland.

Today's the day.

# CHAPTER
## 36

MARA LIES ON a cot in the corner, unmoving. Her long-sleeved T-shirt and maxi skirt are covered in blood. Before I see her face, I take in her belly, round and full. *Goose.* I let out a sob and drop to my knees. "Mara," I whisper. "Mara, wake up."

Her movements are slow, her eyes unfocused. She grips her left shoulder where the shirt's fabric is torn, the skin visible beneath. A bullet wound. She's been shot. Blood has saturated the canvas cot beneath her and drips onto the floor. Without a thought, I pull off my sweatshirt, wincing as I bump my tender wrist.

"We need an ambulance," I say, unwrapping the ACE bandage from my wrist and pressing it to her wound, then propping the sweatshirt under her shoulder in an effort to stanch the bleeding. Mara cries out in pain and reaches out, gripping my hand with her bloody one. On her ring finger is my engagement ring. Though my wrist protests, I don't pull away.

"Help me," she whispers.

I press my forehead to hers and fight back tears. "I'm here. I'm going to get help." I think of the charge at the urgent care. "Is Goose okay?" I ask as I dial 911.

"Yes," she manages. "I was having some pain, but I had an ultrasound. She's perfect."

I grip her hand, which feels damp and too cold. "I'm going to get help, Mara. It's going to be okay." I release a small gasp of relief when the call goes through.

"9-1-1, what is your emergency?"

"My friend's been shot. We're in the basement of an apartment building on—" I can't remember the address.

I take in the white walls, health and safety posters affixed to the plaster—one that says *Choking Hazard*, the other *Safe Lifting Techniques*, their edges frayed and curled in. Around them are remnants of tape from whatever hung there before. Above the desk is a diploma from the Community College of Philadelphia in the name of Francisco Gomez. I'm waiting for a response when the operator repeats herself. "Hello? 9-1-1, please state your emergency."

"Can you hear me?" I call into the line. "Hello?"

"You have reached an emergency line," the voice says. "Please state your emergency."

I let out a sob as I fumble with the phone, pushing buttons. "Hello? Hello?"

The operator starts again. "You have reached—"

There is a beeping on the line, another call coming in, and I quickly disconnect 911 to answer.

"Alexandra?" Terrence sounds worried.

"Terrence," I say, my voice breaking. "Can you hear me?"

"Yes," he says. "Thank God. Where are you?"

I'm sobbing as I speak, praying he hears me, that the call doesn't end, as I rush the words out. "In the basement of Dottie's building. Mara is here. She's been shot. We need medical help, but I can't get through to 9-1-1. Terrence?"

"Okay," he says, his voice calm in a way that makes me cry harder. "I'll get help, I'll be there soon."

"We're in the basement, Terrence. In Frank Gomez's office," I add. When I pause for breath, the line fills with static. "Terrence?"

All I can hear is crackling on the line. I press the phone tighter to one ear and use my finger to plug the other. "Terrence?" I don't hear anything but static. I hang up and redial, but an automated voice tells me to check the number or try again later.

I drop the phone and turn to Mara. "Where's your phone?"

"Upstairs," she says. "I didn't have time—"

"Okay. It's okay," I say, feeling anything but okay. "You're going to stay here while I find help," I tell her, forming a plan. "There are police in the building and a detective, Maxwell, I'll go—"

"No!" Her fingers clench my palm, and the pain in my wrist almost doubles me over.

I wrench my hand away. "Mara—"

"Not him." The skin on her face is almost translucent, her breathing raspy. "Lexi, he shot me."

"What?"

Frantic, she grabs hold of my shirt. "Lexi, he'll kill me. He'll kill us both. And Goose—"

"Maxwell?"

Her nails dig through my sleeve, clawing at my skin. "You have to believe me," she says, each word taking effort.

I think of how Maxwell took over when someone broke into my hotel room, his competence. Then of Maxwell on the stairs, exuding anger like heat. The fact that he'd known exactly how long had passed since Mara ran from Dottie's apartment.

"Pinky swear," Mara whispers, and the words brew a sudden storm of rage inside me. That she would pull out the benign mantra of our childhood, after what she's put me through.

"Really, Mara? I should believe you now, because you've been so honest about everything else? About being married, about never being pregnant? After you took off without a word, with *my* daughter, I'm supposed to just believe you? We're not in high school, Mara. This is real life. There's no pinky swear option here."

"Wait," she cries. "Just listen. He and I were involved. Maxwell." Her voice is a whisper and the pain in it deflates my rage.

"I didn't know it when we started dating," she goes on. "But Peter Maxwell is a criminal—he's on the take for a local dealer."

"Clayton?" I ask, remembering the name Maxwell gave me.

"Yes. He runs the largest drug ring in Philadelphia. He's ruthless, but he hired a lot of the older girls from Lotus. Not me. I wouldn't ever sell drugs, not after Cate."

"Cate?" I repeat. "What do you mean after Cate? I know she was pregnant, but—drugs?"

Mara looks relieved. "You knew."

"I found the notebook in the storage locker."

"You found Gladys."

"Yes. She gave me the key, and I found the storage locker," I say, eyeing the growing pool of blood beneath the cot. There's no time for this. "There was a thumb drive in there? Did you take that?"

"Yeah," she says distractedly. "I should've told you about Cate. I wish I had . . . it was so awful, Lexi."

We shouldn't be talking about this, not now. Later. Once we get out of here, once Goose is safe.

"She needed an abortion. She was desperate," Mara says, clinging to my hand. "My mom had a friend who miscarried after taking pain medication," Mara continues, and I kneel beside her. I hope Terrence is coming. He won't let me down. I just need her to stay calm and awake.

She is calmer now, talking, so I ask, "You gave Cate pain medication to miscarry?"

"Yes," she whispers as tears slide down her cheeks. "It was so stupid. My dad had pills from shoulder surgery."

I picture Cate, wearing her soccer sweatshirt and standing in front of Mara, a hand outstretched.

"You gave them to her . . . and she died?"

"She passed out in the hot tub, hit her head. We didn't get there in time." She averts her gaze from mine and the whites of her eyes, so bright when we were younger, look dull and yellow.

"We?"

"Me and Caleb," she says, and the venom in her brother's name slides the missing piece into place.

"He was the father," I say without question.

"Yes," Mara gasps, sobbing. "We went to that party at Seth Wilson's, and Cate got really drunk. Caleb, he—"

"He raped her?" But I know the answer.

"We don't speak, Lexi. I hate him to this day."

I recall how Caleb said Mara didn't come home when their father died, implying she'd only wanted the money. In truth, she couldn't stand to be near her brother, the man responsible, however indirectly, for our friend's death.

Mara shifts and a trickle of blood streams from the canvas onto the floor. It suddenly looks like so much blood. I adjust the sweatshirt, stunned at the weight of it. I lift its bulk and tie the arms around her shoulder, blood staining my hands before bunching the heavy midsection under the wound in an attempt to lift it higher.

"I ended up here with a friend from the cruise. I worked at Lotus and, for a while, it was good. I wasn't the best dancer, but I made up for it by handling the newer girls and sorting out disagreements. The manager started to rely on me; we became friends. Tom."

The name sends a shock of pain through my wrist and I shiver.

"We left Lotus to start our own club—no exotic dancers. We were going to create a spot for dancing, some live music."

Though I've already heard some of this, I don't say anything. I wait to see how she'll spin the story—if she'll admit to the money she took, the people she screwed.

"I had eighteen thousand dollars saved. Tom had another ten. We found the perfect place and were waiting on Tom's brother who worked in construction. He was going to give us a bid on the work to get it open. Tom was worried someone else would grab it, so he signed the lease and put money down. Turned out the place had fifty thousand dollars of deferred repairs. It was practically condemned. Tom wanted to borrow and try again, but by then, I just wanted out." She's quiet. "He was handling all the money, but he wouldn't give me back my share, said he needed it for the next place. I ended up taking an advance on his credit card to get my share of what was left."

"Five thousand dollars," I say.

Her eyes flash wide. "How did—"

"I met Tom."

"He's not my biggest fan." She closes her eyes. "He was stuck in that lease for five years after I left. But I lost a lot, Lexi. Everything I had. I took what I needed."

I think of my engagement ring on her finger. "I know."

"I found a new gig, and that's where I met him. It was like a dream. I just wanted a dream," she adds, spit bubbles collecting in the corner of her mouth. "Like Dottie and Arthur."

It takes me a moment to realize she's talking about Maxwell now. Dottie had discovered her happily ever after, so why not Mara, too?

Blood pools around the sweatshirt, and I scan the room for something else to slow the bleeding.

Mara closes her eyes, as though her lids have grown too heavy to hold open.

"Mara!" I grab her shoulders.

Her lips curve into a smile. "You have to listen," she says.

"I'm listening," I say, pulling the desk chair close enough to lift her legs onto the seat to keep the blood in her core. It's all I can think to do. It's not enough. I can't stay here, waiting for someone to save us. "I need to get help."

Where is Terrence? I try 911 again but nothing happens—no ringing, no error message. I check the metal desk, but there's no phone. Try the drawers, locked. I empty the silver penholder onto the surface and watch as several pens and pencils, two pennies, and a half dozen paper clips scatter across the desk.

"He was good to me until I got pregnant," she says.

I go still. Her first pregnancy.

"Mac was never going to let me leave," she whispers, her chest heaving.

The name echoes through my brain and creates an overwhelming silence, as though I'm underwater. "What did you call him?"

"Mac," Mara says. "It's his nickname."

Peter Maxwell is Mac. The men who attacked me outside the Lucky Dive used his name. *Mac wants her unharmed.* I feel Maxwell beside me in my hotel room, his hand on my arm on the stairwell. He is in this building. How long before he finds us?

"I just wanted to get away, start over . . ." Mara trembles as she inhales. "So I collected evidence against him. Took pictures of messages on his phone, recorded things he said, forwarded messages from my phone to an email I set up." Mara seems to get a burst of renewed energy as she tells the story, but blood continues to drip under the cot and a sheen of sweat coats her face. How long do we have to save her? To save Goose? I touch Mara's belly, desperate to feel the life inside, but the baby is terrifyingly still.

"I made a list of the people who came to the apartment, got names. Then, one night, a week before I came to Colorado, I followed Mac and watched him and three other guys unload a trunkful of heroin. I didn't know if he was buying it or selling it. I took pictures and video and copied it all onto a thumb drive and left it on his kitchen table with a note that said I had a copy, too, that I'd send it to the police. I put the thumb drive in the storage unit and left the extra key and a note with Gladys."

"And the notebook? Why keep that?"

"Caleb," she says, tears welling again. "I kept the notebook to remind him of what he did."

"Has he seen it?"

She shakes her head. "He knows it exists, but not what's in it."

"Nothing's in it, Mara. At least, nothing about Caleb."

She closes her eyes and shakes her head. "I know. Cate said she burned those pages."

Mara knew her brother was a rapist, and she kept Cate's notebook to warn him that she knew what he'd done. She wanted justice for Cate. Lost everything with Tom, then ended up in danger with Maxwell.

And she escaped.

I can't believe I let this woman carry my child, and yet, this is Mara—the same fearless girl Cate and I loved. The one who tried to help her friend end an unwanted pregnancy, raped by her own brother. The one who wanted to give me a baby when I couldn't have one. She is boldly reckless and she is fiercely loyal. She is a liar, and she is my friend. She can be both.

"He found you in Denver?" I ask.

"He got some alert that I was there. He showed up at your house while you were at lunch. He must've been watching."

Henry and his investigator. That report must have tipped off Peter Maxwell that Mara was in Denver. Tracking Henry's address, he'd found her. There was no local narcotics officer. It was Maxwell all along. "Is he really a detective?"

"He is," she says gravely. "He's a god in Narcotics. Makes him un-fucking-touchable, and he gets a slice off the top to keep away trouble."

"How did you get away?"

"That nosy neighbor of yours was on the street, watching the house. I told him I needed a couple days to get the thumb drive. He was coming back to the house that day—the day I left. I knew I'd never be safe once he'd found me, so I flew back to Philly with the key, to get the evidence and give it to the police, but when I went into the station, I saw one of his friends and I freaked out. I didn't know who to trust."

I remember the hours in the bus station, waiting for her. All along, she'd flown.

"I took your ring in case I needed cash," she explains.

"I don't care about the ring," I say quickly. I could ask what she'd been doing the day Henry saw her in the office, going through our files, but I don't care. "None of that matters. Where is the thumb drive now?"

"Here," she says, reaching an unsteady hand down her shirt. "It's taped to my chest. You have to hide it." She retrieves the device, smearing blood on her shirt. Freeing it from the strip of duct tape, I recognize the shape pressed into Cate's notebook from the storage locker. "Don't let him get it, Lexi. Please."

"I won't."

"I need you to know, I never wanted this to happen. I really thought he wouldn't find me. I figured six months had passed and it was working." She presses the drive into my palm. "I wanted to carry your baby. I wanted to do this for you."

"You did do it for me. You are doing it right now."

I study the round evidence of Goose. Blood drips off the cot more slowly now, and I hope that means the bleeding is slowed. I try to calculate how much time has passed since I entered this room. Since Mara was shot. How much more time will pass before help comes.

"It was my fault," she says. "Cate."

Her chest convulses, and for a panicked moment I think she's seizing, until I realize she's sobbing. She is so frail, so weak, her breathing so slow.

"It wasn't your fault."

"But it was," she whispers. "I gave her those pills. I thought she'd just miscarry, that her parents would never find out, that everything would be okay—"

"You were a kid," I say, smoothing the damp hair off her face. She is pale, so unbelievably pale. I wrap my arms around her gently, desperate to hold the life in her, willing her to stay with me.

When men commit violence against women, we, too, hold the blame. While Caleb and Maxwell might rarely consider their victims, Mara carries them with her. This, I realize, is why she displayed that picture of Cate: as a way to hold herself accountable for what she did, to remind herself of her part in it.

It's also the reason—at least in part—why she came to me, all those months ago. While I didn't know what she had done or how she'd been involved, I knew Cate the same way she did. I am the other piece of the three of us.

And now I feel that blame. No matter how inadvertently, I led Maxwell directly to Mara. He might have found her eventually, but he is only here today because of my call. Mara has been shot because I told her abusive ex exactly where he could find her. I calculate the devastating math of our friendship. Cate died because of a mistake Mara made. Now, Mara might die because of mine.

I imagine something terrible happening to Terrence, that the police or Maxwell have arrested him. "Stay with me, Mara. Help is coming." I murmur the words like a prayer.

"I didn't even tell my parents it was Caleb. I never said anything about what he—"

Her words are cut off by the sharp thwack of a slamming door. Her eyes widen, and we both go silent, listening. The police would be loud, calling for us. Terrence, too. I detect rage in the quiet, a whiff of the rotten cabbage scent of lighter fluid, the sulfur of a lit match.

Maxwell.

I cross the room and hear footsteps. The muted slap of dress shoes. He is coming.

# CHAPTER
# 37

THERE IS NO lock, so I navigate to the far side of the filing cabinet and push it as quietly as possible until it's wedged between the door and the desk. The pain in my wrist is like stabbing knives, but I don't stop. Mara suddenly seems too vulnerable up on the cot, so I lower her to the rug, then drag it to the farthest corner of the room.

"Mara," I whisper, giving her a little shake. She doesn't respond. Her pulse is weak, harder to detect than before. I rock back on my heels and put my palm on the rounded ball of the baby. Lower my lips to whisper to her.

"Goose." There is a slight shift from inside and something brushes under my palm. "I'm here, baby," I whisper, momentarily blinded by tears.

Mara is dying. I scan the room for something I missed, like an escape hatch. There is nothing. From outside Frank's office comes Peter Maxwell's voice.

"I know you're in there, Mara. Come on. Let me in. You're hurt. I can help. You've got your baby to think about."

I hold my breath, don't speak. Goose presses into the smooth skin of my palm, the motion like a spark. Mara moans and I cringe at the noise, which seems to spur Maxwell into action. I jump at the slamming sound of Maxwell trying to enter the office. The filing cabinet holds, but it won't for long.

"Fuck off," Mara shouts, chest heaving once the words are out.

"That's not nice, Mara. Not nice to see you knocked up with another guy's kid either. After all we've been through."

Mara's face flushes red. "Right. You had us all scared shitless, had my friends arrested—because I wouldn't get an abortion," she calls, her voice cracking on the final word, her chest heaving with effort.

"It's okay," I whisper. "Ignore him."

"What the fuck, Mara?" Maxwell slams his fist on the door. "Enough already. Let me in."

"Not happening." Her words are breathy, soft.

I clasp her hand. "Don't talk, Mara."

Her eyes drift closed, then snap open. "Were you so against a baby because Clayton finally cut you in on the big take?" She inhales, a long shuddering breath. "Pretty big coincidence that I got picked up for solicitation a block from where the police stored half a million of uncut heroin same night it was stolen. Right, Mac?"

"That's enough." Maxwell's voice is a low growl.

"I wasn't your girlfriend; I was your goddamn alibi!" She stops, breathless, an expression of pain on her face.

"It's a good story, Mara." He slaps the door. "Now give me the drive."

"I got the abortion, Mac." Her voice is less angry now than resigned. "Just like you wanted."

Mara closes her eyes, and I lower my forehead to hers, her skin damp and cool, clammy. He had her arrested. He set her up. "You're safe, Mara. I'm here."

Maxwell pounds on the door, but Mara breathes deeply and presses a hand to her bump.

"You have to save her," she whispers. "Save Goose."

"We will, but first we have to get you to a hospital," I whisper, knowing full well I'm offering the impossible.

She shakes her head in slow, drunken movements. "Not me. Just

Goose." Her fingers clench mine, tears streaking her cheeks. "Save Goose. For Cate," she says, her grip slackening as she momentarily closes her eyes.

Cate was pregnant. Mara is pregnant. Goose is the baby neither of them got to have.

I can't lose her, too.

"Mara," I whisper. "Mara, I need you to stay with me. The police will come," I say, willing it to be true. "Hold on."

She doesn't rouse. I lower my face to hers, feel the whisper of her breath. I lift my phone to try 911 again, but the phone is dead. I am alone.

"I can wait all day," Maxwell says. "But you're dying in there, Mara. And so is that baby."

I close my eyes and try to block out his words, but he's right. Mara is dying. I have to do something.

Snippets of the birthing videos I have watched dozens of times during the pregnancy play in my head. I imagine the confident hands of those doctors and nurses, then look down at my own—the swollen right one, the purplish bruise, cuts on the other, both streaked with Mara's blood—and I remember the knife in my backpack.

I snatch my pack and turn it upside down, emptying the contents onto the cold floor. The knife tumbles out, first-aid supplies from the bar and the small bottle of vodka the flight attendant gave me.

"Mara!" Maxwell pounds on the door.

Mara has lost too much blood. A C-section will almost certainly kill her. But if I don't try, I lose Mara *and* I lose Goose. I lift the knife with a trembling hand and open the blade, study the edge as I recall how easily it sliced through my skin.

"I can't," I say aloud.

"Lexi," she whispers faintly. "Do it."

I lower the knife so she can't see it.

"Goose—she's moving. I can feel her." Mara reaches for my hand, grip weak as she presses it on her belly.

The flesh twitches and something nudges my palm from inside. I gasp and tears flood my eyes. It's so much more than what I felt before—the gentle movement. This is my child, some concrete part of her body. Her elbow? A knee? I lower my face to the swollen bump and rest my cheek to it, waiting for motion, wishing my baby girl could punch her way out.

"You can do it," Mara whispers. "You have to do it, Lexi."

I lift my head and meet Mara's eyes, her gaze fatigued but focused.

"You were always the strongest one . . . you can do this. Save our baby. I didn't save Cate. I couldn't save my own baby. But you can save Goose." She reaches her hand to cup her stomach, the same protective gesture she started on the day we found out she was pregnant. She has protected my daughter all these months, but she can't protect her anymore.

Still, she's wrong. I'm not the strongest one. But I am the only one left.

Something hard and sharp—a hand or elbow or foot—rises below the surface of Mara's abdomen. My child, just inches away. I picture her pink skin, the wispy damp fur of her newborn body. Imagine sliding my finger into her soft fist and know I must get her out.

Tears fog my vision as I crack the seal on the bottle of vodka from the airplane and pour some onto the hem of my shirt, using the alcohol-soaked cotton to clean the blade and wiping my hands with the damp fabric. I locate the waistband of Mara's maxi skirt and pull it over the baby bump until the stretched globe of skin is fully visible.

The rest of the vodka I pour over the lower third of her belly. Mara gives an involuntary shiver as I palpate her hip bone and strain to remember the exact steps from the videos.

"Tell her I love her." Mara's voice is almost inaudible.

"You hang on," I say. I need to believe I can save them both. "It's going to be okay."

Her lips barely move as she whispers, "I love you."

Trembling, I place the tip of the knife just inside the left hip bone and press the blade into her skin. Mara inhales sharply, but she doesn't cry out. The blade slices through the skin, parting like a zipper as I make my first incision. I pull back as the knife nears her opposite hip. How quickly the blade passes through is unnerving. It feels like it should be so much harder. Mara groans as blood bubbles from the cut and runs down the dome of her belly.

"Mara?" Maxwell cries. "What's happening, Mara?"

Again I pray that the ambulance is en route, that Terrence has reached the police. That someone is coming. I pause momentarily and listen for sirens, but there is nothing. The blood leaves a trail down Mara's side, reminding me what I've done. What I can't undo.

If I stop now, she could live. She could survive.

And Goose would die.

Lowering my unsteady hand to the firm surface of Mara's belly, I make a second incision. A pained cry comes from Mara, and she snaps her mouth closed to muffle the sound.

"Keep going," she whispers to me when I pause.

When we were preparing the birthing plan all those months ago, I never thought to ask Mara about her wishes if something went wrong. She wouldn't have wanted to plan for contingencies. She would have had faith that it would all work out. She might still have that faith.

Through a cloud of tears, I go to work, cutting through the layers of thin protective tissue. Mara writhes, mouth open in a silent scream as tears stream down her cheeks. "Don't stop," she hisses and I look away from her face, give the task my full attention. When I focus on the knife and the memories of those videos, I can almost pretend this isn't real, that I'm not performing surgery on my best friend.

Soon, I can see Mara's abdominal muscles, and I pause. Surgeons don't cut through the muscles but between them, so they can naturally grow back together. I have no idea how to do that. When I press the knife to the abdominal muscles, Mara lets out another cry, one that feels like the knife is also carving into me.

Maxwell beats at the barricade.

"Mara!" he shouts. Through the shelving, I can see a sliver of his face, pressed in the two-inch opening, like Jack Nicholson's character in *The Shining*. "Open this door, damn it!"

Mara has gone eerily quiet. I touch her neck and feel the slow, thready beat of her pulse. She's still alive. I slide my hands into her abdomen, working to part the muscles along the line of my incision. I have to use a sleeve to swipe at my tears so I can see. I barely make any progress on separating the muscle before my vision clouds again. The smell of wet copper fills the room and the band of blood on the rug continues to grow. Every lost moment feels one second closer to a train that will run us all down. A guaranteed death sentence.

With a steadying breath, I tug at the muscles, which give a little under my fingers. Clenching my teeth, I pull harder. A look at Mara's face—I am killing her. I feel the dizzying climb of panic. Cate flashes through my mind. Cate, who couldn't wait to get out of her parents' house, go to college, and start her life. Who died three months shy of achieving her dream. Cate who took those pills on Mara's advice; Mara, who spent years blaming herself.

Mara murmurs something that sounds like *Baby. Cate.*

Focus. I pick up the knife and start again, keeping the cuts shallow as I try to deepen the incision. I'm afraid of pushing too hard, slicing through the placenta. Of cutting my daughter. Goose grows still, as though she senses the danger, but I can feel the shape of her, our skin separated by mere millimeters.

Mara is limp, lifeless.

"Mara," I say. "Mara, wake up."

No response. Letting out a stifled sob, I work faster, ignoring the sharp ache in my wrist as the blade slowly parts the muscles, promising myself Mara has likely passed out from the pain. I create an opening five or six inches long and wonder if it's enough. I'm an idiot to think I could perform this surgery after watching videos online, even if I've seen them dozens of times.

But I cannot lose them both.

There's more pounding, then a scrape as the file cabinet inches across the floor. I fumble to move faster. If I deliver this baby, will Maxwell let my child live? I fight to clear my head and carve the opening larger, struggling to see through the blood pooled inside the incision.

Mara moans, and I cry out in relief at the sound, though she barely moves and a sheen of sweat covers her ghostly complexion. Maxwell slams into the barricade over and over, nudging it slowly across the floor. Each smack is a reminder of the ticking bomb. I lower my head and keep cutting, until the incision stretches the distance between Mara's hip bones, and I can see past her uterus. There's enough space for the knife and my hand as I make a careful, shallow cut. Below, the deep red of placenta is visible. I don't remember this from the videos and I am momentarily terrified that I've taken some wrong step. That I've cut into the wrong place. But then the sack moves; my daughter, announcing herself.

I am touching the last barrier between me and Goose.

Trembling, I press on the placenta with my left hand and slide the tip of the knife between my fingers, inching the blade through the blood-rich tissue. I hold my breath and a moment passes before a rush of reddish-yellow fluid flows down Mara's belly and soaks the rug beneath her. Amniotic fluid.

So close.

A gunshot strikes the steel door and sinks into the metal with a sickening thump. I bend myself over Mara, shielding her torso and belly, and swipe the tears from my face.

"Open this fucking door!" Maxwell yells.

I think of what this man is capable of. There's no way to hide, not entirely, so I use an elbow to flip the cot on its side as a barrier. I have to get Goose out, then work to stop Mara's bleeding. My movements are more assured and efficient than I feel. I'm on my knees, using my teeth to pull my sleeves up my arms before pushing my left hand through the incision to feel for Goose while, with my right, I guide the knife through the placenta. The blade sticks my hand and I flinch but don't stop.

And then I feel it. The warm, wet globe of my daughter's head.

I let out a cry and drop the knife. I use my right hand to pull the incision open as I reach for Goose. It's impossible one-handed, so I slide both hands into Mara's body. I feel Goose's head, run my fingers along the soft jawline, but I don't know how to free her. I can't pull her out by her head. I try to remember this moment from the videos, but there were so many tools, so many hands.

Mara's chest isn't moving and Goose is still stuck inside. She's going to die. I glance around the room in search of something to hold open the incision so that I can use both hands to pull Goose free, but there's nothing.

A second gunshot blasts. Bits of wood rain down on us, but I barely look up.

"Open. This. Fucking. Door."

If I can hold Goose for one minute before I die—if I can just cradle my daughter, imagine what she might look like on her graduation from kindergarten, a floral dress and patent leather shoes. Her graduation from high school, long delicate fingers as she lifts her tassel from the left side of her hat and slides it to the right, pride and joy and relief on her face.

With my fingers splayed on the baby's back, I try to imagine how I can safely pull her free. In the videos, a nurse bears her weight down on the woman's uterus in order to shift the baby toward the open incision. It gives me an idea. I rotate ninety degrees so that I am straddling Mara's waist. Facing the baby, I lean into the bump and slowly push Goose toward the opening.

The globe of her head is almost at the surface, and I slip my hands down past her tiny neck.

"Come on, Goose. Come on, sweet girl."

My fingers brush the silk of her hair as I stretch the opening and try to get a hold of her shoulders. But she feels too soft, too breakable. I am inside Mara almost to my elbows when I feel the baby turn, face down against my left forearm. I stretch my right hand farther down and cup my daughter's bottom, gently raising her to the surface. I peel down the layers of Mara to free Goose's head. At the sight of her gorgeous dark hair, wet and slick, I gasp.

Leaning all my weight into Mara, I pull the baby free.

"Mara," Maxwell booms, but my focus is on Goose as I turn her upside down like they do in the videos, use two fingers to open her mouth and clear any liquid. Before I can get my fingers between her lips, my daughter lets out a wail that is more screeching cat than human. My own cry follows, and I turn Goose in my arms and clutch her to me.

A perfect baby girl.

I use the knife to cut the umbilical cord and tie it off with my hairband, then lift the baby to Mara.

"Mara." The word is a prayer, a blessing. Goose is alive. We are all three here, together. "Do you feel her? She's right here, Mara."

I lower my head to Mara's and touch my forehead to hers, holding the baby between us. I am twisted in so many directions, pulled by so many emotions. I want to yell at her to fight. I want to plead with her not to leave me. I want to beg forgiveness. I touch the baby's head to Mara's lips, like the smell of the child might rouse her.

"She's here, Mara. We did it. Our girl is here."

Maxwell resumes slamming into the barricade. The scrapes are no longer staccato but drawn out as the barricade gives way. On my knees, I crawl to the farthest corner of the room and sit with my back to the wall, Goose in my arms. Folding up the bottom of my shirt, I wrap it around her body and hold her tight to my chest, sliding my index finger through the opening in her tiny fisted hand as she twists her head and sucks on her recessed lower lip. Rooting, but I have nothing for her. A tear falls from my chin onto her face, and I feel an ache to feed her. She lets out little mewing sounds, sucking furiously. I uncurl two of her fingers, amazed by the presence of fingernails, their uneven edges, and push them into her mouth in an attempt to appease her. "You're okay, sweet girl." I turn to Mara, looking for help, for answers. A streak of blood runs along her cheek like a thick slash, her hands empty and open at her sides. I lean over her and sob, letting out years of devastation.

But then, the high whine reaches my ears.

Sirens.

Multiple sirens. The banging stops abruptly. The room goes quiet as the noise outside escalates.

The sirens are on top of us when Maxwell strikes his fist one last time. His voice is low and thick with rage. "There's nowhere you can go that I won't find you, Mara."

The muffled sound of shoes on concrete, then distant voices. Goose sucks noisily on her own fist. Then the quiet is broken by shouting, boots on the stairs.

"Help!" I call out. "Please help me!"

"Are you alone?" a man shouts.

"No," I yell back. "My friend was shot and she's bleeding. It's just the two of us . . . and my newborn daughter," I say, my voice cracking. *My daughter.*

There is a crash and the room fills with officers in full riot gear. They swarm us.

"What happened? Are you injured?" I see the man's gaze slide to the knife on the floor.

"She was shot," I say quickly. "And bleeding out. She begged me to deliver the baby. Our baby," I add then, and it's not a lie. The reality of what I've done strikes fresh, compounding the relief and the terror, until all I can do is lower my head and cry.

Before I know it, paramedics have lifted Mara onto a stretcher. The reality of her limp, bloodied form is shocking, a husk of my fierce, brave friend. They load me into something that feels more like a wheelchair, though it has a tall back and straps, and they tip it slightly so I'm partially reclined. Through it all, I clutch Goose to my chest.

When a paramedic reaches for her, I cry out. "No."

"We're just going to check her," he says. "You want to make sure your baby is okay, don't you?"

Even as I struggle to hold on, the paramedic pries the baby from me. My arms have never felt so useless, so empty. My heart is like a vacuum as I reach for her.

"Please," I say, attempting to stand. "I need her. I need to be with her."

The paramedic carries Goose away. I try to stand, but a man crouches in front of me. He has brown eyes and a beautiful smile.

"It'll be okay," he says, then points to my wrist. "It looks like you're injured, too. What happened?"

Streaks of blood mark my arms to the elbow. "It's from delivering the baby," I say.

"I meant here," he says, lightly touching my right wrist with a gloved hand.

My wrist has swollen almost to the size of my forearm; angry purple bruises, mottled with green and blue, circle it like a band. "Oh. I think it's a sprain."

"We're going to get that looked at," he says as his gaze shifts to my chest. My drab olive shirt is soaked with blood, creating a semicircle of dark green above the line of my bra. I see the balled-up sweatshirt I'd put under Mara's shoulder in a futile attempt to stanch the bleeding. The black hides the blood, but a barrel-sized stain on the rug beneath is bright crimson. There is blood lower on the rug, too—two separate stripes, from where I cut the baby out of her.

"Is she going to be okay? Mara, I mean?"

"She's got good people taking care of her," he tells me, rising to his feet and strapping me into the strange, upright gurney.

If Mara dies, it's my fault. If she dies, I killed her.

# CHAPTER
# 38

*Birthday*

AS THE PARAMEDIC wheels me toward the ambulance, Terrence appears on the street. He looks like he's been awake for three days.

He grabs my hand. "Alexandra, my God. Are you okay? We were scared to death."

"I'm okay." I remember the thumb drive in my pocket and dig it out, cupping his curled fingers for an extra moment. "Are you okay?" I wonder if the police harassed him, if I've inadvertently put him and Damon in danger by asking for his help.

"We're fine," he says. "It took us forever to get the police here."

"She's here. The baby. She's beautiful and she's healthy and she's perfect." I press the thumb drive into his hand.

He opens his palm to see what I've given him but doesn't say a word as he sticks it into his own pocket. "I can't wait to meet her. And Damon will be so excited. That boy loves babies."

The paramedic directs him to step back so they can load me up, and Terrence promises he'll see me soon. I wish he could come with me. After only a few hours in his company, I feel safe with him. Protected. It is such a gift, but there aren't words—or time—to tell him.

A paramedic sits beside me as the ambulance bumps and sways through the streets. I doze as he talks, waking as I'm wheeled down a hall, then looking up at a face in a blue mask and hairnet, a voice asking me to count backward from ten. Different faces, a new room. A weight presses down on me as I try, and fail, to sit up. My tongue is glued to my teeth and my eyes don't want to open.

When they do, I am alone in a hospital room.

"Hello?" The effort of emitting the single word is exhausting, and I let my eyes fall closed again. When I next wake, a woman in purple scrubs is reaching above my head, silencing the bleating sound of an alarm.

"There she is. You slept almost fourteen hours. How are you feeling?"

"My baby," I say. "Mara. Are they—" The words dam in my throat so that I have to cough them out. "Are they okay?"

"I'm not assigned to them," the nurse says. "Let's take a look at you, and I'll see what I can find out."

I try to stay awake while she unwraps the inflatable cast on my arm and gently turns it over to look at the underside, humming as she works. She checks my blood pressure and the stitches on my chest. As she presses gloved fingers into my wound, I think of Mara, of the blood. Picture her resting in a bed like this one, her lips curved in a gentle smile, the right side higher than the left in the crooked way of all her smiles. I paint the image with a ferocity as strong as I can muster, like I can manifest her recovery. As the nurse is leaving, I call out.

"And you'll check on them—Mara and the baby?"

"Absolutely," she assures me.

In the corridor, a police officer sits on a chair by my door. He glances in at me, and I see Maxwell's face, feel myself flinch.

But it's not Maxwell.

This officer is too young, but the intrusive image of Maxwell brings on a fresh wave of terror. I hear the echo of the words he shouted as the police swarmed us at Dottie's building. *There's nowhere you can go that I won't find you, Mara.* I wonder who is guarding Mara's room. Or maybe this officer isn't here to guard me, but to keep me from escaping. If Mara dies, will I be charged with her death?

When I emerge from sleep again, it feels like hours have passed. I sit up in bed, wincing as the sudden motion ripples pain through my chest and spine. I look for my phone—on the bedside table, the tray—but it is nowhere to be found. Only then do I remember the burner phone, its battery dead. I must have left it in the maintenance room. I wonder if the police found it.

A little woozy, I slide the pulse oximeter off my finger and put my feet on the ground, taking a few steadying breaths as I measure the distance from the bed to the small closet across the room. Once my head clears, I rise, careful to keep the IV pole close as I cross the room. Inside the locker is a white plastic bag containing my shoes, underwear, and jeans. Nothing else. I recall the sweatshirt on the floor of Frank's room, soaked in Mara's blood. And my shirt? Did they cut it off me? I wonder if anyone has contacted Henry.

The IV pole in one hand, I shuffle to the door. A new police officer sits in the corridor, the quiet confirming my hunch that it's nighttime.

"Do you know how the others are doing?" I ask him. "The woman who was shot today—or yesterday—and the baby?"

"No, ma'am. I don't have any updates. Detectives should be back in the morning."

"Wait. How long have I been here?"

"The call came in Sunday and it's Tuesday, almost Wednesday now."

I hesitate before asking one last question. "Are you here to protect me or to keep me from leaving?"

He pauses. "It's too late to leave tonight. I'm sure the detectives will be able to tell you more tomorrow." With that, the officer folds his hands in his lap and turns away.

I return to bed, realizing as I settle in that the officer didn't answer my question. Those few minutes of activity have left me winded as I inspect the bandage along my chest, a faint yellow staining the gauze. A deep purple bruise stretches down my right side, but I feel almost no pain. Once I've gotten myself back under the covers, I consider what is coming. The officer said more detectives will be here in the morning.

Surely Peter Maxwell isn't brazen enough to kill me in a hospital. But the thought alone makes rest impossible. While the buzz and hum of the machines lull me toward sleep, other noises jerk me awake—an alarm in a nearby room, a voice, the squeak of a cart being wheeled down the hall, the clunk of the heat switching on. With each sound, I imagine Peter Maxwell entering my room. The police officer in the hallway provides little comfort.

After all, Peter Maxwell is a police officer, too.

When I wake again, there is a nurse at my side.

"Good morning," she says. "I'm glad you're up. You slept quite a while after your surgery."

"Surgery?"

"They had to reset your wrist."

I picture Maxwell drugging me, asking questions, torturing me for answers. Unwittingly, I look at my hands and arms for signs. Only the cast on my right wrist.

"Why did I sleep so long?"

"It can happen after trauma. Totally normal," she says, checking the machines. "But I'm glad you're awake so I can give you the good news."

"What news?"

"Your baby girl is doing great. She's three days old today."

As the words echo in my head, I can feel the weight of her against me, the warmth of her damp skin on mine. The way her eyelids fluttered open long enough to reveal the deep navy of her irises. Goose is alive. I feel an urge to leap out of bed and sprint through the halls until I find Mara. To hold her and scream and cry together. Mara was right. We did it. We brought our girl into the world. I have to call Henry, tell him the news.

"When can I see her?" The words are just out when a man in a suit enters. Not Peter Maxwell. Where Maxwell is maybe five ten, this man is easily six five and Black. He has a gentle face and kind eyes. A woman follows behind him.

"Okay to come in?" he asks.

"Sure."

The female detective introduces herself as Detective Kendall and her partner as Detective Samuels. She motions to the chair with a questioning look, and I nod.

Kendall sits and opens a notebook on her lap while Samuels leans against the far wall.

"Do you have an update on Mara?" I ask them.

The detectives share a glance, and I know immediately that something is wrong. I cover my mouth, tears streaking down my face.

"I'm afraid Ms. Vannatta didn't make it," Kendall says.

"No." I fist my hand into the sheets, grip them as though I might slide off the bed. They're wrong. We brought Goose into the world together. I am determined to find her and show them. I release my hold as I swing my legs off the bed. The sensation of the cold floor on the soles of my feet sends a shock through me. Mara is dead,

"Mrs. McNeil?" Detective Kendall is standing beside me, a hand on my shoulder.

I fight the urge to shove her away, but instead I let her help me back into the bed. I have so many questions. Where is Mara now? How did it happen? Am I to blame? I want to ask if she died of blood loss, if *I* killed her by delivering Goose. But I'm too afraid of the answer.

"The baby is yours?" Samuels asks.

"Yes. Biologically, she is mine," I say. "Mara carried the pregnancy."

As her name comes out of my mouth, I begin to tremble, then sob. No matter what choices Mara made in the last week, she was my best friend. And now she's gone. But there's more than just grief. There's also guilt and shame—for what I did to her to save Goose. For what I believed about her. That I ever believed that she might be a criminal. That I thought she would willingly steal my child.

I remember the morning of Cate's funeral, the way my parents had murmured to each other about whether they needed to attend, finally deciding they should. While they sat in the rear of the church, I had taken a seat with Mara and her parents toward the front. At the burial site, my parents had stood to the side, hands clasped in front of them, eyes dry.

They say children learn to love from their parents, but not me. My parents taught me poise and stoicism, how to control my exterior to mask the interior. But love—along with trust and friendship and loyalty—was something I learned from Mara and Cate.

"I'm so sorry for your loss." Detective Kendall sets a narrow box of tissues atop the thin hospital blanket. The fabric has the same texture of the velour blanket that lived on the couch in Mara's TV room, the one we would crawl beneath to watch scary movies. I rub it between my fingers and think of all the things I wish I'd said to Mara in that basement. How lucky I was to be her friend. How brave she was. How much she meant to me.

"Can you tell us what happened, in your own words?" Samuels asks.

I take several long, hiccupping breaths and start from the beginning —how Mara left Denver, why I came here to find her. Anxious to avoid mention of the crimes I committed, I tell them that Mara sometimes talked about a Dottie Rosen, so she was the first person I sought out upon my arrival, leaving out the rest—Maxwell, the men outside the Lucky Dive, Gladys Knight and Damon and Terrence, Lotus Lounge, Debra, Tom in the alley.

"When I arrived, Dottie's front door was broken down and there was blood on the carpet." An image of Mara, cut open, flashes through my mind. "You're sure my baby is okay?"

"Positive," Kendall reassures me.

"When can I see her?"

"Soon," Kendall says. "We're awaiting DNA results before we can release her to you."

Release her to me. I can take her home. I squeeze my eyes closed and press my palm to my chest, relief almost painful as it burns through me. "How long will that take?"

"We took a sample on Sunday," she says. "A nurse drew your blood for some tests. If we're lucky, we'll hear Friday. Otherwise, we'll have to wait the weekend."

Those moments I held my baby in my arms wash their warm embrace through me—the curl of her damp hair, the plump roundness of her cheeks. The smell that reminded me of baked bread. They say being a parent means a piece of you lives outside your body, but I feel like it's so much more than a piece. That without her, all that remains is a sliver of me, not enough to survive.

"Can we go back to what happened?" Samuels asks. "You found Ms. Rosen's apartment broken into. You saw blood."

I close my eyes and fight the urge to tell them about Maxwell. Who he is, who he works for, his threats. About the thumb drive I gave to Terrence, but I am so afraid. What if I tell them and they don't believe me? What if he somehow gets to my baby? How can I trust these police officers, when one of their own is a liar and a criminal, maybe even a killer? Mara said Maxwell had the full backing of the department behind him. For all I know, the men who attacked me at the Lucky Dive were also police. These two detectives could be accomplices—maybe Maxwell sent them to test me, to see whether I would rat him out, give them the thumb drive.

I can't risk it.

"Mrs. McNeil."

I reach for the plastic cup beside the bed and bring it to my lips, try to swallow. Gripping the cup with both hands, I tell them about going down the stairs and into the basement, finding Mara, delivering the baby. I leave out Terrence and Damon, and Peter Maxwell.

When I'm done, Samuels stands to his full height, no longer leaning on the wall. "Did Ms. Vannatta say who shot her?"

"No," I answer. "She kept saying someone was coming for her, that it wasn't safe. She was terrified. She insisted I barricade the door. But she didn't say who he was." The lying comes more easily the longer I talk. Boldly, I look up and meet the detective's eyes, search for signs that he is lying, too.

"You don't know his name?" Detective Kendall confirms.

"No," I say. "She was barely making sense."

Samuels clears his throat. "The first officers on the scene say it looked as though you delivered the baby in the basement?" His brow lifts. "By cesarean section."

"Mara begged me," I say, crying again. I wish I could ask if she'd been alive on her way to the hospital. Whether it would have made a difference to wait for the paramedics to deliver Goose, if they might both have survived.

"Why not go for help?" Samuels asks.

"Someone was outside, threatening us. He fired a couple of shots, trying to get in. We couldn't leave. I called 9-1-1, then my phone died. Mara was worried about the baby. That if she bled out from the gunshot wound, the baby would—" I can't finish the sentence.

It hits me again that Mara is gone. That she'll never make a joke to cheer me up, never ask for pepperoni pizza and vanilla ice cream. Never hold the baby girl we brought into this world.

"Mara Vannatta has been a person of interest for some time," Kendall says.

"Why would the police be interested in Mara?" It's a question they should expect me to ask, but I wonder if I deliver it believably or if they know I've already heard this. If we're all just playing a game here, if some wrong move will cost me the baby—or my freedom.

"We believe she was working with a man named Clayton," Samuels says. "He's the head of a drug syndicate our department has been working to take down for years."

The detectives share a glance, unreadable to me, and I'm determined to remain silent. I think of how well Maxwell set Mara up as his alibi, potentially his fall guy. Do these officers really not know that Maxwell is the man they want? That Mara had nothing to do with those drugs? I finger the blanket and think of the baby, of my first touch of the warm mound of her head. I didn't do anything wrong. They will have to let us go.

"Please. I need to see the baby," I say. "Our baby."

Our baby. The detectives' expressions soften, and I thank Mara for giving me exactly the right thing to say. Another gift I can never repay. The detectives ask if I ever got a look at the man, and I tell them I didn't. They confirm that they went through Dorothy Rosen's apartment and found nothing.

I mention my missing backpack and they promise to look into it. I'm antsy as the detectives explain the next steps—collecting my fingerprints for exclusion, potential follow-up questions.

"There's no way to see my baby? Just for a few minutes?"

"We'll make it happen as soon as possible," Samuels promises.

"Today?"

A little frown. "Probably not today," he admits. "But soon."

The answer burns like a fresh cut, but I nod. It's close now, the moment Goose will be in my arms. I wrap my hands, white-knuckled, around the word.

Soon.

# CHAPTER
# 39

WEDNESDAY ENDS AND Thursday drags on, punctuated by intermittent visits from hospital staff and a lab tech who takes my fingerprints. Henry finally returns my call from last night. I'd left him a voicemail with the hospital's number, and when I answer the phone in the room, he is breathless.

"Lexi? Are you all right? Why are you at the hospital?"

"I'm fine. I left you a voicemail. Didn't you get it?"

"I just dialed the number you left." His voice is breathy, his words too fast. "I didn't realize it was a hospital. What's happening? Are you okay?"

"It's a long story," I say. "But I'm okay. And she's okay—Goose, I mean." I'm not yet ready to say her name out loud.

"Oh, Lexi. Sweet Goose. Tell me everything."

Three days without holding her seems like forever, but when I close my eyes, I can feel her in my arms in that dank basement. I describe her downy cover and the curve of her cheek, the pucker of her lips that were already sucking the moment she was born.

"She sounds perfect." Henry's voice breaks, and it takes him a moment to continue. "When do you bring her home?"

"I don't know. There's a lot to sort out. Mara . . ." It's my voice that cracks on her name, and I shake my head as though I can relay it all without a word.

"Lexi."

"I'm okay." But we both know I'm far from okay. I promise to keep him posted, and he reminds me that he's still in New York, only a couple hours away.

Not long after we hang up, I get a new IV and the offer of additional pain meds—which I decline, though I feel plenty of pain to warrant them. Every time someone enters the room, sweat collects on my upper lip and my muscles tense, expecting Maxwell. I've been in bed all day and yet my body feels like it's run a marathon.

I cannot leave the hospital without confronting him.

At the end of the day, Detective Kendall returns with my statement, which I review and sign. I feel a fresh desire to tell her about Maxwell and instead ask about progress on the DNA testing. She crosses her fingers and says only, "Tomorrow, we hope."

I have to be patient.

With the reassurances that a DNA match will confirm Goose is my child, I feel a moment of relief. I will be taking her home. I imagine walking back into Henry's house, Goose in my arms. Carrying her as I pass through the yard and into the coach house where Mara last lived.

I settle back into the bed as the rounds wind down for the evening. Dinner is served, and I'm looking down at the unappealing meal when finally, Detective Maxwell enters my room.

---

Dressed in black jeans and a denim button-down under a black leather jacket, Detective Peter Maxwell looks, for the first time, more like a criminal than a police officer. Fitting. Gone is any vestige of the man I'd thought was upstanding, honorable, and I wonder if he can sense my loathing and fear from where he stands. I work to project confidence and remind myself that I have evidence of his crimes.

"You have something that belongs to me," he says, and I wonder how long he's been lurking, keeping tabs on me. "It wasn't in Dottie's place or that basement office, so she must've given it to you."

I imagine him walking among the other officers, searching for the evidence that proved he was a criminal while his colleagues assumed he was on the straight and narrow. Does anyone know what he really is?

He waves his fingers in a *come here* motion. "Where's the thumb drive?"

I am grateful Damon and Terrence haven't been here. At least as far as I know, Maxwell isn't aware of their existence. Unless he somehow identified Terrence from his call to 911. Under the blankets, I shift to feel the comforting presence of the nurse call button below my left thigh.

Hands clasped in my lap, I struggle against the trembling—my legs, my chest, my hands—almost as though I'm coming out of frigid water. "Mara is dead and you killed her. Now, I'm going to take my baby home, and you're going to leave us alone."

He smiles like this strikes him as funny. "And if I don't?"

I sit up straighter in bed, trying to match his formidable stance. "I'll send the contents of that drive to every relevant law enforcement agency in the country, post it on the web, and you'll die in prison."

The muscle in his jaw beats twice. "Give me the thumb drive."

I glance around the room—for a weapon or an ally, but we're alone.

"I know the drive isn't here. I went through this place last night."

The words ignite the fuse of suppressed fear as I imagine him watching over me while I slept. Why not kill me? But the answer is obvious—the thumb drive.

"I'm not an idiot," I tell him. "The thumb drive is in safe hands. But I know what's on it. That evidence will be tough to explain to a jury."

Maxwell steps toward the bed, the bulge of his gun visible under his leather jacket. He wears no wedding ring now, and I assume that detail had been for my benefit, to throw me off his scent.

"You think you can threaten me?" He grips my arm, and I jab the call button as his fingers dig into my flesh.

From the intercom comes the nurse's voice. "Ms. McNeil? Do you need something?"

Maxwell releases his grip, and I watch him until he has taken a few steps back before replying to the nurse. "No," I say. "Sorry about that."

The connection goes silent before Maxwell says, "That nurse can't protect you forever."

I recall what Mara said about Clayton, the man who runs the drug operation. *Ruthless*, she said.

"I understand, Detective." I ignore the throbbing in my arm from his grip, the way it pulses into my fingers. "You could come after me any time."

He seems pleased to hear me acknowledge the seriousness of my predicament.

"But if the evidence on that thumb drive gets out, I'm probably not going to be your biggest problem, am I?" I say calmly. "Do you think you'd make it to trial? That you'd live that long?"

The line of his jaw goes hard.

"Here's how this will go: The police are going to finish with their questions about Mara's death, and I'm going to get my baby. After that, it's yours."

"Assuming your baby leaves the hospital," he says. "So much can go wrong in those fragile little bodies."

I'm transported back to reaching inside Mara to pull her out, the loose skin of her elbows and back that reminded me of a baby elephant, her tiny rib cage that swelled when she cried. The red of her palms as I slid a finger into her half-formed fist. The way she felt tucked against me. The absence of her is suddenly as painful as if he were strangling me with his bare hands.

"You think the nursery isn't armed with cameras? If anything happens to me or my baby, the pictures and video go out—to the FBI, the police, the media. With your name and your position in the department." I speak the words clearly, with authority.

Finally, he hisses, "You better not be fucking with me."

"I'd have to be an idiot to fuck with you, Detective."

Then, Maxwell is gone.

I press the call button with a shaky hand and request something for the pain. I don't really need the medication—what I need is another body in this room to clear out the threat of death, the threat to Goose, the fear that circulates through every cell of my body, and the question that runs with it: What will Peter Maxwell do?

The evening passes uneventfully. The nurse tells me I'm cleared to go home as soon as the DNA comes back. I ask again if I can see the baby, but she defers to the detectives, and they're gone for the day. Maxwell wants what I have, and he knows it's not here—it doesn't make sense for him to try anything else until I've been released. Still, sleep feels risky, so I fight it as long as I can. Until I lose. I wake to a presence in the room, and when I let out a startled cry, the nurse pats my arm.

"Didn't mean to scare you, hon." She motions to a vase of flowers on the bedside table. "These came for you this morning. Pretty, aren't they?"

Morning. It's Friday. The DNA tests, Goose—my mind is whirling before I'm upright.

The nurse hands me a card.

In neat square handwriting, the message reads:

*Get better soon and call when you're ready for pickup.*
*—D&T*

Damon and Terrence. Terrence has written his phone number on the reverse side. When my backpack is returned from the police station later that morning, the cash and my credit card are miraculously still inside. I'm cleared to be discharged as early as this afternoon, and a nurse brings me a scrubs top to wear since my shirt was destroyed. All we're waiting for is the DNA results. Then we're free to leave. I sit in the chair in the corner and flip through the same hospital magazine a dozen times. Finally, a nurse enters with the two detectives.

I leap up.

"She's yours," Detective Kendall says, and before I can ask where she is, a second nurse rolls in a clear bassinet. I cross the room and, in my haste, tangle myself in the IV as I reach for the small pink-wrapped bundle.

She feels so light and also so dense—like the whole of my heart is wrapped in this tiny package. And Mara's, too. I push the blanket away from her face and run a finger along the delicate fuzz on her pink fore-head, kiss her head and her cheeks as tears slide off my face onto hers. My baby. I study the small white dots on the skin of her pink eyelids, the short dark lashes, clustered as she blinks. Her wide eyes gaze up at me, not quite focused. I press my nose to her head and smell the faint-est whiffs of maple syrup and soap.

"Thank you," I say to the detectives, to the nurses.

"She's beautiful," Detective Kendall tells me.

"Do you have a name picked out?" asks Samuels.

"Cate," I say. Probably, I'd known all along. "Catherine Mara McNeil."

"Pretty," the nurse says. "I'll be right back to remove that IV, and we'll get you two on your way."

When the nurse leaves, Detective Kendall confirms my home phone number—I assure her I'll get my cell phone replaced in a few days—then closes the notebook and tucks it under her arm.

"Best of luck to you," she says, leaving a business card on the table by the bed. As Samuels passes, he leaves a card of his own before reaching to smooth down the fine dark hair on Cate's head with two knuckles. "She really is cute," he says, and then he, too, is gone.

The hospital room is quiet, but there is a dull washing sound inside my head, like the rhythmic lull of the sea. I lay my daughter on the bed between my knees and unwrap her swaddling. She wears a onesie, the sleeves pulled down over her hands—to keep her from scratching her face, I read somewhere. Now freed, her legs kick in little frog mo-tions. I press my nose to her neck, smell the milky scent of the formula the nurses have been feeding her. I unsnap the onesie and gently re-move it, exposing her chest and arms. Every perfect bit of her. I lift my shirt and cradle her to my skin, holding my baby close. It's a cliché to say that I loved her at first sight, but I did. I do.

"Cate," I whisper. "Mommy loves you so much."

Her eyes flutter open, the irises a blue so deep they are almost vio-let. I know infants can't see far, but I swear she looks at me and one cor-ner of her mouth ticks upward. Like a smile. I wish I could show her to Mara and Cate, tell them that she will carry us all forward. That, when she's old enough, many years from now, I'll tell her our story. I'll remind her how much her aunties would have loved her.

When I realize what I have to do next—the gamble I need to take—I collect the business cards off the table and fold my palm across them.

It's time to face Mara's demons.

# CHAPTER
# 40

MY DISCHARGE PAPERS have been signed and Terrence is on his way. The nurse sets me up with powdered formula as well as several cans of premixed, two bottles, a pacifier, a small bag of diapers, wipes, and two extra onesies, then shows me how to wrap Cate into a perfect burrito before putting a sweet pink hat on her head. When I come out of the room in a wheelchair (they won't let me walk), Terrence waits at the nurse's station. He grins when he spots the bundle in my arms.

"Thanks for coming," I say.

"Damon is waiting in the van," he answers, leaning down to look at Cate. "She's gorgeous, Alexandra. And be warned, Damon loves babies. I mean *loves* them." Somehow that doesn't surprise me.

"I'm ready," I announce.

The nurse wheels me to the curb where the van idles, Damon peering out from the back seat. Through the open window, he calls out, "Hurry up. I want to see my goddaughter."

I halt at the sight of the van, fresh dread pooling in my limbs. "I don't have a car seat."

"We got you covered," Terrence says, sliding open the van door.

Already buckled into the seat beside Damon is a blue car seat with a plaid cover. "Borrowed it from my sister."

"You're an angel," I tell him, and he blushes.

We get Cate fastened into the car seat and ask the nurse to check that we've done it correctly. When she gives the thumbs-up, I climb into the front and peer back as Damon examines Cate.

"She's the cutest white baby I've ever seen," he says.

"Only the cutest white one?" I tease.

"Top three, all in."

When I raise my brow at Damon, he nods to Terrence. "Hey, I've got to prioritize Big T's nieces, else I don't have a ride."

I laugh and buckle my seat belt as Terrence starts the engine, then confess I don't have a place to stay. There's no shame attached to the admission, and that surprises me. I feel safe being vulnerable with Damon and Terrence, and they have a plan.

Damon says, "No way Ms. Knight would let you take that baby anywhere other than her house."

"It's true," Terrence says. "She insisted you stay there, as long as you need."

———

Gladys Knight provides a warm welcome and the evening passes quickly. While Gladys fixes a big stew, I upload the contents of the thumb drive and make some phone calls—a quick call with Henry followed by a long call with Detective Kendall. Finally, I speak to Henry again. He's booked me a flight home and wants to come down from New York tonight. It takes some convincing to assure him that Cate and I are fine for the night. "I can't wait to meet Cate," he says. "I'll see you so soon."

Despite the nerve-racking conversation with the detective, the calls with Henry are calming. Knowing how soon I'll see him, how it will feel to hold Cate and lean into him . . . how much I long for his company.

When the four of us finally sit down to dinner, Terrence and Gladys take turns holding Cate while Damon moves his chair to sit beside whoever has her.

The last thing I do is text Maxwell from a fresh burner phone to confirm that I'll bring the thumb drive to the diner tomorrow morning.

His response is immediate.

9AM.

During the night, Gladys enters the guest room every time Cate makes a peep. She knocks, waiting for permission to enter, then slips in with an air of competence and joy, talking me through tricks for getting babies to sleep, which mostly boil down to a full belly followed by a good burp and a clean diaper. I promise her I'm okay—adrenaline keeps me wide awake anyway—but I can tell Gladys loves it, so I soak up as much as I can, my single night of training, and imagine a world where my mother had been someone like Gladys.

As the sky brightens behind the yellowed lace curtains, my mood darkens. The meeting will be over in under a half hour, I tell myself while a thousand warnings fill my brain. Then I'll get on a direct flight to Denver. Take Cate home. We'll never have to see him again.

Gladys makes coffee, tries to get me to drink a cup, but I'm already shaking and I can't imagine caffeine will help. I feed Cate at the kitchen table, manage one bite of toast for myself.

Terrence arrives to drive me, and Gladys and Damon stay at the house to watch Cate. It's painful to leave her, and Gladys seems to sense my hesitation. She holds my baby close and puts a hand on my arm. "We'll be right here, waiting," she says. "You hurry back to your girl."

I blink against the tears in my eyes and lean to kiss Cate's plump perfect cheek. A small smile—almost certainly gas—crosses her face, and I force myself to turn away.

As Terrence drives past the diner, I scan the patrons through the front window, wondering if Maxwell is already waiting inside. Terrence pulls up to the curb down the block from the restaurant, and I turn to look at him.

"I'll be right here," he says. There is fear in his eyes, and I feel it, too. He knows what happened to Mara, what Maxwell did. He and Gladys and Damon all know. There was no way to avoid it last night, but they're sworn to secrecy, for their own safety. "You have it?" he asks.

"I do." I slide out of the van and start toward the diner before I lose my nerve. I scan the street, but no one stands out. I tell myself I'm not alone. Inside, there's no sign of Maxwell. Relieved, I take a seat near the front of the restaurant, facing out.

When Maxwell arrives, he hesitates a beat before walking to the table. He is freshly shaven, wearing a button-down and suit jacket. He looks like a detective today, and the reminder of his power, of his official role, is terrifying. The tight line of his lips makes it clear he doesn't want to sit with his back to the entrance, but I haven't given him any choice. His displeasure feels like a tiny point in my favor.

Before either of us can speak, the server arrives at the table. "What can I get you, hon?"

"Coffee with cream for me," Maxwell says.

"Nothing for me," I say. "Thank you. I'm not staying."

The waitress pours coffee for Maxwell and points to the creamer on the table before taking her leave.

As Maxwell douses his coffee with cream, I set my closed fist on the table, uncurling my fingers until the thumb drive falls free.

He snatches it up and slips it into an inside pocket of his coat. "This is the only copy?"

"Are you Lance?"

He holds my gaze. "Is that what she said? Lance?"

There is something different in his expression—a flash of nostalgia or even regret. "I think she cared about you," I say.

His expression softens a beat before he barks out a caustic laugh. "What is this, some sort of trap?" He waves at me. "You wired or something?"

I stand up and remove my hoodie, exposing the thin T-shirt underneath. Run my hands across my chest, pressing the thin bandage to show there isn't a wire. Then, I turn around, pulling the shirt tight against my back so he can see there's nothing there either. Two teenage boys watch from a nearby table, gawking like I'm a lunatic. Finally, I take my seat and unfasten the air cast to show my bruised and swollen wrist. "No wires. I want to know why my friend had to die."

"That's on her—she should have stayed away from Clayton."

"You're not Clayton?"

"Hell no."

"But you work with him—or help him," I say.

He doesn't answer.

I take a sip of water. "I just want to know what her life was like here," I say. "If she was ever happy."

"She was happy."

"With you?" I press.

Maxwell takes a slow look around the restaurant as though expecting that we're being watched. Then he lowers his voice and leans in. "There was nothing illegal about my relationship with Mara," he says, cupping the coffee mug between both hands. "We kept it quiet because of my job."

"Lance?" I repeat.

After a beat, he nods. "My middle name."

I shift the conversation. "Someone told me she was trying to help the women at Lotus?"

"She always had a project—someone who needed her help. Especially those women. That club was a mess."

Anger sparks my tongue. "Is that why you and a bunch of thugs rounded up those women and threatened to arrest them?"

He holds my gaze. "I wasn't there."

"But you did arrest Mara," I say.

"I helped her get back on her feet."

"Until she got pregnant," I say, studying his face.

He looks down in his coffee. "That baby would have put her in danger."

"So you made her get an abortion and then *you* put her in danger."

He lifts the mug and drains it before setting it back on the table. "I don't have to listen to this." He pats the pocket where he put the thumb drive. "This better be the only copy."

I hit the call button on the phone tucked under my thigh, confirm that the call is dialing before I say flatly, "It isn't."

"That wasn't the deal," he snaps.

"I guess we had a different deal in mind," I say with false bravado, my leg muscles tensed, ready for flight.

He lashes out and grabs my right wrist, the cast still sitting on the table between us. The pain launches me backward in the chair and I cry out, shoving him off with my uninjured hand. My phone slides off my seat and clatters to the floor. As diners nearby turn to look, he releases me, smooths the ugly grimace off his face.

"You get any second thoughts about sharing those files and I will find you," he says through clenched teeth.

I offer up a blank expression, hold my chin high and shrug. "What do you mean? What files?"

I feel a cool breeze from the street as the front door swings open, and it is like the first breath of air after a long incarceration. I glance up to confirm they're here before Maxwell leans across the table. "I will hunt you down. Hunt your daughter down."

My hands tremble, and I fight to remain at the table as instructed, though my eyes fill with tears at the fury in his voice.

"Do not fuck with me," he seethes across the table, though the last word is cut short as he seems to sense the presence of the team Detectives Kendall and Samuels assembled—Philadelphia PD, local FBI, and two agents from the DEA. In a flash of movement, his fingers lengthen as he dips a hand toward the bulge in his jacket. His gun. Before he can reach it, the first officers grab him by the elbows and yank him from his seat. They shove him to the linoleum floor, and before I'm out of my chair, they're kneeling on his arms, pinning him down.

"Get off me," he shouts. "I'm with the department. Check my badge." He kicks his feet, twisting his body, but there is nowhere for him to go. "She's lying. She made it all up—some crazy plan to frame me."

I pocket my phone as I walk outside to the sidewalk where Detectives Kendall and Samuels are waiting. Samuels puts an arm around my shoulders. "You did great," he says, and I lean into him, finding an odd sense of comfort under the large man's wing.

"You really did," Kendall echoes.

I spot the van down the block, Terrence watching us. I raise a hand toward him. "It's over, right?"

"It's over," Kendall confirms.

I've told them I won't testify. I won't put Cate's life in danger, and they've assured me they have more than enough evidence with the thumb drive. They've agreed to put it in writing, which was Henry's suggestion. I have agreed to identify the men who attacked me outside the Lucky Dive if they can locate them. But that's my final role.

Samuels reaches out a hand, and I take it with my left and shake it. When I turn toward Detective Kendall, she pulls me into a hug.

When I reach the van, Terrence folds over, resting his hands on his knees. "Thank God. I saw all those cops go in there, and I didn't know if he was—" He waves his hand. "You're okay. You're okay, right?"

"I'm okay."

Terrence drives us back to Ms. Knight's house, and we find Damon and Gladys in the front room with Cate. Damon makes sweet cooing noises and Cate's wide eyes are curious, almost amused. The awe I feel is fresh when I see her.

It's as though I've known her forever—the perfect slope of her cheeks, her rounded nose, the upturned curve of her lips—and at the same time she seems brand-new every time.

"Everything go okay?" Gladys asks, handing me the baby.

"Yes," I say, recalling Maxwell's fury. I wished I'd been able to learn more about Mara, about how she ended up with him, but it's not his perspective I really want. So I settle on the couch with Cate in my arms and ask Gladys to tell me about my friend.

# CHAPTER
# 41

GLADYS FEEDS US soup and sandwiches for lunch, and Cate naps in Terrence's arms while Damon dozes in his chair and I soak up everything Gladys shares about Mara. Finally, it's time for me to go to the airport. I'm happy to take a cab, but the very notion springs them all to life—Damon wide awake and Terrence offering to drive and Gladys insisting. Damon wants to come, too, so the four of us load into the van. Gladys stays behind, but she gives me a hug and tells me I've got a place to stay whenever I'm in town. I kiss Cate on the forehead and buckle her into the car seat.

I text Henry as we start the drive. The mood is quieter, all of us exhausted, but Damon talks to Cate in a soft voice the whole ride to the airport, telling her about the things he'll show her in Philadelphia when she's old enough—the children's museum, which he assures her isn't as lame as it sounds, the zoo, the Phillies, cheesesteak. In the driver's seat, Terrence eyes Damon in the rearview mirror, grinning. I think of what Damon has been through, how he holds himself, his fierce optimism despite his circumstances. I love him for it.

There's a beat of sadness at the prospect of leaving them, these strangers who helped me find Mara and save Cate. Until Henry, the people closest to me were my parents, Mara, and Cate.

All of them are gone now.

How I wish Mara and Cate could be a part of Baby Cate's life. Each of us a would-be mother, in our own ways. But only I, the one who couldn't carry a child, ended up with a baby in my arms. Those last months of Cate's life, she'd been so secretive and sad. At the time, I thought it was about us all graduating high school, about moving away and beginning our separate lives. How much I didn't know then. How much I didn't see.

I imagine her mother's heartbreak when she realized that her daughter had been pregnant. Did she know Caleb had raped her? I'm guessing not—but she must have known that, had she been a different type of mother, her daughter might still be alive. And then there's Mara, who wanted her child but aborted it because the child's father threatened her. For those weeks she was pregnant with Maxwell's child, did she remember Cate? Did she imagine giving birth to a child, naming her after our lost friend?

Home will seem strange and lonely without Mara. I am optimistic about things with Henry, but no matter what, he and Kyle and Nolan are my family. As are Terrence and Damon now, and Gladys Knight.

I wish again that I'd told Mara how much I loved her in those final moments. Told her I forgave her. That none of it mattered. How could it? If not for Mara, I wouldn't have Baby Cate. She made me a mother.

At the airport, Terrence pulls to the curb, and I climb out, planting a kiss on each of Damon's cheeks.

"You're a prince among men," I tell him.

He laughs. I can sense his pride, hope he can hold it close in hard moments. Terrence cradles Cate and hands me my pack, which I pull onto both shoulders. He kisses Cate, too, then hands her to me, and I cuddle her against me, hugging Terrence with my free arm. "I wish you'd let me pay you," I whisper.

"Enough of that," he says.

"I can't thank you enough," I say as he steps back. His eyes glisten.

"And we'll be back in September, remember?" I've spoken to Gladys about asking Damon and Terrence to be Cate's godfathers, having her baptized here in a few months. I want these men in my daughter's life. And in mine.

I hear my name and turn to see Henry emerging from the airport's double doors, relief etched on his face. When we spoke on the phone last night, he asked if he could come down. I was hesitant, but now I'm glad he's here. He raises a hand to Terrence and Damon but stays back while I say goodbye.

"She loves you." I tilt Cate upright so that the two men can see her face. "And so do I."

I can feel the tears coming. Before they fall, I turn and join my husband. He peers at Cate, making no move to wipe his own tears, and soon we are both crying as we walk into the airport.

I lean down and whisper to my daughter. "Okay, baby. Here we go. Mama is taking you home." Henry wraps an arm around my shoulders and kisses my cheek, pressing his face to mine.

I allow the harried travelers to bustle around us. After all, Cate and I have a lifetime.

# CHAPTER

# 42

*May 2008*

Mara is doing homework on her bed and Cate is on the floor, leaning on the wall beneath the window, the notebook open in her lap. She wants to write something profound, but she's struggling to focus. Cate can feel Mara looking over, knows she's checking to see if the seven white oblong pills Cate swallowed have taken effect. She gives Mara a thumbs-up, though the edges of the room seem to be softening. It's pleasant, this feeling. Like floating.

The music is quiet. It is so unlike the hundreds of times they have jumped around this room, shrieking and laughing with Lexi. Cate feels older, but not in a bad way. And she still can't wait for one of their silly dance party nights, which is way overdue.

She tries to picture her mom before she had Cate, and wonders if she was afraid when she got pregnant. If the idea of being a mother was overwhelming. Was that when her mom stopped laughing so much? Or was it later, when she had the twins? Two babies at once. It's hard to imagine any of their parents as teenagers. Lexi's uptight mother and Mara's angry one. What made them that way?

Cate wishes Lexi were here now. Now that it's almost over, it seems stupid to have kept it from her. The three of them are a team, and soon they'll be off to their individual futures.

They haven't talked much about that. Mara isn't planning to go straight to college, but she'll end up in charge of some company, or start her own business. She isn't built to work for someone else. Lexi should be a doctor. Screw her stupid parents. And Cate? Who knows. Whatever she does, she's going to be independent.

There's a tight pulling in her gut, like period cramps, but worse. It must be happening. There's no pain, only pressure, and it's not entirely unpleasant. She laughs, and it must be loud because Mara's looking at her like she's crazy. And maybe she is. Crazy relieved, crazy happy, crazy grateful for this awful thing. It's like how people talk about a near-death experience, how it changes the way you see the world. Cate wants to explain it to Mara, but right now, her tongue feels twisted, like the words wouldn't come out right. She'll tell Mara later.

Mara's phone rings and she answers it. Cate knows by the look on Mara's face that it's her mother. She's angry about something; Cate can hear her voice rising over the line. She thinks of her own mom and stands, in need of some fresh air. Her muscles are sore from yesterday's soccer practice, the one she barely survived without puking again. How nice it will be to practice when this is over, to feel at home in her body again. Maybe she'll get in the hot tub for a few minutes and relax. Mara watches her, frowning, and Cate gives her a smile. *I'll be right back*, she mouths, waving at her friend to go back to the call with her mom.

They will talk about this later, Cate and Mara and Lexi. How it made them all stronger. How clear it is to Cate now how much they need each other, how crucial it is to have people who will catch you when you fall. Mara caught Cate. Lexi would, too. They will talk about how lucky they are to have each other in this world—they'll talk and cry and laugh and dance, just like they always have.

No matter what else happens, they will be friends forever—Cate and Mara and Lexi.

Cate knows they will.

# ACKNOWLEDGMENTS

THIS BOOK—OR PIECES of it—has been in my mind for the better part of a decade. I've never spent so long on a single story, and I've never worked so hard. I've also never been so proud.

First, I want to thank you, the reader, for following Lexi, Mara, and Cate on this journey and for your support of me—whether this is the first Danielle Girard book you've read or the seventeenth. It's because of you—your love of story and character—that I get to do the thing I love most. Thank you.

To AMB, book whisperer and friend. I can still picture us in that sports bar in Minneapolis—you with a dream to help authors create stories, me with a story I'd been wanting to write for years but hadn't found the right way to tell. I'm immensely grateful for the gentle guidance over the many months of writing the first draft of *Pinky Swear*. I can't wait to do it again.

To my incredible agent, Danya Kukafka, who saw something in *Pinky Swear* and knew exactly how and when to push to help me realize its potential. You are the ultimate professional and your humor and enthusiasm make even the toughest bits of the business a joy. I am so grateful for our partnership.

To Sarah Grill, my wonderful editor. From our first conversation, I knew *Pinky Swear* was in the right hands. Your care and compassion for the story and the characters has made this book what it is. Thank you for taking it on.

Thank you to the entire team at Atria: my publicist, Sierra Swanson; marketing, Zakiya Jamal; Davina Mock-Maniscalco, for interior design; managing editors: Paige Lytle, Shelby Pumphrey, and Sofia Echeverry; Liz Byer, production editor; and Vanessa Silverio, production manager. And to Jimmy Iacobelli and Chelsea McGuckin for the stunning cover.

Big thanks also to the team at Trellis Literary Management for handling all the details and foreign bits, especially Tori Clayton and Allison Malecha; and to my UK team; my agent, Stephanie Glencross of David Higham Associates; and Jennie Ayers, my editor at Hera Books. I'm thrilled that *Pinky Swear* has a home across the pond.

The years between my last book and this one have been big—in some ways awful and in some truly magical. If wealth is measured by the people in your life (and I think it is), then I'm a rich, rich woman. To my hometown crew who have picked me up and let me lean, especially during the toughest times: Albee Willett, Christy Delger, Christine Smith, Sarah Cawley, Aunge Thomas, Allison McGree, Shannon Agee-Jones, Whitney Pritham, Elise Sheehan, and Chris Garton.

The thriller community is made up of the most ridiculously talented and supportive people who exist, and I'm very fortunate to have so many amazing friends there. To the Dirty Work Wives: Hannah Morrissey and Tessa Wegert; my killer couple cohort, Daniel Palmer; the Thriller Thursday gang: Lauren Nossett, Greg Wands, Tessa Wegert, Carter Wilson, Kimberly Belle, Vanessa Lillie, and Alex Segura. To the members of the Rhode Island retreat that never was: Jaime Lynn Hendricks, Vanessa Lillie, Jennifer Pashley, and to the SMA lovelies: Danielle Trussoni, Catherine Baker-Pitts, and Christina Baker Kline. And to the other authors whose writing I admire and who have touched my life and my work, thank you, thank you, thank you. There are too many to number but the list includes: Jeneva Rose, Lee Matthew Goldberg, Connor Sullivan, Don Bentley, Lou Berney, Rachel Koller Croft, Ashley Winstead, Jennifer Hillier, Wendy Walker, and Anne-Sophie Jouhanneau.

Over the past few books, I've been lucky enough to get to know a number of fabulous bookstagrammers. Your enthusiasm and love for books and authors makes what I do so much more fun. I'm grateful to you all, but a few deserve special mention. First, to my New York ride-or-die, Dennis Michel, @scaredstraightreads. Also, for all the love in person and online, thank you to Magen @bonechillingbooks, Candice @candice_reads, Kristin @k2reader, Sonica @the_reading_beauty, and Diana @dianas_books_cars_coffee, to name a few. If you're a book lover, I encourage you to find and follow some bookstagrammers, who make discovering new books both easy and highly entertaining.

Thank you, too, to Kerry Schafer, friend and producer, who keeps the *Killer Women Podcast* from going off the rails. What began as a pandemic project has blossomed into a passion one, and as I write this, we are approaching episode number two hundred. I'm eternally grateful to the talented women who have come onto the show and spoken candidly about the unique joys and challenges of being a thriller author and of balancing the job with all the other aspects of life.

They say family is complicated, but mine does not feel complicated. It feels, quite simply, like the solid foundation from which I have been able to pursue this dream and also the stabilizing force when everything else is in turmoil. My dad is ten years gone now, but I'd like to think he'd appreciate this book more than most, as it touches closest to the work he did to help women realize their dreams of motherhood. Mom, Nicole, Tom, Steve, and also Blake, Jabe, Kelsey, Luke, Will, and the newest member of the Girard family, Eddie, there aren't sufficient words to thank you for all the ways you have and do support me and for the joy you bring to my life. I love you.

Finally, for Claire and Jack, nothing I ever create could hold a candle to the two of you. From where I sit, you are the sun, the moon, and all the stars. Even twenty-something years into this motherhood thing, you continue to amaze me. I love you both so much.